DREAMING BEAUTY

DREAMING PRINCESSES, BOOK 1

ISBN: 978-1-961733-03-9 (paperback)

Cover design by: Arcane Covers

Published by Bursting Box Publishing
BurstingBoxPublishing.com

For the dreamers and their dreams.
"Don't quit your daydream." - Anon.

"For it is very probable . . .
that the good fairy, during so long a sleep,
had given her very agreeable dreams."
-   *La Belle au bois dormant*
(Charles Perrault, 1697)

Map of Somnus
and surrounding kingdoms

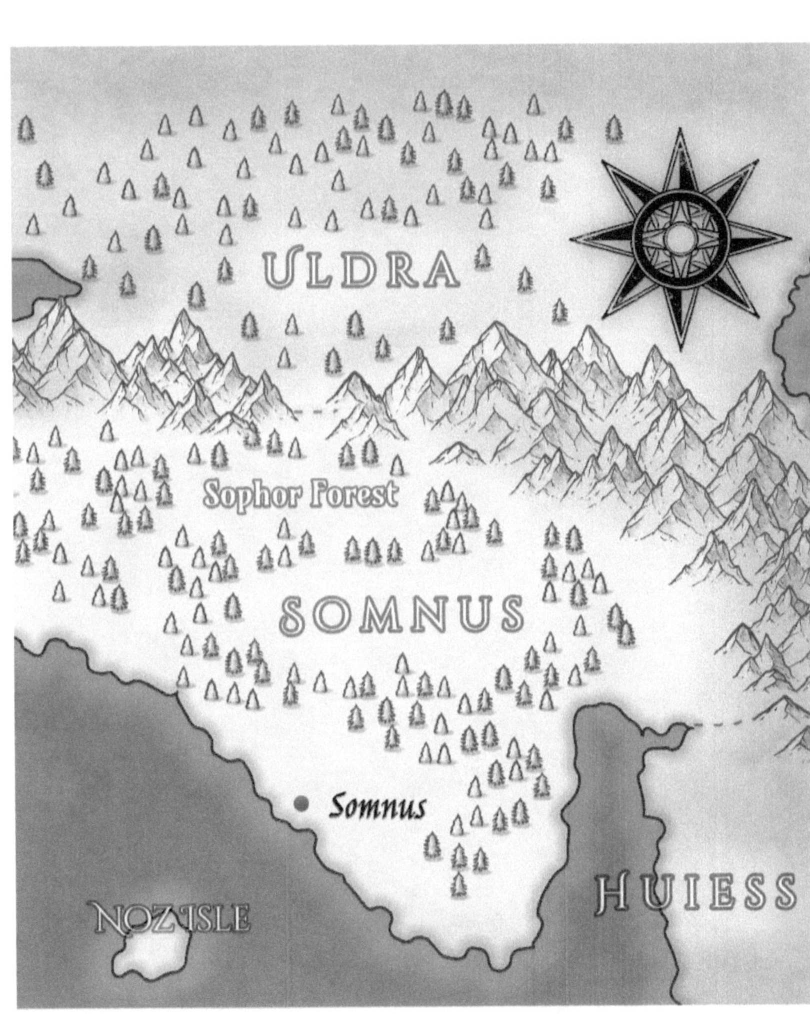

ULDRA
Sophor Forest
SOMNUS
Somnus
NOZISLE
HUIESS

DREAMING BEAUTY

DREAMING PRINCESSES, BOOK 1

C. RAE D'ARC

Chapter 1

I never liked needles. Whether sewing, knitting, mending, or embroidering, I disliked the frustration of stabbing the thread through the eye, the tediousness of weaving back and forth, and the piercing pain of accidental pricks.

All the same, I never expected a single prick from a spindle to be my demise.

Everything was supposed to be perfect for my sixteenth birthday celebration. I had planned the ball and feast down to the napkin folds. From the truffle appetizers to the elaborate fish entrées, from the spring green drapery to the star floral arrangements, and from the dance-worthy music selection to the hour candles to keep the schedule, I organized it all. This event would prove to my father that I could lead, that I could see projects fulfilled, and that I could be like my eldest sister, Garnet.

Garnet and I were physical opposites, making my dreams to be like her almost silly. At twenty years old, she was a female version of Father, the King of Somnus, with her ink black hair, strong and sharp facial features yet motherly figure, a mouth that seemed most comfortable in a cunning smile, and dark brown eyes that could take on the world with all of its challenges and worries. I, however, took after Mother with my round face, sandy blonde hair, emerald green eyes to inspire my name, and features that required emphasis to call them feminine.

Garnet stared suspicious eyes at me, the perfect image of frustration if she wore a frown instead of a teasing smile.

"Emer," she said, "how can you expect me to help you if you lock me out of the ballroom?"

I responded with my cheesiest grin. "Your persistence to help me is precisely why I barred your entrance to the ballroom. Your schedule is busy enough as it is. I expect nothing more of you than to enjoy the celebrations tonight."

Garnet's smile twitched as her eyebrows went high. "Do you realize how backwards this is? Most people wish to be surprised on their birthdays with a festival that was planned for them, not to be the one frantically planning a surprise event for others."

"I know," I said, "but what I want for my birthday is to see you and the others enjoying yourselves."

Garnet pinched her lips tightly, her tired eyes growing sad. "I suppose I will try. Very well. You have full responsibility of this event."

"Perfect." I grinned.

Garnet's joy was my short-term goal for the night. Long term, proving myself worthy to lead could let Garnet and Father give me more responsibilities. Then I could lighten the burdens on Garnet.

She was perfect for someone who was born and bred to someday rule over Somnus, but she was imperfect for someone who had to make hard decisions. I was a personal witness to her love and concerns for our people. I was also a personal witness to her anxiety attacks before festivals and after battle reports.

The only times I saw my eldest sister truly happy were during our secret midnight masquerades. With that in mind, I had planned a masquerade for my birthday celebration.

Garnet sighed in resignation and turned to leave. I watched and waited for her draping red gown with golden embroidery to disappear around the corridor.

Finally.

I ran to the kitchens. The chaos inside mimicked my insides as every chef and baker bustled about, calling orders and services to one another. The heated room smelled of flour, fish, and spices. I skipped around the preparation tables, careful not to dirty my dress or shoes.

My other older sister entered from the castle's side entrance. Aquamarine (known as Marin among friends and family) had Father's black hair and Mother's rounded face that made her look younger than her eighteen years, and her eyes were a green and brown mixture of hazel. She wore her usual outfit for visiting her husband at the docks; a simple surcoat over a tight white shirt. The surcoat had wide arm holes for easy movements and was made elegant by its bright blue color, pink flower embroidery, and a pink sash knotted around her waist.

"Ah, there you are, Emer," she said, gesturing for people behind her to come forward. Her husband—Admiral Ranae Irving of the Somnus Navy—and five muscled dockworkers rolled three large barrels into the kitchen. Rolling those large barrels was no easy feat. I waited by surveying the horned fish entrées, rolled with grains and a thin layer of sealeaves. The men situated the barrels and unstopped a hole to pour a glass of deep purple wine.

My brother-in-law smacked a barrel. "Three barrels of Ormio wine, as requested."

"Perfect," I said, gesturing to the castle cooks to complete the fish entrées with their herbal sauce. I was about to turn away to my next task when Marin's voice caught me.

"Is it perfect?" Marin asked, turning her face away from the dead fish. "So much life taken to serve the hunger of guests who may not even come. I heard that you invited the royalty of Ormio and Huiess, but do you truly think they will come?"

The stress clawed into my stomach, and I whispered back, "Even if the kings and queens refuse to come, the princesses know how to sneak away from their parents as well as you and I. Have hope." Leaning away, I said, "Concerning the fish, there will be stuffed mushrooms for others like you who observe a meatless diet, but what is worse? Killing a few extra fish or insulting a guest by miscounting the dinner plates?"

Marin opened her mouth to answer, but her husband jumped in. "You should not ask questions when you know you will dislike the answer." To Marin, he said, "Come now. Is it time to change into that gown you were dying to show me?"

My sister blushed and gladly took his arm to escort her to their chambers. I smiled, thinking of her beautiful blue-green bliaut with sleeves that draped to the floor. Her transformation between a simple dock lady and extravagant princess always took me by surprise.

I glanced over my own gown. Beshrews. In all my frantic planning for the event, "tattered" described my insides and outsides. My brown dress was rumpled from my day's activities, including a dusting of flour on my bodice. How did that get there? At least my elbow-length blonde hair remained contained in its morning updo. It usually liked to poke free from the bows like birds fleeing the nest.

The sun hovered over the horizon. There were a hundred more items to check off, but guests would arrive any moment. Time to make myself look as perfect as the rest of the evening, as if no sweat or tears were shed behind the curtains.

I dashed from the kitchens to my bedchamber, passing the ballroom.

The servants were still arranging the florals? They were behind schedule. I considered helping, maybe stealing a moment to smell the star tulips, but there was no time to instruct them in the proper hanging of garlands. No time, no time.

Maybe I should have allowed Garnet to help—no. This was my problem, not hers. I would show Father that I was capable of difficult and last-minute decisions. Still, I prayed to the goddess of time that the sun would sink slower, allowing me more time before guests arrived.

I found my two younger sisters, Pearl and Tanzanite, preparing for the celebrations in our shared bedchamber.

Pearl was impossibly beautiful for a fifteen-year-old. She had Father's midnight black hair and Mother's round brown eyes and milky face. On me, I thought the round features made me look overfed. On Pearl, they made her look youthful and innocent. She also had a figure that could wear a potato sack and still turn heads. For all her beauty, however, she was as naïve as a fawn. Some called her the Light of Somnus for her beauty and unsuppressed charity for others.

At twelve years old, Tanzanite was my youngest sister and the youngest princess of Rezhina Valley. My sisters and I called her Tanzi. Her blonde hair was striped with black and her dark green eyes had tones of brown in the right lighting.

As soon as I entered the room, Tanzi jumped from her chair and ran to me.

"Emer!" She cupped her hands around my ear and whispered, "Pearl said something mean to me, so you should look at her and laugh like I said something funny about her."

I leaned back, but instead of laughing, I stared in shock. "Tanzi! How rude!"

First of all, I had a hard time believing that Pearl said anything mean. Second of all, where did Tanzi learn such a trick? Every year, she seemed to grow more and more devious.

She pouted at me. "Beshrews."

Shocked again by her language, I rocked back. At least, I tried to. Tanzi stood on my dress, pulling me off balance. An ugly rip tore through my dress and my heart.

Everything was supposed to be perfect. The brown bliaut gown was the perfect shade to emphasize my green eyes. It was the perfect length to make me look tall and not baggy. It was the perfect fashion of elegance, with a high queen's collar and lace sewn around the openings. I came to my bedchambers hoping to freshen it with a wet rag over the wrinkles and flour dusting. Instead, a rip of twelve centimeters rose from its broken hem.

"Oh," Tanzi said, looking at her accidental alteration. "Oh no! Was this your evening gown?" Her hands went up to her horrified mouth. "Forgive me, I am so sorry! Can we mend it?"

Was there time? I had no other gowns ready. Too late to customize another gown. Too late even to shop for something premade. Too late, too late.

Pearl knelt at my feet to examine the rip. "It may be easy to mend." Turning her eyes to mine, she stood and wrapped her arms around me. "Everything will be alright," she said. "Let it out. Mother says that holding back tears only causes headaches."

Was I crying? It was only a rip. Only a rip in my perfect dress on my perfect day when a hundred other things piled on top of me. I hugged Pearl back, allowing myself a few seconds to breathe and pretend that everything was still perfect.

No time to pretend. No time to breathe.

I squeezed my little sister before stepping back, sniffling and wiping my eyes. I had to be strong. How could I keep Garnet from breaking down if I did too?

"Tanzi," I asked, "will you fetch Elisa to meet me in the weaving room?"

Tanzi nodded and slipped out the door to call on the castle seamstress.

I thanked Pearl and sent a prayer to the goddesses that the rest of my plans stayed above the manure trench. A quick scrubbing removed the flour and smoothed the wrinkles before I ran down the stone stairs.

Midway through a corridor, I spotted an elderly maid with more grey hair than black.

"Elisa!" I called. "Did Tanzi send you?"

The seamstress blinked. "No, Your Highness. I haven't seen Princess Tanzanite."

Grumbling, I beckoned her to follow me anyway. I showed and explained my ripped dress as we walked to the weaving room. Tanzi stepped out just as we arrived.

"Oh!" she said. "You found her! Elisa, Emer needs—"

"I already informed her," I said, hurrying past my sister. "Thank you, Tanzi."

"Do not worry," she said, stepping away. "All is going according to plan." Her attention lingered on me with a curious expression, but I had no time to speculate.

A large loom appropriately took up half of the weaving room. The other half was occupied with washing and dying buckets, filling the room with scents of soap and stagnant water. Our interest was in the corner, where a strick of flax sat beside an empty spinning wheel and a cabinet with dozens of drawers that contained buckles, thread, and snippets of lace and fabric.

Elisa began picking at my dress and pinning the ripped edges together.

"Will it be done in time?" I asked.

"Yes," she said, "as long as there is enough thread on the spinning wheel. Could you grab it for me?"

"Of course," I said, reaching for the bobbin of freshly crafted thread. When the weather forbade me from visiting the gardens, I often came to the weaving room to watch Elisa spin at the wheel. She sang songs to keep her spinning rhythm and wrapped her flax with blue ribbon to symbolize her happy marriage. I had watched her remove the bobbin on occasion, but never tried it myself.

"How do I take it off?"

Elisa spared me less than a glance as she busily picked at the threads of my garment. "Loosen it from the maiden."

Right…what was the maiden? I grabbed at the bobbin and the parts around it, then pulled. Nothing. I pulled harder until the wood cracked and my hand slipped. I grabbed the next closest part of the spinning wheel for support. My finger caught the needle top that was usually covered by unspun flax.

Pain shot through my index finger, jumped up my arm to my heart, then burst to my head and fabric-laced toes.

I fell into a dream and I dreamed of falling. My hair slipped free from its pins to flutter like tongues of flame around my face. Each wild flutter made me want to cry out. My sixteenth birthday was supposed to be perfect with no hairs out of line. The shimmer of my gown dimmed as I fell into nothingness. The force of the fall put me in a fetal position, pushing my lighter legs and arms above me as my back raced towards the ground.

At least, I assumed there was a ground.

All I could see was the tunnel of blackness growing around me as the hole of light shrank to a pinprick, then faded, faded, faded. The darkness swallowed me, yet I continued to fall.

A voice echoed in the blackness. It came from… somewhere. From the light? Or somewhere below? I concentrated on the sound only to recognize my name.

"Emer…"

Only my sisters and close friends called me Emer. My parents called me Emerald, and everyone else called me Princess Reo of Somnus. The harder I listened, the more distant it became. The whisper faded to a thought, then to a memory.

I fell, but surrounded in darkness, I had no perspective to gauge my speed or distance. All I had was the air rushing around me. Eventually, I managed to twist myself to face the rushing air. I continued to drop into darkness as silver dots appeared below. They grew into spots with a sinister shine. A few of the shining dots grew larger and closer. My heart caught as I realized what they were.

They were the points of needles. My pulse quickened. I fell with uncontrollable speed towards the sharp ends of gigantic needles.

I wanted to spread my arms to slow my fall, but I also wanted to curl into a ball to hopefully avoid the needles. I struggled to angle myself away from their stabbing tips. Swimming through the air did nothing to change my position.

With every second that I fell, more and more dots appeared. More spots with sinister shine. There were too many too close together. I could not avoid them. The air rushed faster past me as the needles came closer. My heartbeat hammered in my ears.

A wicked gleam shone on a dozen needles directly below me. Their deadly tips reached for me like teeth. I saw my reflection in them, then shut my eyes, terrified of the impact.

With my eyes squeezed closed, the rushing air around me shifted. It blew from multiple angles and softened.

"Hey," an unfamiliar masculine voice scoffed.

I dared not to move. The needles. Too many needles below. I kept my eyes shut in darkness, tensing for the pain.

"Hey, girl," the man drawled. "You awake?"

What a disrespectful cad.

My eyes snapped open. The needles were gone. Instead of never-ending darkness, I sat on wildflowers beside a dirt pathway, wearing an odd purple chemise

12

that cut below my shoulders and knees. Two men stared down at me from the path. Beyond them, the grassy field dropped to a flat blue horizon.

The men looked about a year or two older than I was. Their long-sleeved tunics, if I could call them such, cropped at their waists and were made of some glossy material. Their heavy boots were likewise made of strange leathers and appeared new and sturdy, despite the amount of mud crusting their thick soles. The packs on their backs were also strange. They had a strap for each arm, rested on the shoulders, and had a variety of outside pockets—one containing an odd tubular waterskin.

One man stood closer to me and captivated my attention. His face was sculpted as if by the goddess of mankind, perfectly chiseled and smooth. Ink-black hair swept along his youthful hairline, and a trimmed beard defined his angular jaw. His eyes were the lightest of blues, like a cloudless day. Staring up at him was like staring at the sun.

"So, she's alive," he said. His baritone voice was warm, and he slurred his words…He was the disrespectful cad?

A corner of his mouth lifted into a devilishly attractive smirk while his eyebrow on the opposite side arched high. He straightened and pulled back a long stick.

Had he been about to prod me with that? The nerve of him!

Before I could accuse him of disrespecting his royal highness and warn him with charges, he turned away to speak with his companion.

"Do you think anyone's searching for her?"

The second man leafed through a booklet. His handsomeness played less with chiseled angles and more with gentleness. He had youthful wide eyes and round cheeks, despite his muscled figure. His dark brown hair had prematurely receded a couple centimeters, and his nose had probably seen better days. His small mouth puckered as he concentrated on the pages.

"She's probably just lost, Caden. Can't blame her, considering these trails."

"Or drunk."

"Excuse me?" I asked the chiseled Caden. "I am not intoxicated." Shuffling to my feet, my little wobble argued my declaration.

Both men stared at me, a little surprised. Caden failed to retain his doubtful smirk.

"Oh yeah?" he asked. "What's your name?"

I frowned. "Are you so lowly that you have never seen depictions of the royal family?"

The two men raised their eyebrows. "Royal?" the second man asked.

I huffed. "I am Princess Emerald, third eldest of Queen Reo, daughter of His Royal Highness, King of Somnus."

The two men shared a quick, wide-eyed glance, then Caden burst into laughter.

He became less and less handsome with each insult.

"Well, welcome to England." He laughed and dropped into a mocking bow. "Now, come on, we'll take you back to town. I'm sure they have some good sobering drinks for you at the pub."

"I am not drunk," I snapped.

"Oh yeah?" he challenged. "Then what's your real name, and where are you?"

"My name is Princess Emerald Reo, and I am…" I looked around myself. Where in Somnus was a well-worn dirt path between sheep fields and a sudden drop to—was that water crashing onto the rocks below? Never before had I seen so much that it stretched to the horizon and curved beyond sight. Considering the men's strange slang and slight blending of words, they reminded me of Uldrans from beyond the valley.

A roar in the sky took my attention to a strange white bird that flew high in the air without flapping its long wings or fish-like tail.

Where was I?

I stumbled as my vision tilted.

"Whoa, there." Caden caught me by my hand and around my back.

"Do not touch me," I commanded, taking a step for balance. Not only was it inappropriate, but also wildly confusing as his muscled arms offered no

15

support or warmth against me. I felt nothing. Nothing felt right.

His hands snapped away. "Pardon. We only mean to help."

"Your help is unnecessary," I said automatically.

The handsome devil shrugged off his worries and spoke to his companion. "Come on, Mica. She says she doesn't need our help."

"And you believe her?" Mica asked. "Miss, you're unsteady. Let us help you into town."

Before I could repeat my independence, Caden scoffed. "So she can scam us? The prettier they are, the bigger the scam. By the looks of her, we'll be asking for alms when she's done with us."

"Excuse—"

"Caden," Mica chided his deceptively handsome friend. "This isn't Paris. She obviously needs help."

Caden rolled his eyes, but did nothing more to persuade his friend one way or the other.

Mica took careful steps towards me, as if I was some feral animal.

"Look," he said with slow enunciation, "we're only trying to help. Let's get you back to town."

Surely, I could make my own way down this path, but what town was it? I had no idea where I was or how I arrived there. As little as I desired their aid, I momentarily depended on their knowledge.

Hoping not to sound like a lunatic, I carefully worded my question, "Where would you take me?"

16

Caden gestured with a nod up the path. "Boscastle."

I knew all of the towns in Somnus. None were named Boscastle. Another confirmation that I was outside my father's kingdom. As if the vast expanse of water and lack of mountains on every side said otherwise.

How did I come here? Had I traveled thousands of kilometers while unconscious?

A worrisome thought returned as Caden offered to help me stand.

"Do not touch me," I said again. Why had I not felt him when he caught me? Why could I not feel the warmth of the sun or the strong breeze that bent the long wildgrass? Why did I feel only a concept of what it should have felt like and…wool blankets? The whole world passed through me as though a dream.

Goddesses above! I was still dreaming!

My vision tilted again as I struggled with the truths I knew. This was a dream. Yet it seemed as real as life. The details of every salty wave, every fresh blade of grass, the dimples in Mica's cheeks and the crispness of Caden's laugh went beyond any dream I ever had. But I felt nothing.

Mica frowned. "Miss, if you don't mind me asking, were you robbed? What do you remember before we found you?"

I remembered falling in darkness, rushing towards a thousand needles. I shuddered.

Mica muttered to Caden, "We can't leave her like this. She's traumatized."

"What do you expect—whoa!"

I collapsed to the ground, losing consciousness within a dream.

Chapter 2

When I regained consciousness, it was still within a dream. This time, I woke in a bedchamber. It was a decent size, with its own fireplace, wardrobe, and writing table. The bed was large enough for Pearl and Tanzi to join me, but its texture was the same as the wool blankets of my own bed in Somnus. I sat up, wearing the same oddly cropped chemise that I had worn at the cliffside. A pair of short boots and stockings were the only items in the room's wardrobe and closet. I put them on, confused that even the leather boots felt like wool. A small water closet joined the bedchamber, too small for a bathtub. Instead, metallic knobs broke through the glossy wall…which also felt like wool. Back in the bed area, I peered out the window, bracing my hand on the wooden sill. More wool. A hillside of wild grasses blocked my view of this strange dreamworld.

Stepping from the bedchamber, I spied through a window that searched the opposite direction. This view showed off the other side of the deep gulley and a creek that flowed through the middle. A quaint village of large and sturdy homes faced the small stream. The buildings were solid enough to be parts of a castle, yet they were each unique, with a variety of maintenance, as if cared for by different people. The stream in the middle was also a bit of a mystery. A couple meters wide, it was shallow enough that its bed rose above the water level in some areas. Its edges were also perfectly straight. Unnaturally so. Was it carved out by people? I knew of no such stream in Somnus. Where was I?

No one else occupied the hallway outside my bedchamber, but the walls were lined with locked doors. What kind of place was this?

I made my way down a grand set of wide and carpeted stairs to what seemed to be an entryway combined with a dining room and lounge area.

The deceptively handsome devil named Caden sat in an armchair in the lounge. He held a small glowing box that went black the moment he saw me.

"Ah, she wakes."

"As it appears," I said, rubbing my eyes. How could I collapse in a dream? How was I still dreaming even as I woke? "Where am I?"

Caden stood and offered me a strange clear bottle of water. There was no cork and the bottle crinkled under my touch. Not glass? It was extra tricky to determine the material when it felt like wool in my hand.

"When you collapsed on us," Caden said, "we brought you here, to Boscastle Cottage. We had the suite booked, and, honestly, we had no idea how to help you. Mrs. Priddy said you just needed rest and liquids. Do you want help with that?" He gestured to the not-glass bottle.

No, I did not want his help, but the odd bottle was a puzzle.

I clenched my jaw and passed it to him. He opened the bottle with a simple twist and crack of the top, then returned it to my hands. The irritating man made it look easy.

Unsure what else to say, I said, "Thank you, Mr. Caden."

"Seaver," he said with a little shuffle. "The Honorable Seaver. My father is Lord Seaver in Parliament. My friend Mica is the son of Lord Wright. You were fortunate that we found you and not someone else."

I scoffed. "As you say it."

"Look, er—" he rubbed the back of his head "—we need to get on the trail again, but I'd like to make sure your needs are met. Do you have any contact information, or way for us to check on you?"

"All I have is my name," I said. Normally, my title was enough to earn respect and basic accommodations. Considering his response the first time I gave my name, I offered my nickname instead. "Emer. Emer Reo of Somnus."

"Emer. Brilliant." He pulled out his small box again that glowed when he touched it. I had never seen such magic before. Magic itself was a lost art in Rezhina Valley. While it was common belief that the valley was created by magical goddesses, their powers of creation had become diluted with every generation until they had disappeared entirely.

Caden was handsome enough to be a descendant of the goddesses. Did he have a power of creation? Then what was the glowing box/tablet/contrivance? No stories mentioned the goddesses using artifacts for their magic.

I tried my best not to look like a wide-eyed lunatic. I knew dreams were strange sometimes, but how had I come up with that bizarre item?

Still fingering his glowing box, Caden asked, "How do you spell your hometown?"

I spelled Somnus for him as he tapped away on his box. His thumbs moved fast enough that I expected he was trained with the device. "Er, is it in England?"

"It is in Rezhina Valley."

His box chirped, and his eyes darted over a quick read. "Hey, Mica's wondering if you're hungry."

I stared at the glowing box. The small magic item worked as both a map and messenger? And a rude devil like Caden could master the tool?

Before I could say anything, my stomach answered Caden's question with a growl. I cringed. How many times would I be humiliated before this man?

Caden grinned and gestured for me to follow him to the elegant dining area with many small round tables covered with white linens.

Several people sat and ate in the room that smelled of butter and pastries. As naked as I felt in my single-layered cropped dress, it seemed that the styles of this kingdom were far more scandalous than any in Rez-hina. Caden wore blue trousers, brown boots with laces, and his strange tunic was unbuttoned to reveal his green undershirt. Another man wore a simple black shirt that featured a morbid picture. The women wore trousers like the men, usually skin tight with holes in strange places. I tugged at my dress again, but accepted the limited modesty this strange dream bestowed me.

We found Mica at the bar, thumbing away on his own glow box. He greeted us with merely a glance away from his device. "Hey. I ordered our food already."

Watching him work with his little box, I could not contain my questions any longer. "Are you two traveling wizards, or are those glowing boxes of yours some other kind of magic?"

Caden slowly turned towards me and blinked. "What?"

"May I ask about your glowing boxes, or are they too sacred to discuss publicly?"

"You mean my phone?" He laughed. "You're trolling me."

I was familiar with trolls—had even met a couple —though I was unfamiliar with the species used as a verb. Hoping to clarify, I asked, "What kind of troll?"

Mica's mouth dropped a little, and Caden gave me an askance look. "Maybe we should take our food outside."

Without confirming with Mica or me, he stepped away to the back door. Mica addressed the barkeep to ask, "Can I get my order to go?"

Still thoroughly confused, I ran after Caden. Once outside, I was surprised to find how large the building was. "What a strange castle," I said. "It has absolutely no fortifications other than its walls."

"That's because it's a hotel," Caden said. "Seriously, you're unreal."

"*I* am unreal?" I balked. "I am the only real thing here."

"I beg your pardon?" Caden guffawed.

"You are only figments of my imagination. Truly, my mind is quite commendable for creating such exquisite details for strange places and irritating people."

"You can't be serious." Caden gaped. "You think I'm the irritating one? Look, even if you are the daughter of a king, being a pretty little princess doesn't excuse you for acting like an upstart."

"Can't I leave you two alone for two seconds?" Mica interrupted.

I consciously stepped away from Caden as he straightened his posture, blinking like his lean towards me had been unconscious. Mica passed each of us an egg, sausage, and cheese sandwich and smirked. "Are you two done huffing and puffing? It's starting to get a little steamy."

What did he mean by that? Based on Caden's angry flustering, I supposed the saying was suggestive.

"She's crazy," Caden said. "She thinks she's dreaming and we're just parts of her brain!"

"Sounds like an interesting story," Mica said.

Caden released a little laugh that was somewhere between unease, incredibility, and suppressed irritation. With a pointed gesture at his friend, he said a firm, "No. No, this isn't the story I've been looking for. Speaking of such, we need to move on if we want to reach Trebarwith Beach before nightfall. Emer—" he offered me a simple wave between his hurried flustering "—it was a pleasure to meet you. If you need anything, Mrs. Priddy is the host of Boscastle Cottage. Warning: she grew up in London and enjoys confusing people with her overdose of cockney. Good day."

With that, he grabbed Mica by the arm and began down the path. What odd men. Most irritating was the fact that they never answered my questions about their strange glowing boxes.

I remained on the back porch of the hotel as I ate my sandwich. The flavors were paradoxical, as if the cooks had added extra spices to make up for the dulled natural flavors.

With Caden and Mica gone, I returned inside to find some answers.

A woman stood as host behind a counter. I approached her, noticing her thinning grey hair cropped as short as a man's, and her wrinkles that could rival a bulldog's. She wore a label on her chest with the name "Mrs. Priddy."

"Day's a-dawning," Mrs. Priddy greeted me with a warm smile. "Good to see you're looking a bit less Terry Maguired than when you arrived. Did you want a tiddlywink or Rosie Lee?"

Sifting through her odd phrases, I said, "Yes, thank you for allowing me to stay the night."

The elderly woman tilted her head sideways like a pup. "No inconvenience on my part since the young lords paid for your stay. They checked out this morning, but hung around like strays, waiting for you to wake. Darling, you were out like a basin o' gravy. They said you mighta hit your lump o' lead."

I struggled to translate. I remembered my fall, but the memory of the vast expanse of water and the two young men felt more dream-like than reality.

"Normally," Mrs. Priddy continued, "I have suspicions of babblin' brooks bringing in women who're nearly needle an' thread, but The Honorable Seaver an' Wright are factually honorable lads. You can't be too careful these days, but I helped them take you up the apple an' pears. I can assure you, they didn't cop a flower pot or pull any penny-come-quicks. Their biggest fault was paying too much for you to stay here."

Understanding only the vague meanings of her words, I said, "That was very kind of them. If you may excuse me, do you have a map?"

"Sure," she said, gesturing to a few different brochures. "Here's one about the hotel, not that it's easy to lose yourself, but we take pride in the history of our establishment. This one's of Boscastle, including some light an' darks, near an' fars, and tourist stops. Here's one for the sheep paths leading to Tintagel."

Based on the lack of mountains, I assumed this dreamland was beyond the valley of my homeland. Or had my mind created another world entirely?

"Do you know which way is Rezhina Valley?" I asked.

"Where? Speak to my good ear." The elderly woman leaned forward with an ear turned.

"Rezhina Valley," I repeated slowly.

Mrs. Priddy shook her head. "I've lived here all my life, but I never heard o' any place called Rezhina. The young lords said you mighta hit your head. What do you remember from before they found you?"

I remembered the needles and shivered.

"Blimey." She reached over the counter and took my hand. Such a familiar action to a princess would be reprimanded in Somnus. But I was too startled by her touch that I froze. Her wrinkly hands felt like the wool of a blanket.

"You take your time," she said. "If you don't make a mess o' things, the young Seaver paid enough for you to stay the week. That should be plenty o' time for you to find your bearings again."

As if my bearings were the only things I had lost.

I wandered around the hotel, amazed by the luxuries of the place. While its purposes resembled the inns of Somnus, the architecture and decorations were closer to my father's castle. Marble columns and archways supported the open rooms with cushioned chairs and couches. The fireplaces were left unlit, but no one shivered in their limited clothing. The candles on the chandeliers burned without smoke nor melting nor flickering, yet they illuminated the rooms like tiny suns. Two types of peculiar harps—one upstanding, the other horizontal on a desk—sat in the main room.

There were many potted plants throughout the hotel. Each plant had a little tab stuck in its pot with its name and care instructions. Clever. I scavenged through the building to find and read about every little plant, fascinated by the types of trees, ferns, and flowers of this dreamworld. No such flowers or trees grew in Somnus, though I wondered if these plants looked differently when thriving with life. Despite their care instructions, many of the indoor plants of Boscastle Cottage were wilted and dried. I snatched a

28

pitcher of water from a dinner table to nourish each of the neglected plants. A cook caught me when I replaced the empty pitcher. He said nothing, but raised a confused eyebrow.

The next morning, I "woke" again to this strange world. What a frustrating surprise. If this world was a dream, why could I not wake up? How could I go to sleep in a dream? Garnet could consciously control her dreams, but try as I did, I could not will my surroundings to change to Somnus or will Caden and Mica to appear and tell me more about their strange magic boxes. I had no control over this dreamworld.

The sense of uncertainty was incredibly irritating.

After breakfast, I grabbed another pitcher to attend the plants again.

"Where d'you think you're going with that?"

I stopped and turned slowly towards the voice, keeping the water leveled. "Mrs. Priddy," I said, "your plants are in dire need of sunlight and water."

Mrs. Priddy gave me a sideways look. "Alright. But if you break or kill anything, it's coming out o' your room and board."

I smiled, certain that I could do no more harm than had already been done to her plants. Sure enough, after a single day's worth of watering, rearranging for best sunlight, and some compliments, the plants around Boscastle Cottage wilted less and sprouted a little greener. Their quick turnaround surprised me, but perhaps that was how plants worked in this dream world.

On my third morning, I woke but remained in bed. Why did this dream continue? What was happening in Somnus? Did I need to accomplish something or help someone else to wake myself?

With a goal in mind, I joined my hostess as she cleared the tables from the residents' breakfast.

"Mrs. Priddy," I said, taking a stack of plates from her, "you need more assistance. You can hardly run this whole establishment without more aid."

Even if Boscastle Cottage was a fifth of the size of my father's castle, we had far fewer residents and ten times as many footmen, maids, cooks, and valets. I was unfamiliar with the general workings of an inn, but surely Mrs. Priddy needed help.

"You already rearranged my plants," she said. "Now you want to lemon squash my dishes? That's not a one-time fix. Just how long do you plan to stay? You didn't come with a crowded space. Are you duck an' diving?"

I clenched my jaw to keep from biting my lip, refusing to show how uncertain her confusing phrases made me feel. "I am unsure what that means, but I will not allow myself to be a burden. I will make myself valuable to you and your estate for as long as I stay."

Mrs. Priddy raised both eyebrows. "You wanna work here?"

I inwardly winced. As much as my father insisted that my sisters and I learn the basics of laborious work—to appreciate our peoples' labors, recognize their skills and capabilities, and understand the markets in our economy—we only shadowed the craftsmen and servants for a day or two. "Working" at Boscastle Cottage would require much more than simply caring for her plants. If I wanted to stay in control of my labors, then I had to suggest them myself.

"I may be your gardener," I said. Of all the labors I had learned, I enjoyed gardening the most. After my days of shadowing the gardeners, I continued to wander among the fruits of their labors, asking questions about how they created such beautiful landscapes and the temperament of various plants. "I know a fair bit about plants and agriculture," I continued. "I will continue to care for your indoor plants, though I offer my assistance to develop your grounds as well. The grass is dying in spots, and I can make a flower bed."

Mrs. Priddy's raised eyebrows went higher. "Our grass isn't dying, it's just got male-patterned baldness. We only have a Lord Lovel and grass trimmer for gardening."

"I can do it," I said. I had no idea who or what Lord Lovel was, but all I needed was a hoe and some seeds. Their grounds consisted of nothing but stretches of grass. Adding a flower bed would be simple enough.

Mrs. Priddy directed me to a room with several large white metal boxes and a small collection of gardening tools, including a shovel and a strange machine with long handles and rotating blades. Simply learning how to use the grass trimmer took most of the afternoon. I went to bed that evening half hoping this dream would end and I would never need to work the strange device.

When morning broke, I sighed but dressed in the purple chemise that barely covered my shoulders and knees, as if I had any other option, then headed down to begin work. The morning air left frost on the grass, though I felt no chill or wet dew brushing against my ankles. Only wool.

First things first, I surveyed the ground and what I had to work with. There was a strange satisfaction in claiming my own project. It would thrive or die by my hand and my hand alone. If only Father could see my work and understand that this little garden could represent what I could do with our people.

If only I could wake up and talk to him again. I shook my head to clear the wistful aspirations. Apparently, I could daydream within a dream.

Chapter 3

I walked all the way around the hotel, imagining different plants at every corner and entryway. With ideas in mind, I took my next big step in immersing myself into this dream world. I headed up the hillside towards town.

Without money, I simply looked around and surveyed the town. Instead of horses and carriages, the roads were occupied with strange enclosed vehicles on four wheels and people sitting on narrow contraptions with two wheels. Instead of a designated market with stalls, the main road was lined with buildings for established businesses. Boscastle was a nice place with everything a fisherman, sheep herder, or traveler could need. I crossed no dedicated flower businesses, but I barely skimmed the town's amenities.

What I really wanted was the wild flowers I had spotted during my stroll. I found them again, standing high with yellow petals and white seeds like little balls of fascination. Picking a few with their roots intact, I carried them back to the hotel. I analyzed their roots to gauge how deep to dig, then began my excavation at the hotel's front entrance.

They had good sunlight, and I made sure to water them properly. I even talked idly to them as I made a meter wide bed from the hotel. By the end of my first day, I had half of the front wall dug out, and the little planted wildflowers looked settled into their new home.

Mrs. Priddy stepped out to observe my work. "What the blazes are you doing?"

I twisted on my hands and knees, surprised. "I cleared the area for a garden."

"And you planted *dandelions*? Nobody *plants* dandelions!"

"Why not?" I asked. "They have bright colors and multiple stages of growth to add variety."

"And they explode like Derry and Toms. Take those out. Here's ten quid. Go buy some proper early hours like pansies or something that's hard to kill and takes fisherman's daughter with the pleasure and pain. I don't want them needle and thread the moment you go short of a sheet."

I frowned. Piecing together her tone and bits of phrases, I figured she wanted something that survived my absence. Fair enough. Who knew if I would be around by next season? She handed me a bank note with beautiful art and the number ten on it.

A little miffed that she disliked my flower choice, I dug them out. Even if they were wildflowers, it saddened me to toss them away. Going through the rubbish bin, I found a small container made of the strange material that this dream world called plastic. Poking some holes in the bottom, I replanted my first little flowers in the cup, then took them upstairs to my room.

At dinner time, Mrs. Priddy tried to wrangle me into helping the cooks. They kicked me out for "safety precautions" after I made the mistake of grabbing the strange coils that they called a stovetop. All I felt was wool. Only when they screamed at me to let go did I notice the blistering burns on my left palm. My brain played catch up and triggered memories of burns to make the image less jarring. Ouch.

Determined to make myself useful, I instead played on the upstanding harp for diners. My fingers were limited due to the bandages on my left hand, but I managed the melodies. In Somnus, I had performed a couple times for Mother and guests, though never on a harp with so many strings. These guests seemed to appreciate my simple tunes, sometimes asking for their titles or wondering if I wrote them. It seemed that no one in this dream world knew the songs of Somnus. How tragic.

The next day, I went to the town again and found a little flower shop. They had more arranged bouquets for lovers than seeds, but I managed to purchase pansies as Mrs. Priddy suggested.

Mrs. Priddy scolded me again for digging too deep next to the hotel, worried that I would hit piping. I then peppered her with questions about their strange pipes that ran under the ground to transport their water, sewage, and other luxuries.

Fascinating. If I could only wake up and suggest these methods to my father.

I slowly learned my way around the hotel, with its strange rooms and stranger customs. I noticed more people carrying those glowing handheld devices like Caden and Mica. Guests entered with them, pointing and studying them as they asked about directions, nearby places to eat, and various facts about the area.

Eventually, I asked Mrs. Priddy about the peculiar devices.

"You mean my dog?"

I blinked. "How did you turn your furry loyal animal into a glowing brick?"

Mrs. Priddy laughed. "Here's a lump of ice: learn some cockney. It's slang for phone."

"Then it is not your hunting or shepherding companion?" I asked.

She laughed again. "No, but I love my phone and take it everywhere with me just as a dog loves his bone. Phone and bone rhyme, turning the phone into a dog."

"Clear as mud," I muttered. "What is a phone?"

Despite all my efforts to appear sane in this strange world of quick-growing plants, that simple question rewrote Mrs. Priddy's understanding of my background.

"Oh, oh dear," she flustered. "Maybe that explains why I couldn't find your eastern foam. Somnia must be very remote."

"Somnus," I corrected. "Where might I acquire my own phone?"

"You can buy one online—you can borrow the hotel computer. For heaven's sake, you don't know what a phone is. Do you know what a computer is?"

"Something that computes?" I guessed.

"Oh, dear." Mrs. Priddy wrung her hands and glanced around for help. "The Honorables didn't say you were a Luddite. Are you anti-technology, or just a lump of school?"

I was unsure how to answer that. She said that she loved her phone, and I did not want to offend her. "I thought your phones were magical."

"Oh." Mrs. Priddy's shoulders relaxed. She then took on the responsibility of teaching me everything she knew about computers, which she admitted was minimal. Not to mention many of her explanations became lost in translation between her strange phrases. What I eventually understood, I still doubted. Their strange little phones and computers shared information across the world in the blink of an eye? Yet she insisted it was without magic. How?

We spent the next few days that way. I gardened in the mornings, spent time with Mrs. Priddy learning about this dream world's technology, then played the harp during dinner. When I laid down at night, I dreamt of memories—of Somnus, the people, my friends, but especially my sisters. Every time that I "woke," it was to this world of sloping green fields that dropped into the endless water. Sometimes, I lay in bed for a few extra minutes, trying and failing to return to sleep and my memories of Somnus. There was also a hint at the edge of my waking thoughts each morning that only a magical place would wake me. Whatever that meant.

Mrs. Priddy gave me another bank note to buy myself a second garment from town. I chose a light yellow "maxi dress" that went down to my ankles, perfect for changing into after gardening and stretchy enough to play around the upstanding harp. When Mrs. Priddy saw me working barefoot in the developing garden, she lent me a pair of her own slippers. They were pink, small, and worn, but dependable.

I accomplished the task of removing the dead tips and returning through the side entryway when masculine voices echoed around the hallway. I stopped and hid behind Arthur, a potted tree with large leaves who had showed a great deal of improvement since I moved him closer to the window. I recognized the voices, somehow keenly aware of the lower, warmer voice beside the playful lighter voice. They were the first voices that had greeted me in this strange dream world almost two weeks ago.

The low and warm voice said, "We heard you've employed the young runaway we brought last week? I think her name is Emer?"

"Honorable Seaver," Mrs. Priddy said, "you brought me a force o' nature with that one."

"What do you mean?"

"She's as a yet-to-be storm. Unpredictable, stubborn an' unyielding, yet an expert o' arrangements an' getting things done. There's also a strange mood about her that makes people both terrified an' awed at her at the same time."

The playful voice whispered loudly, "Maybe she's royalty after all."

I stepped around my hiding place and walked into the room.

"Ah, here she is," Mrs. Priddy waved me forward. "Emer, darling. You remember these men?"

"Of course," I said. How could I forget the chiseled devil and his minion?

"Emer?" the devil asked. "It's good to see you're doing better."

Mica, the playful minion, stepped forward to whisper, "I think you've inspired him. He's been distracted ever since we left you here. He even sharpened his razor of wit a little."

Caden's neck burned red. How appropriate for a devil. "I just switched out the blades a little."

Mica scoffed. "Yeah, you were definitely using those one-time-use disposable razors before."

"Mrs. Priddy," I said, interrupting their confusing banter, "give me an audience alone with these men."

Mrs. Priddy scoffed and whispered loudly to Mica, "See my meaning? She bosses me around with the manners of a once a week."

Shaking her head, she left us alone in the entry-way.

As soon as she turned the corner, Caden started, "I see you've made—"

"What is this nonsense about me being a runaway?" I demanded.

"Oh?" He raised an eyebrow. "Did you remember your real home, or are you still pretending that this whole world is only a dream?"

"It is a dream," I said. "Everything I touch is wool like the blankets of my bed. As I told you when we first met, I am Princess Emerald Reo of Som—"

"Yeah, about that," he cut me off. "Your land doesn't exist, even in the past, and I highly doubt you're from the future. Not even Google recognizes your fabled land, and that's saying something."

"Yes, Mrs. Priddy told me a little about Google. Who is this Google, and why does everyone presume he knows everything?"

"Confirmed," Caden said. "You're either a cert-ifiable lunatic who needs serious medical help, or you're a runaway making things up. Assuming that you didn't want to be locked in a white cell, I told Mrs. Priddy the runaway story."

"I am *not* a runaway," I said through clenched teeth. "My father is a king and is probably furiously worried about me, wondering why I refuse to wake or if I am dead while I labor as a gardener among these exotic plants, helping them to grow strong and fulfill their potential while I sit cooped and trapped—"

"Caden—Caden!" Mica tapped his friend with quivering hands, then pointed over my shoulder.

Caden jumped back as his eyes imitated Mica's wide stare. "What the—"

Turning around, I jumped too. The tree behind me moved. Arthur's limbs stretched forward, reaching for me like a snake looking for a place to rest.

I stood still as Arthur's branches grew an extra five centimeters to slide up my cheek with a fond caress. While I knew that the plants grew faster in England than in Somnus, the tree's reaction to my distress was almost…thoughtful.

"What on Earth is going on?" Caden shouted.

I stared at the plant, unsure what to say to the men. Instead, I apologized to the plant. "Forgive me, Arthur, if I caused you any distress."

The men gaped.

"Has this happened before?" Mica asked.

"Not to this extent. The pansies have bloomed faster for me when I felt lonely, and the lavender flowers smelled more potent when I struggled to sleep the other night."

"Whoa, hold on." Caden raised a hand to slow me down. "What's really going on here?"

I shrugged. "Is this not how all of your plants react in this world?"

Mica shook his head, and a slow grin grew on his face.

"Mica," his friend scolded. "I know what you're thinking. Tone it down. Emer, if this is a trick, it isn't funny."

I scoffed. "If someone is using their magic to make my plants listen to me, they are a master of subtlety and wasting their talents."

"Magic," Caden said without emotion.

"Magic?" Mica asked, nearly breathless and swelling with bridled excitement. "Caden, she has magic in her world. She thought we were wizards. She asked us about trolls. Do you know what this means?"

"Calm down." Caden hushed his friend, then asked me, "Can you make them grow again?"

"They grow on their own. What influence can I have other than to care for them?"

"It reacted to your words and emotions. It was definitely you."

"Perhaps Arthur is special?" I offered. "Your world has a remarkable variety of plants."

"Alright," Caden agreed. "Let's test it with another plant. Mrs. Priddy said you've been planting a garden around the hotel. Let's try our theory with those."

42

We stepped out to the little garden where I showed them my little pansies.

"I thought the plants simply grew faster in this strange dream," I said. "I planted these flowers only a few days ago."

"They don't look very big," Caden said.

I frowned back at him. "I planted them as seeds, your lordship."

He raised an eyebrow at that. Did he question my slight mockery of his status or my truth about planting these flowers only a couple days ago?

"Alright," Mica said, rubbing his hands together. "Show us what you can do."

"All I do is talk to them," I said, kneeling beside my little plot of pansies. Did they need water? Usually, I tested the soil with my finger, except the beshrewing wool kept me from feeling any dampness.

"Then talk to them again," Caden said, "because what happened in the entryway was not normal."

I huffed. How was I to know what was "normal" in this dream world? Unsure more than ever, I turned back to the healthy garden beside me. "Hello again. These young men want me to talk to you."

Nothing happened.

"Put some emotion into it," Mica suggested, "like you did with the tree. Encourage it to grow."

As much as I wanted to demand that he not tell me what to do, his boyish excitement and smiling attention were difficult to disappoint.

"Little garden," I said, "will you grow for me? Please?"

Again, nothing happened. So it seemed. The growth crawled millimeter by millimeter. I pointed out the growth, but Caden frowned with doubt. Mica yelped, noticing the little blooming flowers, branching out for more buds. Grass poked between the flowers.

"Oh," I said. "Little grass, this section is ill fit for you. Would you mind pulling back and blooming all the more lovely in your section?"

The men stared as the grass slowly shrank back into the ground, then the surrounding grass brightened its shade of green.

"That," Mica said, "was awesome!"

Caden and I frowned.

I asked, "If your glowing boxes respond to your words, why would your plants be any different?"

"Because," Caden mumbled, "plants aren't programmed."

"Let me get this straight," Mica said, "you're a magical princess from another land, and you're trying to wake up?"

"I have said as much."

Mica turned to Caden with an excited grin.

"Mica, no."

"But what if this is it? We came out here looking for adventure. What greater adventure is there than rescuing a princess?"

Caden fumed. "She's an acting opportunist!"

"I am not a liar," I argued. "Simply not of this world. I seem to be in a deep sleep."

Mica, however, continued to grin at me with wild wonder. Apparently, Caden was not excited enough, and Mica poked his friend insistently, as if to stab him with energy. "Caden—Caden!"

"What—would you stop that?" Caden slapped his friend's hand away.

"But this is it! This is the adventure we were looking for!"

"No," Caden snapped. "This is a trick. I don't care how pretty she is, she's crazy as King George and pulling one over on us."

I blinked, surprised to be called *pretty* and *crazy* in the same breath.

"Come on!" Mica urged his friend. "She's a magical princess who's lost her way home! Can you spell 'adventure' any more clearly? How much more obvious can it be? It's just like one of your books!"

"Maybe it's too obvious," Caden argued. "Someone's duping us. How many people know about our trip? With all those pictures you've posted on social media, any number of our friends could have arranged this."

"Excuse me," I said. "Would you please explain yourselves? Mrs. Priddy said you are sons of lords. Yet you say you are seeking adventures. Do you have no duties or obligations to your fathers or to lordship?"

Mica shuffled uneasily, and Caden rubbed the back of his head. "Being a lord doesn't mean the same thing it used to. Besides, being a lord is my father's dream job, not mine."

I frowned. "What do you mean?"

Mica answered, "He's a dreamer who thinks he can be a bard instead of getting a real job like the rest of us."

"Dare you to say that to J.K. Rowling," Caden retorted with a little shove. "Besides, an author isn't the same as a bard. I don't sing. And you're one to talk, Mr. Photographer."

"That's a hobby," Mica said, resting a hand on a strange device hanging around his neck like a black millstone. "I don't have delusions about earning a living with my camera."

Caden grinned. "Yet here you are, seeking stories and new sights in Boscastle instead of studying law and history in London."

"I'm just saying," Mica said, "that our trip is almost over and you still haven't found your muse. Now a *magical princess* needs our help, and you say no?"

I folded my arms, still confused. "Saying that I 'need' your help to wake myself is a hyperbole. Why would I need the help from someone who refuses to accept their duties? You have the opportunity to lead, yet you throw it away to chase dreams? Then, to top it all, you think to take advantage of my lost state by turning my situation into some profitable product?"

Everything about Caden infuriated me. How dare he throw away the opportunities I scrambled for? How dare he use my helplessness for his own selfish desires? How dare he look so handsome even as he frowned?

He turned his frown on me. "You obviously don't understand the burden of expectations. Can't say I'm surprised. Mrs. Priddy said you're a luddite and as lost as an unmarked sheep. If you honestly wanted to return home, then you'd be begging us to help you and bring you along."

My hands went to my hips. "Does that mean you *can* help me back to Somnus?"

Caden and Mica responded at the same time.

"No."

"Yes!"

Mica pouted at his friend. "Even if it is a prank, what harm could it do? We go on a silly adventure—like we wanted—and laugh about it over drinks when it's all over."

Caden set his jaw as his eyes bounced between Mica and me. "Fine."

"Yes!" Mica said with two bouncing fists.

"Only if," Caden added with a point, "we have her permission in writing. I won't allow any mis-construed notions of abduction if she joins us."

I raised my eyebrows. "You are right to assume that I am fully capable of drafting a contract. I am now sixteen years old and accountable for myself—"

"You're only sixteen?" Caden did a double take. "Er, you look older."

"I beg your pardon!" My mouth dropped open in offense. Mica frowned in confusion while Caden shrank with an embarrassed little cough. "I admit, I have passed my time of accountability, yet my birthday ball was meant to introduce me to potential suitors. Princes from all over the valley and beyond were coming to call on me."

Mica slurred out a confused sound. The red around Caden's neck spread up his face, and he held up his hands to stop me.

"Whoa, alright. I'm sorry. I meant it as a compliment. Sixteen is still considered a minor in our society. Blast, it's a good thing we didn't take you to the hospital or anywhere without multiple witnesses."

"Emer," Mica asked, "what's the life expectancy in Somnus? How old do you expect to live?"

I frowned at his random question. "About sixty harvests, supposing one survives their first seven. Why?"

"Ah," Caden said, his face cooling. "Right. See, Mica and I expect to live at least eighty. With our technology and medicine, that's normal for our society. It also means that we have more time for growing and maturity. Our age of majority is eighteen, which makes you a minor."

I gaped. What a marvel to lengthen their lifespans!

Mica fingered his chin in thought. "Even if you're new here, is there anyone you could consider a guardian to sign off this adventure? Maybe Mrs. Priddy?"

"I suppose she is my employer," I said. When Caden raised an eyebrow, I explained, "Unofficially."

The men followed me through Boscastle Cottage to find Mrs. Priddy.

"You're leaving already?" she asked. "Should'a known not to hire a tenant. Now you're leaving me Jack Jones. Do you need some sausage an' mash before you hit the frog an' toad? You earned a couple days' worth if you need to hit the cab rank."

I never knew words could be so confusing.

Thankfully, Mica picked up the translation. "Yes, we'll be off to help Emer find her home, so she's unlikely to return." Turning to me, he asked, "Would you like your paycheck in bank notes?"

"If possible, yes," I said. "Thank you, Mrs. Priddy. Your generosity is unparalleled in this land."

Mrs. Priddy went behind her counter to withdraw a single bill with one hundred on it. "That should do it. Go buy yourself some more clothes. That dress needs a lemon squash."

I looked over my cropped purple dress to guess her meaning. No idea. Unsure how to respond, I gave her a thankful smile.

Mica beamed. After a little huff, Caden blessed me with a grin that faded before reaching his irritated eyes. "Consider us your tour guides. Where to, princess?"

Chapter 4

I opened my mouth, thinking to ask again about finding my homeland. Except they were unable to find it with their highly technological boxes. The only way to return home was probably to wake myself. Maybe there was something I needed to accomplish or some place I needed to go to end this dream. The fleeting memory of my morning thoughts said I needed a magical place to wake me. Either way, I needed to know more about this world.

Straightening my back and shoulders, I made my first request to the young men. "If Somnus is not within riding distance, then perhaps I may travel there by magic. Do you know of any witches who live nearby? Or perhaps there is a place especially known for breaking spells?"

Caden groaned and slid a hand down his face. Mica grinned all the more.

"I don't know about witches, but maybe St. Michael's Mount could interest Your Highness."

Caden snorted, a jarring sound to come from such a dignified face. "Are you cutting our backpacking trip short? I'm not walking all the way to Penzance."

"Don't be ridiculous," Mica scoffed. "We wouldn't make it there before your party. Call up your driver. We set off on foot to find an adventure. Now that we have our adventure, we can drive."

Caden grunted. "Miles has been shadowing us this whole trip. He shouldn't be far."

He made his mobile glow again and lifted it to his ear. After a quick greeting, he smirked.

"Don't play dumb with me, Miles. I know my mother had you follow us in case we did anything truly stupid. We need a lift to Penzance."

When he hung up, he scoffed. "He'll be here in five minutes. Go figure."

Shortly after, one of those strange horseless carriages that Mrs. Priddy called automobiles stopped in front of us. This one was particularly shiny and black. A man in a crisp black and white outfit stepped from the carriage and opened the back doors for us. He was middle-aged—by Somnus's standards. According to Caden and Mica, thirty-or-so harvests was still young. He walked with a slight limp, and an unfortunate scar marred the right side of his serious face. He greeted Caden with a bow and said, "Young Master."

With no explanation, Caden offered to help me into the carriage. "The drive's an hour and a half, so get comfortable."

My hand rested in his, though I felt only an impression of wool. I stepped inside, amazed by its luxurious seating.

I wished that I could sense the cushions and leather materials. Just how rich were the lords in this world? These carriage seats could rival the comfort of my father's throne. I stared out the window as the road passed by with blurring speeds. I was unable to soak in the beautiful countryside of this world. The vehicle drove faster than even the Sesso horses. Maybe Ormytha's unicorn could give it competition. Maybe.

The carriage also had temperature control. All this without magic? I thought it was impossible, but Mica began to describe an overwhelming scientific process. My sister Marin might have understood more than I did. Caden quietly took notes each time I asked how their world worked. Each time I pestered him to know what his notes said, he frowned and threatened to drop me off the side of the road. I would rather keep my questions to myself than give him the satisfaction of teasing me with his notes.

I huffed and stared out the window at the zipping scenery. We passed fields of sheep, sprawling towns, and narrow roads framed with arching trees.

I focused my eyes outside and my ears on the two men across from me. They nudged each other with quiet shuffles and grunts. That particular dialect of men was lost on me.

Eventually, Caden sighed, then cleared his throat.

"So, princess," he said, twisting the cap off of his translucent water flask, "what do you think of England?"

"The towns are beautiful," I said. "You have so much space."

Caden sputtered on his drink. "What?"

Mica smirked at his friend. "Give her a break. She hasn't seen London or its suburbs."

"Somnus is one of three kingdoms in a single valley," I said. "With the mountains surrounding us and the lake and rivers separating us, we have no space to grow. We have little room to farm and raise livestock, and keeping the water stocked for fishing is a struggle." My voice drifted as I thought of the lake, the fish, and my sister Marin, who loved both.

Caden tilted his head and his eyes blurred as if he stared into a space no one else could see. "What about beyond the mountains?" he asked.

I shrugged. "We send trappers and explorers, though little is known about Uldra and the other kingdoms beyond our valley. The most fearsome rumors return to us about malicious ogres and nobles with powerful magic. Nothing like the magic this world seems to possess."

Caden's gaze remained unfocused as he withdrew his little notebook and pen from his coat pocket.

"What are you writing this time?" I asked, curious. Caden said nothing, and Mica smirked.

"See?" Mica asked his friend. "Aren't you glad we picked her up?"

Caden continued to ignore us and scribble in his little notebook.

"Is he alright?" I asked.

"No," Mica chuckled. "He has a terrible ailment of the mind called 'author.' He writes fantasy books. Do you have those in your world?"

I pondered. "Books about imaginative worlds and impossible situations?"

"Sure," Mica said. "He finished a series and felt lost about where to go next. He wanted to start a new series, but didn't have the first idea where to begin."

"I had lots of ideas," Caden muttered, still absorbed by his notes.

Mica snorted. "But nothing that made you *want* to write. So we went on an adventure to be inspired."

I raised my eyebrows. "You were in Boscastle looking for inspiration for a fantasy?"

Mica nodded. "Writers get to do odd things and call it work."

Caden smirked back. "On the outside, it isn't much different from what my father does as a lord in Parliament. Research my brains out, stare into empty space, write like mad, then try to network my words into making a difference."

"True, true," Mica laughed. "Either way, Caden felt choked in the bustle of London. We needed a holiday. So we planned a backpacking trip along the coastline and the setting for the legendary King Arthur, Knights of the Round Table, and Merlin. We even considered camping in the Sherwood Forest next week if this venture failed to inspire him. As it is—" Mica gestured to Caden as the writer flipped another page in his notebook to expand his thoughts. "I think he already found his muse." Leaning towards me, Mica mouthed a clear "Thank you."

I smirked. "Do you dislike camping?"

Mica's eyes bulged as his head vibrated side to side. Then his smile broke free.

"Well," I said, smiling back. "I am glad we can help each other then."

Our vehicle slowed as we reached another city along a completely different shoreline. Where Boscastle had been a small town on the edge of rocky cliffs and the mouth of a narrow river, this new town spread against a long and sloped beach.

Mica reached over to tap Caden's knee. "Hey, we're here. Should we stop for lunch first?"

Caden's stomach answered for him. Reluctantly, he pocketed his pen and notebook. "I could go for a pastry right now."

"Excellent!" Mica pressed one of the many buttons on the door. "Miles, we'd like to stop for lunch in

Penzance. Do you know of any good places for Cornish pasties?"

The funny carriage stopped, and the driver came to open our door. Mica stepped out first, then Caden. The first nudged the latter, then gestured to me. Rolling his eyes, Caden reached back into the vehicle to assist me.

"Thank you," I said, surprised. I placed my hand in his, though felt only wool blankets as I raised myself from the deep seat. I misjudged the distance when stepping from the low carriage and nearly fell back. Caden caught me with an arm at my waist, stepping close to pull me up. Still a little wobbly on my own two feet, I found my balance, then found my attention on Caden standing close enough to embrace. His blue eyes met my green as he helped steady me. His nearness gave my knees a new reason to wobble. He was far too handsome for his own good.

"Are you alright?" he asked, his voice a little husky.

My own voice came out more airy than usual. "Yes, thanks."

He stepped back to a proper distance as Mica gave us a gracious bow.

"Welcome to Penzance," he said. "A city most famous for its pirates, and just a hop, skip, and jump away from St. Michael's Mount."

I watched for him to hop, skip, and jump like a secret passageway, but he walked normally.

Apparently, it had been a figure of speech. I asked, "What is so special about St. Michael's Mount?"

"What's so special?" Caden repeated. "Not only is it a historical castle with botanical gardens, but it's a place of folklore galore. Legend has it as the place where the giants lived that Jack slew. Crossing over is a trick of its own, as it changes with the tides."

Mica tapped away at his phone again as if looking up a magic spell. "Ah, we're in luck," he said. "The tide's out. We can walk over, but we'll need to boat back if we're there longer than an hour."

Caden smirked. "You can't set a time expectation for adventures. We spent over an hour to get here, we might as well spend twice that to make it worth the drive. Miles, could you arrange a return trip?"

"Yes, m'lord."

"First," Mica said, "let's eat. I'm starving, and if we're in Cornwall, I want a Cornish pasty."

We picked up some delicious pastries with meat and cream filling, then wandered towards the docks. The men found a bench to sit while they ate, and I stood at the dock railing. A large ship with red sails drifted by, and great ships floated in the distance like little islands, proving the great expanse of the water. I truly wondered how I could dream of such a landscape when no such sights existed in Rezhina. The greatest body of water I knew was our Imazhin Lake. Yet this seascape stretched on, with no end in sight.

Caden joined me to lean against the railing.

"How far does the water go?" I asked.

"From here? Not that far. If you go south-east, the narrowest point of the English Channel is about thirty-five kilometers. Athletes like to swim across it. From here, though, if you look directly south—" he pointed and leaned closer to my perspective, bringing a desirable scent with him "—you'd run into Spain. Then the Americas are somewhere across the pond."

"Pond?" I asked incredulously.

"Sorry, that's slang. It's an ocean. Takes a few hours to cross even by plane."

I asked, "Plane?"

"Airplane," he said, as if that would explain everything. I was fairly certain that Mrs. Priddy defined those as the giant birds that roared across the sky, though I had hoped for Caden's confirmation. I huffed when he said nothing more. Insufferable man.

He did, however, take my rubbish to the bin for me. One mark for courtesy against…I had lost count.

Mica led us back to the automobile to drive a little farther. We probably could have walked, considering the short ride. Mica helped me from my seat that time, and I found my footing more easily.

We walked down a long sandy beach. A brick pathway stretched between the beach and St. Michael's Mount. Even from a distance, I could tell the island was unique and magical. A beautiful castle sat atop the mount, surrounded by greenery. It was like a little piece of home in the middle of the vastly unfamiliar ocean. Caden explained how the pathway was only available during low tide. Amazing, how oceans could move so much in so little time.

We began our tour of the island with the gardens. Mica happily pointed out the Giant's Well, and another sign labeled as "Giant's Heart."

"Giants?" I asked. "You have giants in this world?"

"Probably not in the way you're thinking," Caden said.

We wandered up the battlements, passing several dusty cannons that looked unused for decades.

"This is a time of peace?" I asked the men.

Caden shrugged. "For the most part. There are always wars going on, revolutions, and riots, but we don't use cannons anymore. This place hasn't been tainted by war in a long time."

"Like Noz Isle," I said. Despite the disputes and battles between Rezhina's three kingdoms, the island in the middle of Lake Imazhin was neutral ground. That was why they held the midnight masquerades, and how my sisters and I became friends with the daughters of our parents' enemies.

After a short jaunt through the castle, we came to the back gardens that were sculpted like my hair for a festival and packed with beautiful and unique plants. Mica paused to take pictures of a variety of purple flowers, each one completely different from the next. Then he became fascinated by a variety of white flowers and an odd stalk that stretched as high as a tree.

60

How imaginative could this dream be? St. Michael's Mount might have looked like a slice of Somnus from a distance, but each plant and flower was beyond anything I knew. Even Caden seemed amazed by the place. More than once, he pulled out a notebook to sketch a flower and scribble a note.

"Are you feeling inspired?" Mica asked his friend.

"Hush," Caden said. "I don't want to lose this thought."

Mica chuckled and leaned over to me. "Take that as a yes."

When Caden finished his thought, he shifted towards me and tapped his notebook. "So, you can make plants grow. What else can you do?"

"I cannot say," I said. "As you saw, I was unaware that I was influencing the plants until we tested it. I am unsure if it was just the plants around the hotel, or a power of my own."

Caden smirked. His face should have been outlawed for looking handsome while he mocked me. "Nothing about that hotel is magical, believe me. Mrs. Priddy confirmed she's never experienced any oddities with her plants, and she's never heard anything from her guests. Knowing the eccentric kinds of guests she gets, she would have heard. So that leaves us with you."

"Emer," Mica said, "are there others like you in your world? Others who can control or affect plants?"

"No," I said. "There are rumors of people who can wield magic from far beyond our valley, but magic is lost in Rezhina. It is a marvel that my eldest sister can perform a sleeping drought."

Caden grunted. "So we can't even guess what else you can do based on the powers of others."

"Did you say a sleeping drought?" Mica asked. "Could she be the reason you're sleeping and can't wake up?"

I gasped. The mere suggestion from anyone outside of the royal family would be treasonous. But...it was possible. "I had not thought of that before," I said. "For what reason would my sister put me to sleep though? She has only ever used it to help us rest after fitful days or on guards stationed outside our bedchambers. A harmless prank, at most."

Caden jotted down a few notes and leaned forward. "She's your eldest sister? So, she didn't put you to sleep to take your position as heir or anything?"

"No," I said. "She is the natural heir to my father's kingdom."

"She could still feel threatened by you," Caden said.

I had no response to that as the possibility sank with a queasy feeling in my gut. As hard as I worked to prove myself as a capable leader, I never meant to replace Garnet. Did Father think otherwise? Did Garnet?

"If she did," I said, "she hid her animosity towards me. She was kind as always."

Caden gave me a knowing look. "People can surprise you."

Chapter 5

We continued our tour inside of the castle, which seemed…fake. As if someone had taken my home and played House. The furniture was wrong and even the wash bin seemed more decorative than functional. This castle was beautiful, but it was no home.

Even more befuddling was the way the tour guides spoke of the castle. Everything was referenced as hundreds—sometimes thousands—of years ago.

What a strange dream of some far-off future, where people used glowing boxes for everything, and they only theorized about the intricacies of castle life.

Mica lingered in a hallway with glass-covered pictures and more hanging shields than one family could ever need. Mica rotated slowly around the room with his glow box, then pointed his larger camera at various objects and angles. As much as I wanted to ask what he was doing, his wide eyes and pursed lips said that he was concentrating and too busy to be bothered. Caden also had a scrutinizing expression as he studied each room and took notes in his notepad. He found particular interest in a reading room with books lining the walls and framing the doorways. A cut out cubby seat held more books than my father's study. More books with flimsy binding sat on little end tables between arm chairs with fat padding and vibrant red hues.

When I read Caden's notes about the room over his shoulder, I could hold my tongue no longer. "You do realize that this room looked differently during its occupation, right?"

"What do you mean?" he asked, hardly glancing up from his notes.

"Have your people always had such technology as your little phones?" I asked.

"No," he said, a hint of a question in his voice to encourage me on.

"Did they have these smokeless lights back then?"

Caden's eyes flicked to the lamps above and hanging on the walls. "No."

"Did they have these exact glass windows?"

"No."

"Did they have these vibrant colors of fabrics?"

"Maybe. Hard to say. What are you getting at?"

"What I am getting at," I huffed, "is this room—this whole place—is…wrong. It is too clean, too bright, and too full. It is nice, and I am considering possible upgrades to my father's castle, but it feels…"

"Staged?" he offered.

I tilted my head. "Staged…like an arrangement for a play? Yes, I suppose that is appropriate."

Caden set down his notepad and truly looked at the room for the first time. "Yeah, I guess all of those bookshelves were added later. Books were rare commodities back then. And the game table doesn't have a single scratch on it. It's been stained and polished with materials they probably didn't have in the sixteen hundreds. As you said, the windows were probably warped and foggy, and the rooms would have been heated and lit purely by fire from candles and fireplaces. This room would have been a cold and smoky mess."

Finally, someone understood my frustration with this unsettling room.

"My father has always kept our people as his highest priority. Even our castles were built as fortifications for them if enemies ever attacked. The castles are only large enough to occupy every family in residence."

Caden raised his eyebrows at me. "How did you become such an expert on castle life?"

I scoffed. "I told you, I am a princess. I live in a castle. Ormio's stronghold is larger, and Huiess has more castles—smaller, mind you—but my father takes pride in the defensive build of our home."

Caden set down his phone to lean casually against the smooth wall. "Is that so? What else can you tell me about your kingdom?"

"Anything you want to know," I said.

"Alright, let's start with the basics. How many people live there?"

66

"In all of Somnus? That is what you call a basic?" Truly, these England people were too complicated.

"You mean you don't know how many people you rule over?"

"I do, I just…give me a moment." Arithmetic was not my strong suit and I preferred to use an abacus. "Let me see, I believe we number around sixty-four thousand."

Caden raised an intrigued eyebrow. "Sixty-four thousand? Is that so? How do you figure?"

"It is impossible to know exactly as we mostly count by families. Our average families have five individuals, and we try to balance the duties of one hundred families between every lord. We have one hundred and twenty-nine lords who report to the king, so that makes sixty-four thousand and five hundred people."

He let out a little snort as if disappointed. Had he thought to catch me in a lie?

"Alright, if I was to visit Somnus, what would you say is a must-see?"

"Hmm," I thought. "That would depend on your interests. Do you prefer sporting or artistic events? Exploring the afternoon markets or traversing the untamed pathways? Playing it safe with the noble balls or venturing for the fabled monster of Imazhin? We have it all."

Caden smirked. "Really? Interesting. Would you mind if I took notes on a few things you said? They'd make for an interesting story. But, of course, I won't write it if you've already written it. You'd have to be a renowned storyteller to weave such a setting. And an actress on top of it all to personify a princess from that world."

"I am a princess of Somnus," I huffed.

"So you say," he said, taking out his pen and note-pad again to scribble some more thoughts. "Though, now I wonder if the character of my story should be a real royal or just disillusioned."

"I am not disillusioned," I said, annoyed enough to stamp my foot like a child.

Caden raised a devilishly handsome eyebrow and corner of his mouth. "Oh, really?"

"Yes. How else would I know about the real life-style of castles? Even your historians have it wrong."

"Who's to say our history is the same as yours? You claim to know more than our archeologists? I think you're simply making things up to sound smart. Spoiler alert: it isn't working."

My face grew hot as I rolled my shoulders back, straightening my spine and stretching my neck to raise my chin to my tallest posture. All this and he still casually stood a few centimeters higher. How could his mere height be audaciously irritating?

"Believe what you will," I said. "When I return to Somnus, I will spread the tale far and wide about how insufferably ignorant you were."

I stepped closer to prove that I would not back down from my words. Caden, however, smiled wider.

"You'll make me infamous in your world too? Why, Emer, it almost sounds like you'll miss me."

My lungs swelled in preparation to burst with words I would surely regret. Mica's laughter distracted me.

"I don't know whether to separate you two or give you a room. Seriously, guys, these sparks flying are bound to set a fire of one kind or another."

Caden's mouth snapped shut while the fire in his eyes shifted from teasing to annoyed.

I likewise turned my line of fire on Mica.

"Being handsome cannot excuse his selfishness and disrespect!"

Mica raised his hands in defense. "I'm just calling it like I see it."

"Wait—" Caden turned back to me "—you confess I'm handsome?"

I huffed again and turned my heel on him. As much as I wanted to stomp angrily, the best way to convince him that I really was a princess was to act accordingly. Caden lingered through the tour and I was less than eager to lose myself in this strange place, sticking me in the same room as Caden recorded his imaginative thoughts. Ridiculous writer.

Irritated, I sat before the clean fireplace on the floor, bending my knees to hide most of my legs under my short purple dress. The hearth was far too clean. It looked unused for years. Caden and Mica said this place was one of their most magical. I mourned for their world. Sure, they had amazing devices of information and vehicles that transported us a day's journey within hours, but where were their fairies? Where were their dragons, unicorns, and half-kinds? Their most "magical" place was a corpse of a time long lost.

Shh-k.

I turned, surprised by the sound. Caden and Mica stood nearby, staring at Caden's phone which he held between me and them.

"Smile," Mica teased. "You're on candid camera."

"Excuse me?" I asked.

"Sorry," Caden flustered. "You just—the scene was perfect. I wanted to capture it."

"Capture?" I asked, still waiting for an explanation.

Caden flipped his phone around to show me an image of myself. The picture was no painting with brushstrokes, and clearer than even a polished silver mirror. I could see every detail as I sat at the cold fireplace, my face sad and forlorn.

Mica nodded appreciatively. "Put a mellow filter on that with some reflective quote, and you could make a viral post."

"A—"

"Ignore him," Caden said, smirking. "Social media's not worth the trouble of explaining."

We wound our way up to the outlook tower to oversee the cannons (which also looked too clean), and the great expanse of water. Mica captured a few more "candid" images of me as I peered over the balcony, pointed at the distant ships, and faced into the wind to keep my hair from whipping my face. Once he even asked me to pose before a locked gate that led to a mossy set of stone steps. It was another testament of how old this place truly was.

"You said legends surround this place?" I asked.

"Jack and the Beanstalk, or Jack the Giant Killer," Mica explained.

"Basically," Caden said, "Jack climbed up a beanstalk to the land of the giants, where he caused all sorts of trouble."

Mica gestured to a tree. "What do you think, Emer? Can you make a plant grow tall enough to reach Somnus?"

I looked up to the clear blue sky. "I hardly think Somnus is up there."

Mica shrugged. "Maybe it's invisible?"

Caden snorted. I took his disbelief as a challenge.

"Alright. We shall find the tallest plant and make it grow."

We wandered back through the gardens until agreeing that the tallest plant was one that grew upward like an outstanding stalk of four meters.

Mica lingered back at the fork in the garden path to watch for anyone who might try to stop our experiment. I had to leave the safety of the pathway and step through some ferns to reach the particular stalk. It grew precariously close to the ledge of the cliffside. Its base was fern-like with large leaves, then it was bare until halfway up, where it branched out with limbs like a candelabra. The ends of the branches even bloomed large cups of yellow petals.

"So you know," Caden said, "these gardens have gone through years of cultivation, and that plant could be older than you. If you break it or injure anyone—including yourself—my father's position as lord can't protect you."

"Oh?" I asked, wrapping my hand around the strange stalk. The texture surprised me. I had forgotten that everything I touched was wool, even this stalky plant. It was thick enough that I needed both hands to reach around it, but it seemed only sturdy enough to hold its own weight. "For what cause," I dared back to the young men, "will you claim this misadventure?"

"For science!" Mica called from his lookout.

Caden grinned. "Just don't do anything too stupid."

"Too late," I muttered, wrapping myself around the stalk. "Alright, strange stalk," I began, "I need you to grow for me. Can you do that? Grow tall and strong, taller and stronger than anyone else in your family. Do you see the top of that castle? I want you to race it to the sky. Grow."

72

The stalk did grow beneath my grip. It stretched like a waking person, creeping its way upward. I kept my grip firm on the stalk, and by the time I finished speaking, I had to stand on my tippy-toes to reach the same spot.

"I-it is working," I said, excited and terrified at the same time. "Am I supposed to climb it?"

"Whoa." Caden stared in awe. "It *is* working. Just hold on, and let it take you up."

"Let it…let it take me up…right." Easier said than done. That meant letting go of the safety of the ground. That meant trusting my weight (and possible life) to a plant that I just convinced to grow to the sky.

"Alright, stalk of the heavens," I said, hoping to encourage the plant as much as myself. "Please, stay strong as you grow tall."

Its progress continued slowly. It had grown maybe a meter since I first talked to it. Gritting my teeth, I climbed up to its strange branches, raising me above the ground. The stalk continued to stretch upward.

I made the mistake of looking back to Caden. I was already two meters above the ground. Abandoning this insane idea was still an option.

Caden frowned. Was that worry in his eyes? "Don't look down," he said. "Keep talking to it. It looks like it needs encouragement."

Indeed, the plant began to wilt a little under my weight.

"No-no-no," I said. "Keep going, keep it up-upward. Keep going up. You can do it. Please? Please, do not fail me now. Stay strong and take me home. You can do that for me, right?"

The plant continued to grow, but also continued to lean.

"Put some trust in it," Caden said. "People stand taller when they have purpose."

"Alright," I said, "I trust you to hold me. I trust you, great stalk. I trust you to grow tall and stay strong." I hoped it was deaf to my lies. My heartbeat quickened and my voice wavered.

"I don't think you were very convincing," Caden said, worried.

"If it looks so easy, then you come do it," I snapped back.

The plant snapped too.

"Emer!"

Looking back, a large crack splintered in my stalk around the spot of its original height. Looking down gave me a sight that was equally shattering. Rocks. A long fall to jagged rocks below. Sharp as needles.

"Emer!" Caden shouted again. Mica joined his side and dug through his pack. "Hold on, Emer!"

An insane little chuckle escaped me. "As if I was about to let go? I think we need to abort this plant—I mean plan."

The stalk cracked again.

"Grab this!" Mica shouted, throwing a thin white rope to me.

As much as I wanted to get off the breaking stalk, I feared letting go to grab the rope. I missed Mica's throw. The men stood at the base of the cliff, only three meters away. How could such a short distance seem impossible to reach?

"Please, please, please," I whispered, half to the stalk, half to the men behind me.

Mica pulled the loose rope back and aimed to throw again.

"Here, let me." Caden took the end of the rope. Instead of aiming at me, he aimed higher. He threw with all the strength and muscles of a javelin fighter, sending the end of the rope over me so that it landed across my back. I grabbed it.

Same as the plant, the rope was as soft as a wool blanket. What I saw and what I felt jarred my mind, and I almost let go.

"Wrap it around yourself," Caden said. "Then try to climb back to us."

"Right," I said, forcing my mind to cooperate. With one arm desperately clinging to the breaking stalk, I used my other hand to finagle the rope around my back and under my arms. I breathed a little with the small assurance that the rope would save me from a fall to my death. Instead, I would swing back— hard—into the side of the cliff beneath the men's feet.

The jagged cliffside was only less threatening by its closeness.

"Climb back to us," Caden repeated. "Slowly now."

As if I could sprint?

I wiggled backwards, shuffling back to the safety of the gardens. The stalk creaked again.

"Please," I repeated. "Do not break now. Hold strong." Half to the stalk, half to myself.

"You're doing great. Don't look down," Caden said.

Since the strange stalk only felt like wool, I could not simply feel my way back. I had to look back to slide my legs down.

"Keep coming. We're not going to let you fall."

Slipping back on my stomach caused my short dress to slip up my legs. I stopped for a second as I debated what was worse: death by drop onto rocks or death by shame?

The stalk cracked and fell. I screamed as the stalk disappeared from beneath me. Caden shouted my name again, and Mica yelped.

I fell.

For a second, I was back in that nightmare of falling in darkness, falling forever, falling towards needles.

The rope tightened around my chest, then swung me back against the cliffside. My mind transferred the sight of pain to my nerves. Ow. That bruised, for sure, and my dress ripped behind my shoulder. Arms reached for mine and lifted me up. Caden and Mica pulled me back to the garden and away from the cliff edge. We all lay on the path for a moment, panting, basking in the glory of safe ground beneath us.

After sufficiently catching my breath, I sat up. "No matter if that is my only way back to Somnus, you cannot convince me to do that again."

"Agreed," Caden said, then threw a dubious look at his friend. "You just happened to have a length of rope in your pack?"

"You said to pack for an adventure."

"And you took it literally?"

"You have my gratitude," I said. "I cringe to think of what would have happened if you had not."

"Yeah, see?" Mica said, puffing out his chest. "I'm the hero." He finished his gallant little moment by sticking out his tongue at Caden.

We continued to explore every room and pathway open to the public, but if there was a way to return to Somnus, it was nowhere on this island.

"So," Mica asked on our walk back down, "other than the beanstalk fiasco, what do you think of St. Michael's Mount?"

"It was educational," I said.

"That's it?" Caden frowned.

"And beautiful," I added. "I learned a lot about this world from this trip. I thank you for your help, though I doubt this is the way back to my world."

The two men shared glances, shrugs, and thoughtful looks. "Maybe," Caden said, "we're going about this the wrong way. We came to St. Michael's Mount hoping for some beanstalk to climb back to your world or hole for you to jump through. But you say you're dreaming? You look awake to me."

I shook my head. "I do not feel awake. I can see the flower details, smell the salty air, taste a flakey pastry, but I close my eyes and sense myself lying in my bedchamber between my wool blankets. All I feel is wool. I even accidentally burnt my hand because I was unable to sense the heat."

Caden frowned. "Interesting. Maybe we need to look into tactics to wake you."

"How?" I asked. "My instincts tell me that a place of magic will wake me."

Mica shrugged. "Let's get back to town and discuss it over dinner. I'm starving. Then we can start fresh tomorrow."

The sun began to set as we made our way back down the mount. We stopped at a restaurant at the shore of the island for dinner. I had no idea what to eat, and allowed Mica to order a sandwich for me. Caden also bought a couple bubbly drinks that were far too sweet and tangy for my taste buds.

"Emer," Mica began while his eyes frowned at his phone. "You said you have no sense of touch?"

"Yes," I said. "Everything feels like wool, or my blankets. This is how I know that I am sleeping."

"I Googled it—"

"Let me guess," Caden interrupted, "Google says she has cancer."

"Actually, no," Mica said, sounding surprised. "It's called hypoesthesia—"

"That's probably pronounced hypoes*the*sia," Caden corrected.

"That's what I said."

"No, you said—"

"Gentlemen!" I huffed. "You were saying, Mica? This has happened to others?"

"Yes," Mica said. "It says common causes are arthritis, brain tumors—oh, that's cancer—"

"Told you."

"Caden."

"—diabetes," Mica continued, "or there's a whole list, but considering the state we found you in, your case is probably from trauma or blow from a fall."

Caden frowned. "You're saying it actually makes sense?"

"I'm saying it's possible." Mica slid his finger up and down his phone screen.

Caden folded his arms and leaned back in his seat. "Then it's possible Emer's not dreaming, just sensationally numb."

I mimicked his doubtful and irritating posture. "You still refuse to believe me?"

"Except," Mica said, "there's also her plant magic. Maybe it's because she's dreaming that she can control them, like the way some people can control their dreams."

Caden grunted. "Recognizing that they're dreaming is half the work for controlling a dream. Emer seems to have no problem with that."

I shook my head. "I cannot control this world. If I could, it would be far less confusing, I would know the way home, and people would properly respect me."

"Respe—"

"Let's theorize," Mica interjected over Caden's retort. "You're dreaming, and you want to wake up. What do you do?"

"Movies would say to kill yourself," Caden said, "but I don't feel comfortable suggesting that."

I shuddered. "No, thank you."

"What if," Mica asked, "we could scare you into waking?"

"How would we do that?" Caden asked. "It's not like one of us could turn into a monster and start chasing her down a long hallway."

"Or make her teeth fall out." Mica cringed. "I hate those dreams."

Caden turned to me. "Obviously the scare of falling from a breaking beanstalk wasn't enough to wake you. What nightmares have woken you in the past?"

Falling in the dark…needles. I shivered. Sure, I allowed these men to drive me around their land and guide me through their world, and they had recently saved my life. But telling them about my nightmares involved a different type of trust.

"Caden," Mica muttered. "Tact?"

The handsome lord grunted. "What do you expect? I'm not a shrink. You want me to maneuver my sentences into gaslighting her? Give me a month to write a story, and I'll make you laugh, cry, throw the pages out the window, then lovingly pick them up to read again. Right now, I'm in my own little nightmare, completely out of my schedule and out of control. I don't know what else to do."

"Hold on," Mica said, "Emer's a princess."

"So she says," Caden said.

Mica nudged his friend to be nice again, then spoke slowly with emphasis. "She's a sleeping princess from a magical land. She's just like a storybook fairy-tale! She needs someone to kiss her awake!"

"I beg your pardon?" I sputtered. "How is someone pressing their mouth to mine supposed to revive me?"

Caden smirked. "Ever heard of CPR?"

"It's true love," Mica explained. "True love breaks spells."

I frowned. "Sorcery is rare in my world, thus I know little of it, but I do know that spells generally consist of magic words and tangible elements such as potions and rituals. How could love—an intangible concept—break such a power?"

Caden raised his eyebrow. "Is love not a power of its own?"

I shuffled in my seat, uncomfortably shy about Caden's attention as he spoke of love. "Suppose love is the answer. How do I find my true love and convince him to kiss me when my consciousness is here? I have no way to contact Somnus."

"Maybe he's here, in England," Mica suggested.

"That would suck," Caden scoffed. "What kind of true love only exists in a dream?"

"Oh. Right." Mica deflated. The men said nothing more for the meal, lost in thoughts that failed to work. Their sadness proved how much they wanted to help me.

"Forgive me," I said, "but I keep having the impression that a place of magic will wake me. I know not where, and ask your forgiveness for complicating your travels. You have both been more than helpful. If you desire, I may find my own means from here—"

"Don't be ridiculous." Caden's words, to my surprise. "You have no money, no identification, and no clue where you are. We might be completely out of our element by helping you, but let us try. Besides, what's an adventure that stays on the path every step of the way?"

As little as I wanted to burden them, and as much as I wanted to figure this out on my own, I grudgingly agreed. Every word he said was true. I would be completely lost without them. Out loud, I muttered, "Thank you. As long as it is no inconvenience to you."

The tide had come in, leaving boats as the only way to return to the mainland. Their boats moved not by sail or oars, but roared forward by the same magical "engine" that Mica said propelled the horseless carriages. Fascinating…

We drove back to Penzance, where the lords registered for a hotel for themselves, their driver, and me. They gave me my own room right next to theirs, which I appreciated. When I thanked Mica, he said it was actually Caden's idea.

I said another "Thank you" anyway, then cringed when I walked into the luxurious room. It was one more instance of feeling like a burden when I—the princess—was supposed to be the one to provide and accommodate for others. Especially to those who already provided so much to me.

Chapter 6

Sleep evaded me, which was ironic when I thought about it. If I was dreaming, why did I need to sleep at all? Other than the fact that when I "slept" in this world, that was when I remembered my life in Somnus. Oh, how I missed my family and friends.

Restless, I left my bed and wrapped a blanket around my shoulders. Perhaps a walk around the hotel would help. I stepped from my room, and my door's horrible screech announced my departure. Oops. I cringed and waited in the hallway to see if I had woken anyone. After a minute, I continued down the hallway, worrying less about stepping carefully. My footsteps would wake no one who slept through my door's racket.

At the end of the hallway, a double door opened to a second-story balcony. Maybe the fresh air would calm my mind. Stepping out, I inhaled the salty night air as an intangible breeze brushed my hair back. A road passed below me, but just beyond that was the shoreline. A few lingering city lights spotted my view to the right, and my left horizon was framed by the stretching bay. Straight ahead was a view I never could have created on my own. Moonlight glistened across the great expanse of water, sending little waves washing on the shore.

Marin would have loved this view. No, she would have been *in* it, riding a sailboat across the bay. Pearl would have been the one to stand beside me to admire the stars, while Garnet and Tanzi would sleep peacefully for the first time in too long.

I blamed the salty air as my eyes began to water and my nose tickled.

The door opened behind me, and I jumped. Caden stepped through. He wore baggy trousers and a skin tight shirt for pajamas. I tried and failed not to stare. Apparently, the goddess who chiseled him had not stopped at his face.

"There you are," he said, rubbing his face awake and squinting at me. "You probably shouldn't wander off alone."

"Why not?" I asked, wiping away any evidence of tears. "I can take care of myself."

He scoffed. "You're a pretty young woman wandering around alone at night. What could possibly go wrong?"

I blushed from his compliment and embarrassment at the truth of his words. "I could not sleep."

"Neither could I, not after your door alerted the town like a Blitz siren."

"Forgive me," I said, accepting the fact that his metaphors were only half as confusing as Mrs. Priddy's cockney.

He smirked back. He really was too handsome for his own good. "It's alright. I wanted to enjoy this while I could."

"Enjoy 'this?'" I asked. Did he mean my company? I blushed deeper.

He gestured to the view. Right. Of course he meant the view.

"You don't see the stars in London," he said, looking up. "If it's not raining, it's cloudy. If it's not cloudy, it's smoggy. The only reason I see the sky at all between the townhouses and skyscrapers is by living in Notting Hill."

"Excuse me," I asked, confused. "Do you live in London or Notting Hill?"

"Both," he said. "Notting Hill is just a section of the greater city of London. Even still, the closest thing we have to this is Brighton, which is always crowded with travelers. Sure, Penzance gets tourists too, but it's not suffocating."

I blinked, trying to organize his words and my thoughts. This world was truly a marvel. How did it have such grand country sides as Boscastle, towns like Penzance, and cities within cities? Perhaps their lack of mountains helped give them variety, though my curiosity was piqued.

"If I may, I would like to see this London."

Caden raised his eyebrows, then shrugged. "Sure. I'm not sure what you expect to find there that will help you back to Somnus. It's not exactly magical unless you count the stories of Sherlock Holmes. Even in Peter Pan, they escape the city to Neverland."

"Is there truly nothing magical about such a large city?" I asked.

"I suppose London has a lot of museums, libraries, and colleges. Maybe we can research dreams or possible options to your hypoesthesia. I could look up my contacts at Oxford or Cambridge to widen our research." He yawned and rubbed his tired face again.

I grimaced. "I *am* sorry for waking you."

"It's fine. I don't mind the opportunity to stargaze while I'm here, and I had some dreams I wanted to write down anyway. You can go back inside, but I plan to stay out here for a bit."

"Dreams?" I asked. Even the people in my dreams had dreams?

"I don't normally share my dreams with people."

I gave him a downward stare. "This is all a dream to me. You are literally sharing a dream with me now."

Caden shuffled uneasily. "I guess that's how you see it. Mind you, my dreams can be super weird. This one was actually more normal, which is why I think it's a possible story for a novel."

I buckled down and waited for him to say more.

"Alright, hear me out. It's a story based on a chess game. Wait, do you know chess? It's a board game with kings, queens, knights, and pawns?"

"Is the goal to capture the king? We call it Kings and Peasants, or Kings for short."

"Yes. Well, I had a lucid thought to set a book based on a chess game. Each piece is a full-rounded character and they move across the land or city as they would around the board. It's not a full story, but it would simulate the plot and give some basis on important characters and plot moments, such as the queen's sacrifice."

He used a lot of unfamiliar phrases, but the one that caught my attention was, "Queen's sacrifice?"

Caden nodded. "The queen is the most powerful piece for her mobility. Sometimes she's used as a sacrifice to pull away another piece, creating an opening—oh! The transformation of a pawn into a queen would make a good ending twist. I need to write this down."

He pulled out his glowing phone and began typing away with his thumbs. He reminded me of my father talking about hunting, eyes lit with plans and ideas, a small excited smile, and energetic hands ready for action. My involvement in the matter was about the same as well. While my father would go off with his hunting friends (in conversation or on a literal hunt), I would sit back and simply wait for their change of subject or return from the hunt. Caden was likewise lost in his thoughts, plotting a world of characters, scenes, and ambushes of his own.

"Are—" I hesitated. I could go back to my room and struggle to sleep, or… "Would you mind if I kept you company? You do not need to entertain me; the view is enough to preoccupy me."

He took a couple seconds to think it over, then shrugged again. "As long as you don't mind if I write down some thoughts. I'm not a great conversationalist."

"I know," I said, then threw him a playful grin.

He chortled, then slipped into a porch chair to thumb away with his phone. "Careful. If you keep talking like that, you'll end up as one of my characters."

"Mica called me your muse. Am I not already one of your characters?" I asked. He remained quiet and kept his attention to his phone as he thumbed down his thoughts. "You write a lot. Have you finished any stories?"

"I've finished a few," he said. "I published my first novel last year. A fantasy of little boy adventures. I'd give you the pitch, but my critics called it bore."

"I like fantasies," I said. "According to you and Mica, I live in one. Tell me about your story."

Despite his attempt to appear cocky with his raised eyebrow, his subconscious rubbing on the back of his head revealed his nerves. "It's about a young prince who doesn't want to rule, so he runs away to a distant land where he goes on quests, falls in love, and finds his own way to make changes in his kingdom."

I tilted my head at him. "Sounds almost auto-biographical."

He scoffed. "What is fiction if not a retelling of non-fiction? You know, some of my closest friends read the whole book and didn't catch what you did with my summary."

"Perhaps they have not seen this side of you."

He shrugged. "Maybe. I'd like to think they're all sides of a true me, that I'm more than one dimension."

I smiled back. "I feel like every conversation with you reveals a new side."

He returned to his phone instead of responding, and I turned back to the view. The silence was surprisingly comfortable. Peace rolled through me as I listened to the waves stretch up the shore, the breeze whistle through the trees, and the occasional vehicle rush by. I turned my vision upward to the stars Caden said he would miss. With no mountains blocking the horizon, the wide expanse of sky awed me. It was particularly interesting to study the arrangements of stars. Additional confirmation that I was on another world, and this was not some twisted future of Somnus. These stars were strangers to me.

I turned back to Caden to find him staring into the distance. Hopefully that meant I could distract him from his writerly thoughts.

"Caden? Do you name your stars?"

90

His face snapped to mine, clearly disrupted from some imaginations, but the hint of his smile said that he was fine with my distraction.

"I know scientists have names for every visible star," he said, "and I don't know even a handful of those, but we have constellations, if that's what you mean."

He stood from his seat to join my side at the balcony. "Let's see—" he scanned the sky "—it's actually harder when there are so many. Oh, there's one." He pointed just over the waterline. "That's Pegasus, the winged horse."

"Where?" I asked.

Caden leaned closer to point. I yearned to know if he was warm despite his lack of proper clothing. I focused my eyes on his pointing to keep my blush from rising again.

"There," he said, tracing his finger from one star to another. "Those two stars make his legs, and those three make his long neck or tail, depending on whether you say he's going to or away from Perseus, who is…somewhere in the Milky Way. It's hard to pick out with so many stars—"

He cut off as he finally seemed to notice the proximity that set my nerves in a frenzy. His eyes locked on mine.

"Er," he mumbled and consciously leaned away. "I don't think I can pick out any others."

"Oh," I said. Hopefully he missed the disappointment in my voice. "Well, thank you for showing me the winged horse. It has been a while since I saw one."

Caden raised his eyebrows, then let out a little laugh. "We should probably get some sleep."

"Yes," I said, stepping back to the double doors. "I will see you in the morning."

"Sleep well," he said, then added, "Princess."

I returned to bed with a smile on my face. It took an embarrassing amount of time to settle the fairies in my stomach, but when I eventually fell asleep, a chiseled face invaded my memories of Somnus.

Chapter 7

I dreamed of the pranks my sisters and I had begun last year. It was Tanzi's idea, the little schemer. She accompanied Marin to the docks one day and heard about the midnight masquerades through Renae Irving, Captain Irving at the time. Then she convinced Garnet and me to play matchmaker. We all saw how much Marin liked the captain. The midnight excursions were an excuse for her to spend time with him on his boat and the water that she loved so dearly.

Then we discovered the true freedom of the masquerade.

Anyone could attend. Royalty, nobles, craftsmen, and bondmen from Somnus, Ormio, Huiess, or even the kingdoms beyond the valley if they made the journey. The only requirement was that no judgments set foot on Noz Isle. No politicking. No expectations. No warring kingdoms. Just freedom.

My sisters and I danced freely with the sons and daughters of our parents' enemies, surprised yet joyous when masks were removed and friendships made.

Marin and Ranae began to court openly, but we still snuck away from our rooms every Saturday night to join the festivities on Noz Isle. We joined the sister princesses from the other kingdoms until we all became known as the twelve dancing princesses. Every week, we danced the night away, returning home before anyone noticed. The only evidence of our nightly escapades was the obvious wear and tear on our shoes.

Father hired person after person to discover why our shoes were ruined each week. This encouraged Garnet to practice her sleep hypnosis. Before we ran away to dance, she poured our chaperone a drink, then sang them to sleep. We escaped night after night, dancing freely, laughing as our parents grew more and more confused.

I dreamed of the midnight dances we attended. I dreamed of the other princesses. Oh, how we teased each other when one of us danced with the same man night after night, or even multiple times in the same night.

My memories blurred as a certain young man passed me. Despite his mask of a wild cat, I sensed a familiar attraction to his dark hair and chiseled jawline. We caught one another's gaze for the briefest of seconds, then both turned away, suppressing smiles. My heart pounded with happiness and anxiety. Such strange sensations he stirred in me.

I danced with other men while my eyes wandered for him. We locked gazes again during a dance. This time I recognized his sky-blue eyes.

Caden.

I excused myself from my partner to approach him. "Caden?" I asked to be sure.

He grinned and removed his mask. It was definitely Caden. But…

"What are you doing here? I only dream of memories," I said.

"But you dream of England, too," he said, offering his hand. Even as he spoke, my dream blurred. The music and conversations mixed and faces became indistinct. This dream was no memory, but a true dream of beautiful chaos.

I placed my hand in Caden's, surprised when my mind created a sense of skin beyond the ever-present wool. I expected him to lead me to the dance floor. Instead, he pulled me through a doorway that appeared from nowhere. We were suddenly outside, dashing through gardens and up to a private gazebo.

This was my dream. I was in control. I could act without fear of consequences, and there was no one else around but me and Caden.

I wrapped a hand around Caden's shoulder and kissed him. While my heart leapt with joy, my lips felt…nothing. Not even wool.

Pain struck the tip of my index finger—the finger that had scraped against the spindle. The pain zapped through my arm to my heart, then shot from me to Caden. He jumped back as though I had shocked him. He coughed, doubling over and hugging his stomach. It was not enough. He fell to the ground, coughing for air until none came.

"Caden!" I screamed.

Was this not my dream? Could I not control the consequences here? I willed Caden to breathe and stand again. Instead, he choked and turned his eyes on me as his attempts to breathe waned. He stared at me, betrayed. Then he stopped moving.

"No!" I cried, falling to my knees. "No, Caden! Why?"

"You kissed him," a smooth voice replied. Words of a sister I once knew to be loving. Her voice was too hateful to recognize exactly. Where was she? I could not see her or anyone as the darkness of the night-time garden swallowed my vision. All was black outside my dim gazebo with Caden.

"You were poisoned," my sister continued. "Now, you *are* a poison. Anything as much as a kiss will kill them."

Her last words echoed through my mind, bouncing back and forth in the walls of my skull, overlapping, whispering, "A kiss will kill them—Anything as much as a kiss—a kiss—Anything—will kill them."

No! No, I would not let it happen! I could not!

⋆   ⋆   ⋆

I woke with a start. The sun had barely poked its head above the flat horizon. I lay in the bed, waiting for my heart to return to a restful pace. I knew sleep would deny me though. Eventually I stood and considered dressing.

No matter how much I boasted of my independence and capabilities to accomplish tasks on my own, I was helpless without my handmaid. With only the simple purple chemise or yellow maxi to wear, I flustered over ideas to freshen my wardrobe. A proper second layer of a bliaut would be nice. Except I had no such garments available, and I could not ask one of the men to fetch one for me. Not only would it defend the opinion that I was helpless without them, but I doubted they would be up to the task when bliauts were out of fashion in this world.

I wanted to appear flattering to Caden, but my sister's words haunted me. "Anything as much as a kiss will kill them." Even if Caden intrigued me, what could come of it? He was not real, right? There was no use in falling for a dream, especially if the consequence for expressing my attraction resulted in his death.

Although, considering the many wonders of this world, I could no longer say for sure that it was a mere product of my imagination. Either way, I could not control this dream world nor its consequences.

I had to suppress my feelings for Caden. Either he was real and in danger of heartbreak or death if we developed affections, or he was imaginary and a hindrance to my mental and emotional growth.

Giving up on my gown, I styled my hair in a curling updo before heading next door.

Mr. Knightly opened the door as a proper butler.

"The young lords hoped you would join us. They had breakfast brought to their room."

Caden greeted me with a heart-stopping smile, and I stumbled.

His smile flickered with amusement. "I once knew a man who could turn any stumble into a push-up. I never knew anyone to trip so smoothly. You should try it sometime."

My own smile almost responded, but the words of my sister haunted me. "Anything as much as a kiss will kill them." I had to distance myself. I had to remain aloof from Caden's charms. For his own safety.

Caden and Mica were almost finished with their meals. Mica bent over his glowing box, mumbling about times and schedules.

I sat at their little round table as Mr. Knightly brought a plate of eggs and pancakes for me. They smelled divine.

"Good morning, Emer," Mica said. "Did you sleep well?"

"Eventually," I said, struggling against the impulse to glance in Caden's direction.

"Oh good," Mica said. "We have a five-and-a-half-hour drive back to London. If we head off soon, we'll be back before teatime."

"London?" I asked. "Already?" A frightening little panic rose in my chest. Caden had not confirmed or denied whether I could join them in the great city. As much as I hated to burden them, I appreciated their guidance and companionship. Would I ever see them again?

"Forgive us," Caden said. "We have previous engagements to attend."

I gathered my poise and straightened my back to make my next words believable. "No matter. Surely, I can manage without you."

Caden frowned. "I thought you were coming with us."

"Oh, yes." I shuffled, uncomfortable with the number of emotions waving through me: relief not to be left behind, irritation at that relief, excitement to see London, nerves to spend more time with Caden, and frustration with those nerves as my sister's voice warned me. Swallowing back most of it, I said, "The city you described sounds magnificent, but I mean not to impose. You have done plenty for me already."

Mica took Caden's arm to step aside. Their whispered conversation spelled their concerns. Without hearing them, I knew their words summarized with, "Taking her home with us is a different matter than traversing the countryside."

"Please," I said, "I do not wish to burden you further. If this city is as grand and full of opportunities as you say, then perhaps it is where I will find my answers to return home. I have already benefited from your hospitality, and I understand if I exceeded your limits of generosity. I may find another way to London. How far is it to walk?"

Caden scoffed. "It's over four hundred kilometers. Walking would take weeks. Come on, Mica. You were the one to convince me to help her. She still needs our help."

I frowned. When did the tides turn?

Mica folded his arms and shifted his eyes everywhere except towards me. "I want to help her, but…what are your parents going to say?"

Caden winced. Apparently, he imagined unfavorable results. "Let me worry about them."

His friend raised his eyebrows, unconvinced.

Caden shrugged. "What's the worst that could happen? They refuse to let her inside and think that we gave a homeless person a free ride across the country."

Mica smirked and turned to me. "Are you alright with that?"

"I suppose," I said, suddenly nervous to go to London…and meet Caden's parents.

"Alright," Caden grinned. "Do what you need to pack up. We leave in an hour."

I spread my arms wide. "This is all that I have."

Caden blinked. "Right. Sorry. But if we're sharing the same vehicle for five hours, please give us the courtesy of bathing first."

Mica punched his friend in the arm. An ironic way to remind his friend to be nice.

"What? I can't have the windows rolled down if I'm writing, and bringing a strange woman home will be hard enough to explain to Mother. A change of clothes wouldn't hurt either."

Mica groaned in defeat. I huffed and stomped back to my room. This society continued to boggle me. They seemed obsessed with cleanliness. The next fifteen minutes were spent searching my room for instructions on how to use the shower. Mrs. Priddy had explained the basic mechanics of indoor plumbing, though this room had none of the same knobs as Boscastle Cottage.

A little more than timid, I stepped back to the honorables' room and knocked.

"Occupied!" a voice called back. Was it Mica or Caden?

I knocked again, calling, "This is Emer. I cannot figure out the water system."

The door opened, revealing Caden with no more than a white towel wrapped around his hips as he scrubbed a washcloth through his wet hair. His whole body glistened from a recent wash.

I blushed and turned away. "Forgive me, I was unaware that you were preoccupied."

"I just finished my shower. What did you need?"

"I—" What did I need again? My eyes kept flickering to the sight of perfection in the doorway. "The shower confuses me. Am I supposed to bathe in the ocean?"

"Oh, right. One moment." He stepped away to grab a robe from a closet, slipping that on and letting his hip towel drop to the floor. Even if he was more clothed than before, my mind stuck on the idea that he was naked under that robe. I kept my eyes averted as he walked over to my room. Without any introduction or instruction, he made his way to my lavatory, then pulled at some knobs on the wall. Water sprayed from a faucet above.

"This one is cold, this one is hot. Turn them this way when you're done. Clear?"

As clear as could be from observing outside my lavatory. I felt scandalous enough to have a nearly-naked man in my chambers. At least the technology was a good distraction. Their bathing fountains never ceased to amaze me.

"You know how to use soap, right?"

"Of course," I said, slightly insulted. "I am civilized."

"Good. Shampoo and conditioner are like soap, but for your hair. Lock your door behind me. I'll be back with a change of clothes for you."

With that, he left. I locked my door as he suggested.

102

I preferred the luxury of relaxing in a bath, though the water running down my back gave me memories of playing in waterfalls with my sisters. The concept of shampoo confused me until drying my hair after. It was truly softer and shinier than I had ever remembered. I dressed in my own robe that looked soft and fluffy, yet felt like wool. A knock sounded on my door.

Caden's voice shouted through. "Emer?"

"Yes?"

"Are you decent?"

"No," I called back. Considering his robe visit, he might have argued, but I was not ready to reveal myself according to this world's standards.

"If I leave this bag here, will you come get it?"

If he left it and no one else was around to spot me… "Yes."

"Alright. I hope it suits you."

I waited all of five seconds for his footsteps to fade away from my door. I cracked my door open, then swiped the bag into my room. Inside, I unfurled a white garment that worked well enough for a chemise and shined like silk. The top garment was made of a lavender material that looked soft and incredibly light. The silky under layer covered my shoulders and my knees, though the top garment draped down to my wrists and ankles. Caden had added a gold necklace with a twelve-pointed star pendant that hung nicely within the frame of the circular neckline.

I swiped my hands down the gown, half to smooth any wrinkles and half to brush off any hints of my sweaty hands. I was not nervous to see Caden in this dress he provided. Why should I be nervous?

A couple things went wide after I knocked: the door, then Mica's mouth and Caden's eyes.

"Well!" Mica grinned at the doorway. "Aren't you picture perfect?"

He reached his hand forward to take my hand. As soon as I placed my hand in his, he pulled me into the room with a twirl, flaring my dress.

"Yes, that's perfect!" Mica released me to raise his hands into a viewing frame. "Wait right there. Let me grab my camera."

He dashed to their bedroom, leaving me alone with Caden. He had switched out of his glossy tunic that opened in the front and boots that looked sturdy enough for war. Caden stood before me wearing trousers that matched his tailored grey tunic without sleeves. The hip-high tunic angled into a V shape to a column of buttons down his chest. His fitted white undershirt rose up around his neck and the skinniest scarf I ever saw held it tightly with a little knot. His black leather shoes shined more than pitch in the sunlight. While the whole style confused me, I had to admit it was rather attractive on Caden.

"Mica seems to approve," I said. "Thank you."

Caden spared a quick glance, smile, and nod. His reddening neck said that he had a lot more on his mind.

Mica returned with his camera, fiddling with its many knobs and scopes. He likewise wore a blue-grey tunic that matched his trousers and opened in the front with two columns of buttons. His skinny scarf that tied around his neck was a deep blue and fashioned a bit wider than Caden's.

"Where did you get that outfit, Emer?" he asked.

"Caden brought it to my room."

"Did he now?" Mica turned to give his friend a knowing look. "Why, Caden, I didn't know you had such an eye for women's fashion."

Caden coughed as if the sound could distract from his blush. "I picked it off a mannequin."

"That actually makes sense. Emer, will you give me the honor of posing you to capture your essence?"

"Do we have time for this?" Caden frowned. "Miles is waiting for us, and we have a long drive ahead."

"Do you tell your writing inspiration to wait?" Mica asked, guiding me by the hand to the balcony. "You can never predict when inspiration will strike, when a muse enters your life and begs to be expressed through art. It took us months to plan this trip and Emer's only here until she wakes up." He gently arranged my hands across the balcony railing, then turned my shoulders and chin to uncomfortable angles. "Hold right there." He stepped back to snap a couple of pictures, readjusted, then snapped a few more. "Caden, we may never get this chance again. We must seize it while it's within our grasp. Now look out to the ocean, Emer. Chin down just a little. Beautiful. Don't look at me, look at the ocean. One more."

Mica moved me around like a doll for the next five minutes, directing me to twirl, to lean against the doorframe, or reach towards the ocean as the wind billowed around me. Caden observed from beyond the camera's view, silent, watching, and occasionally jotting notes. A small smile twitched every time his eyes met mine.

My mind whispered the haunting message: "Even a kiss." I forced myself to turn away from Caden.

"Alright," Mica said, scrolling through his recent pictures. "We're running late. Come on! What are you waiting for?"

Caden rolled his eyes but smirked at me to share the tease. "And we're off, like a bale of turtles."

The secretive smile and teasing eyes plucked at my heart strings. It would be a very long ride, indeed.

We stopped for lunch before leaving Penzance, taking part in a ritual that I never heard of before: fast food. It was like a restaurant, except we stayed in the vehicle and Miles delivered our orders to a speaking sign. Then the exchange of money and food was through a window. How odd. The food itself was oily like I had never known. We passed around paper napkins with abundance.

"I just had a thought," Mica said.

"Hope it was good," Caden said around his sandwich. "You only have so many per day."

Mica stuck out his tongue at his friend before continuing. "We'll pass Stonehenge on the way back to London. Do we have time to stop? Maybe the monument is the place that'll wake up Emer."

"A monument?" I asked. "Is it magical?"

"Some say it is." Caden shrugged. "If there's a story to be told about those rocks, it's been told. From astronomers and archeologists to concerts and drug addicts, it attracts all sorts of attention."

Mica explained, "It's one of the oldest man-made structures that still stands, shrouded with myth and mystery."

"Intriguing," I said. "Do we have time?"

Caden called up to our driver, and Miles responded with a positive nod. Caden began a series of phone calls to arrange a guided tour of the monument. We needed a guide? Just how extravagant was this monument?

As much as I flustered and worried about the long car ride, I made a plan to pointedly ignore Caden by staring out the window at the expansive countryside and sleeping. After so little sleep last night, I was truly tired.

Chapter 8

"Emer," Caden's voice woke me like a whisper. After immersing myself in the feeling of laying down with wool blankets all around me, "waking" to the dream of sitting in a car with Caden and Mica jarred my mind. Perhaps my nap had been too short for dreams, for no memories of Somnus accompanied my sleep. Rubbing my eyes awake, I stretched my arms and back.

"Sorry to wake you," Caden said, then thought twice about his words and smirked. "But I guess we're trying to wake you, right? We've stopped at Stonehenge. Would you like to see it?"

I nodded as Miles opened our door. Caden took my hand to help me out of the vehicle, making me wish once more that I could feel something other than wool blankets.

We entered a visitor's center that showed maps and pictures of the monument of stones. Most fascinating were the pictures that theorized what the place looked like when it was first built compared to what remained standing.

Caden, as usual, scribbled away in his little notebook.

"You take a lot of notes," I said. "Do you prefer your phone or your notepad?"

"I prefer my notepad because I'm more likely to remember my thoughts if I scribble them down—which is the whole point of taking notes. The shortest pencil is greater than the longest memory."

"I suppose," I said, surprised by the little tidbits of wisdom that escaped his mouth sometimes.

A short bald man walked over to us, pocketing some wired device and adjusting a thick necklace of fabric with a plastic tag at the bottom.

"Welcome, Lords Seaver and Wright. My name is Gabriel, and I'll be your guide today. If you have any questions, you can ask me or one of the security guards around the stones wearing the yellow vests. Follow me."

We passed a small grouping of huts made of clay and thatched roofs. They reminded me of the Huiess houses built from the limited materials of the Sesso Desert.

Caden chuckled when I broke away from the guide to take a closer look.

"Emer," he said, "those are just recreations. The main attraction is this way."

"Nothing magical about them?" I asked.

"They're as magical as plastic."

I raised an eyebrow at him. "You have no idea how magical that strange material is. Its many uses and durability is astonishing."

Caden scoffed. "Ecologists hate it for its durability and production factories."

Ah, then Marin would hate plastic. Interesting.

I jogged to meet them again on the grassy path towards the large rings of stones. The closer we went, the bigger they became.

Our tour guide walked backwards to face us as he talked. "We normally only allow people inside with tour groups. The only real rule is this: do not touch the rocks."

"Are they cursed?" I asked.

"What? No, they're just one of the oldest structures of mankind."

"How old are they?"

The tour guide smirked. "Do you want the short version or the long version?"

"Short," I said, as Caden said, "Long."

Our guide chuckled, then pointed to me. "3100 BC." Turning to Caden, our guide launched into a dialogue about the bluestones being arranged first, something about the ditch, and…he lost me.

I leaned over to Mica to whisper, "What does BC mean, and how long ago was 3100?"

"Stonehenge is about five thousand years old."

I gaped. I knew of nothing in Somnus that old. Even our prehistoric folklore was only two thousand years old.

"Are these ruins of a building? Your people had technology to put this together even five thousand years ago?" I asked.

"Apparently." Mica shrugged.

I frowned. "What do you mean? You do not know?"

"That's what makes this place extra special. No one really knows," Mica said. "That's the great mystery and magic of them. When humanity had little more than the wheel for technology, they somehow found these massive boulders, chiseled them into blocks, then stacked them. They're so heavy, we don't even know how they got here, let alone stacked them. There are lots of theories and legends about how these stones were created and placed."

"Please explain. Were your people not always so skilled to create large structures such as St. Michael's castle?"

"Definitely not." Mica gestured at the guide. "How about we ask Gabriel?"

Hearing his name, the tour guide looked our way, returning Caden's attention to us.

"Can you tell us the origins of Stonehenge?" Mica asked.

"Of course. There are many. The oldest legend involves the devil himself throwing these stones into place. One stone—I can show you which—struck a friar's heel, naming the stone as the Friar's Heel." He pointed to a single stone near the walkway. "That same stone marks the point of the sun's rising position during the summer solstice, causing more theories about the site being built for astronomy purposes.

"The same folklorist," he continued, "also wrote the most widespread legend of Stonehenge's origins, saying the stones were brought from Ireland by Merlin himself. Before they were in Ireland, they were supposedly healing stones brought all the way from Africa by giants to memorialize the nobles who were killed nearby. They had fifteen thousand men who defeated an army, but they couldn't move the stones. It was only with Merlin's help that they were able to relocate the ring."

To my surprise, Caden nodded. "Geoffrey of Monmouth was quite the storyteller."

Gabriel pointed. "There's some probability to it. A modern archeologist says there's evidence in the blue stones that they could be the same as the Waun Mawn stone circle in Wales."

"That doesn't mean they're from Ireland," Caden said.

"Fascinating," I said, studying the boulders. The longer I remained in this world, the more convinced I became that this dream-world was no imaginary place. They had oceans, history, and even legends that extended beyond anything I knew.

112

We finished walking around the outside of the stone ring, and Gabriel invited us to step over the short rope fence. The terrain became less trampled, and my feet stumbled. Apparently, having a sense of touch really helped with balance.

Caden stopped in his tracks to offer me a supporting arm. "You're alright? If you're an actress, it seems you perform your own stunts."

"I—what?"

Mica chuckled. "Come on, I thought we were past that disbelief."

Caden gave me a wink before raising his phone to take a few pictures. Mica likewise pointed his larger camera at the stones. If I thought the stones were large from the perimeter, they were massive when standing beside them. The various colors of moss and mold were enough to say that these stones were older than anything in Somnus. I also expected them to be moldings of multiple materials. No, they were single stones, making their massive size all the more impressive.

Our guide wandered over to one of the security men and pulled out his phone to joke over something on the screen. Looking at their glowing boxes that worked magic for commoners, I wondered, could Somnus have such technology in a thousand more years?

Mica turned his camera on me again and directed me to stand in front, between, and behind a few of the monoliths. Caden stood beside his friend and watched, his piercing blue eyes on me.

"Nothing's happening," he said. "I don't think your mere presence is going to activate anything. Maybe you need to do your plant-growing thing first. To invite the magic or something."

"Plant-growing thing?" I asked. "I thought writers were supposed to be eloquent with words."

"Words are hard," he mumbled, then added, "Especially as a writer. I know the limitations of words."

"Talking is hard," Mica agreed, snapping another picture of a monolith. "That's why I prefer pictures. A single image is worth a thousand words."

Likewise, I found talking to my plants much easier than talking to people. Plants actually listened. Surveying the area, the only plants available were grass, grass, and more grass. "You think that my magic will invite more?"

Caden shrugged. "Nothing else has worked. It wouldn't hurt to try…unless the security catches you. Don't let them think you're up to anything shady, or they'll fine you. Seriously, don't touch the stones."

"Alright," I said, but still hesitated. Maybe it was my nerves about this mysterious place. With so many legends and unknowns about the stones, who knew what would happen if I brought magic to the place?

A growing part of me had to admit that I was nervous to leave. After experiencing such marvels and wonders in this world, I hesitated to say goodbye.

Goodbye to these rolling grasslands with no mountains to stop the horizon. Goodbye to that rushing gray ocean and wide expanse of endless water. Goodbye to the fascinating plants and flowers with their variety of shapes and colors.

Goodbye to Caden and Mica.

Caden bowed his head closer. "You're alright?"

I swallowed back the majority of my emotions. "What will happen to me when I wake? Will I disappear from here forever? Will I ever see this dream again? What if I forget?"

His beautiful blue eyes slanted upward. "I don't know. Sometimes you can repeat dreams. Maybe you'll come back."

"And if not? How will I thank you?"

Caden's eyes remained sad, though one corner of his lips raised into a little smile. "You don't need to thank us. Mica might want a thank you, but you've given me plenty to think about. Not just by inspiring my writing; I don't think I'll ever forget you, Emer."

I matched and raised his smile. Yes, I could leave with that hope in my heart.

My next objective was to decide where to test my magic. At the assumed entrance of the monument? Or near the top, where two particular stones stood side by side, in perfect symmetry with the most complete section of the ring? Or in the center, where several smaller boulders lay fallen on the ground?

The whole area was neatly trimmed, though the grass around the smaller center stones grew tall. I stepped to the middle of the stones, careful not to touch them. There was just enough space for one person to walk between. I crouched and stroked some of the longer blades of grass.

"Hello," I said. "I need to wake up and return to my home. Can you help me?"

The grass remained the same.

"Come on," I urged. "Out of all the places we visited, you are supposed to be most familiar with legends and magic. There must be something you can do."

Did the grass stretch a little taller?

"Look at you, so tall and healthy. I hope you know how beautiful you are—indeed, you might be some of the most beautiful grass I have ever seen. I would wager that the gardeners here take care of you with just as much thought as those of St. Michael's mount."

The blades beneath my hands shivered. A few of them reached for me. I reached back, urging them with magic that I barely understood.

Several of the green blades straightened, standing tall and pointed…like needles.

I gasped and shivered.

"Emer?" Caden asked, too far to the side to see exactly what happened.

Sunlight gleamed on a particular blade of grass. Before I could pull back, other blades of grass snapped at me, curling around my fingers, wrapping like coils up my hand. They grabbed me, pulled me, as if to retreat deep into the ground and take me with them.

Terror flashed through me with a small piece of hope. Was this the way home? I willed them to take me home.

I fell forward and instinct took over. I reached for the closest item of support. A boulder. While the stone felt as soft as wool, another sensation flashed through me. As much as I wanted to feel something other than wool, this feeling was worse. A throbbing sting struck on the tip of my index finger and echoed to my wrist.

I snapped my hand away from the boulder and grabbed my tender wrist with my other hand, crying out.

"Emer!" Caden yelled, and the closest security guard dashed to me.

"Did you touch the rocks?" the guard shouted.

"Forgive me," I said, "I was falling. It hurt me. Am I cursed for accidentally touching it?"

As if this dream state was not already a curse. The stinging pain ebbed away, but my hand still pulsed with pressure.

"What's going on?" the security asked.

"We were, er—" Mica shrugged "—watching the grass grow."

The security raised a dubious eyebrow. "There's a fine for touching the rocks."

"I know," Caden grumbled.

I panicked. "Please, forgive me. It was an accident, and Honorables Seaver and Wright had no part in my fall."

The security eyed Caden and Mica when I mentioned their titles. "We'll let you off with a warning this time, but I must ask that you leave now."

"Of course," I said with a humble curtsy.

"Thank you," Caden said, then beckoned me away. "Come on. I don't think anything else is going to happen here. We should be back in London soon."

I sighed. Frustrating as it was that I remained asleep, a small part of me was relieved and excited to continue this dream. If only the throbbing in my hand would go away.

I flexed my fingers and shook out my hand, but the only cure seemed to be time as we returned to the vehicle and the road.

Chapter 9

As much as I wanted to remember Somnus, I feared Caden invading my dreams again, of watching him die again, removed from his future without even a goodbye.

Thankfully, no dreams stirred my sleep while I napped in the automobile. The sun neared the horizon by the time I woke, but the sun and horizon were the least of my interests when I looked out the window of the speeding vehicle.

A city had swallowed us while I slept.

It was more of everything than the cities I knew. More buildings, more people, more sounds, and more smells. Every turn revealed something new and extraordinary. The roads were lined with buildings so close that they shared walls. Brick and stone buildings of multiple floors sat on colorful businesses made with advanced materials. One section was blocked with glossy fabric on the lower level as construction scaffolds rose above. Trees and bushes grew in the middle of walkways, and we passed almost as many two-wheeled contraptions as four-wheeled.

The streets were far more complicated yet organized than those of Somnus. We stopped, sped forward, and made sharp turns without any rhyme or reason to my understanding. At least our driver understood the rules behind the chaos. Our vehicle crowded among others, many were black and round, while several others were red and tall enough for two levels of seats. Both of these types had banners of striking pictures on their tops or sides. Crowded as the roads were, the walkways were equally busy with pedestrians.

I gaped out the window, almost oblivious to Caden's repositioning to lean beside me. Almost.

"Emer," he whispered close by. "Welcome to London."

"There are so many people," I said.

He chuckled. "It's the evening rush hour. Everyone's getting off work and heading home or to their favorite pubs. Emer?"

"Yes?" I turned from the window, surprised to find him close enough to smell mint on his breath.

"Before we return to my family's estate, we should address the elephant in the room."

"Elephant?" I asked.

Mica chuckled, and Caden took my hand.

"Things are a little different in the city," he said. "I know it's an insult to refer to a princess as a lady, but it's the smarter option for your time in London."

"Why is that?"

120

"Well, princesses aren't common here," Caden explained. "Claiming to be one causes a bit of a stir. Whereas there are lots of ladies, and no one will question your status if you claim to be a lady of, say, New Zealand or somewhere in the Commonwealth. No one will pester you for your mysterious situation."

"I understand," I said. "People dislike the idea of being figments of my imagination, thus I should refrain from telling them the truth about my dreaming state and royal status. I will follow your suggestion."

Caden smirked. "Something like that."

The vehicle stopped and went silent. Between all the stops and turns of the city, I was unaware that we reached our destination in the middle of a street.

"Miles," Caden asked our driver, "please see the Honorable Wright home."

Mica grinned and punched his friend in the shoulder. "Don't have too much fun without me. If you go exploring in the city, be sure to invite me."

Footmen approached the vehicle and opened the door for us. Caden stepped out first, greeted by a well-dressed servant.

"Honorable Seaver, welcome home. Was your trip satisfactory?"

Caden smiled and reached his hand back into the car to help me.

"Yes. I went on an adventure so grand that I was unable to finish it. So I brought it home with me. Have the Satin Room readied to welcome Lady

121

Emerald Reo from New Zealand. Arrange a handmaid to see to her comforts."

I stepped onto the pavement and took in the five-leveled townhouse. Made of red brick and white columns, it was ornate and well-kept. The tall home was smashed between two more on either side, making it difficult to estimate its depth.

A footman's eyes widened a bit from Caden's words. "Yes, m'lord. Where shall I relocate Lady Elmsworth?"

Caden's attention on me paused. He dropped my hand with a small cough. "Right. I forgot the guest list. One loses track in the country. Arrange for Lady Reo in the Velvet Room then."

"I will see it done, m'lord."

With one last glance at Caden, I followed a footman inside. After a small marbled vestibule, the home opened to a spacious green carpeted lounge to the left and a long hallway to the right. Going forward, I could choose to go upstairs via an elegant wooden staircase that continued for at least four levels, or continue on the same level down a stretch leading to what looked like a dining room. The footman guided me to the right, down the hallway and up a separate set of carpeted stairs to the third landing. With a door on the left and a door on the right, the footman unlocked the door on the left and carried my luggage through. A narrow hallway separated a bedroom from a living room with a small kitchen space. The whole flat was nicely furnished with soft colors against the old brick. Everything in the kitchen area shined like the purest metals.

The footman set down my pack and bowed. "Dinner will be served in two hours. We will have a handmaid assigned to you soon. Does your ladyship have any requests for your handmaid, dinner, or accommodations?"

I tried not to stare like a doe-eyed fool. What was I to do there? "When may I see the Honorable again?"

"The young master has some duties to attend, though I expect he will be present at dinner."

"Thank you," I said. "You may be excused."

He bowed once more then left. Odd that his mannerisms would make me feel more at home than the surroundings of St. Michael's Mount.

Unpacking took all of ten minutes as I explored the space that was apparently left to me alone. Unlike the hotels of Boscastle and Penzance, I had free access to my own fireplace, kitchen with confusing gadgets, and a water closet with a toilet and shower.

I was in the middle of freshening myself with a sample of perfumes when someone knocked on my door.

"Lady Reo?" a matured female voice asked.

"Yes, coming," I said, failing to tuck an errant strand of hair back before opening the door. A woman of about forty harvests stood before me in a humble curtsy.

"Good afternoon, Lady Reo. My name's Jessabelle. I'll be your handmaid during your stay with the Seavers."

I gestured for her to rise. Her black hair, eyes like onyx, and skin tones of the healthiest gardening soil reminded me of the people of Huiess.

"Thank you for your kind welcome, Jessabelle," I said. "Do we have time for a tour before dinner is served?"

"Yes, m'lady," she said, then guided me from my living space.

She explained that the East Wing was mostly for guest rooms. Apparently, there was a basement for the kitchens, laundry, and servants' rooms. The lord had a meeting room on the main floor before the dining room and a separate study room on the second floor.

"Do you have a favorite room?" I asked her as we headed up the stairs again.

"The loft."

"May we go there?"

She smiled and gestured up. "As long as you don't mind a bunch of stairs. It's at the top."

I leaned over the railing to look up through the stairway. Caden's house was as tall as my father's castles. No problem.

Four flights of stairs later, we came to a landing with a small water closet and spare room. The room was crowded with heirloom furniture, including a bassinette, hope chest, rocking chair, and wardrobe.

"This was the nursery," Jessabelle said. "I practically raised the young master up here. This is where I read him stories of Peter and Wendy, Jim Hawkins and Long John Silver, and Tom Sawyer and Huckleberry Finn. When he was older, he'd come back up here to read Pratchett, Tolkien, and Herbert. He'd read in that bay window with his favorite blanket and pillow, asking me to bring him a cup of tea. Even still, if he's nowhere to be found, I'll find him up here, sitting on that window sill with his writing pad or phone."

Though the stories and names she used were unfamiliar, I easily imagined Caden sitting by the window with a book or his favorite little notepad. Every piece of the picture made me smile.

"Thank you," I said.

She smiled back. "Thank *you*. No other guests ask to see this room. It's not usually included in the tour since it's not commonly used anymore, and few want to walk all the way up here."

"It was worth the effort," I said.

On our way back down, an open door on the second level invited my curious eyes. Inside, I found a wooden ballroom with a small elevated stage and strange light fixtures on the ceiling.

"Ah, yes," Jessabelle said, following me into the room. "This is where the party will be held this weekend. I assume you're attending?"

I smirked. "I hope to be invited. If not, I have snuck into dances before."

"So, you're a serial party crasher?" a male voice asked.

I spun around. Caden stood at the door.

"I should warn you," I said, "that I have stolen away to midnight dances far too many times to remain cooped in my room."

He blinked at me. "I don't mean to lock you away, but I don't want you to feel embarrassed or out of place from the party. Londoners probably dance differently than you're used to in—er, New Zealand."

It was my turn to hesitate. I knew dances from all three kingdoms, though this world was more foreign than any of those. "Oh. Then I suppose you will need to teach me."

He laughed. "You're stubborn. If you're determined to attend no matter what, then it's my public duty to teach you enough not to make a fool of yourself and my family. Miles," he called to his valet in the doorway, "can you be our maestro?"

Miles nodded and went to play with some knobs and buttons situated in the wall.

Caden brightened. "We should probably start with footing and positions."

I raised an eyebrow at him. "I know how to dance. Simply not your dances. Probably. What is the most common?"

"That depends on the event," he said. "For this upcoming party, it's the waltz. If you dance as much as you say you do, then this should be easy." He nodded to Miles, and suddenly the air filled with the simple notes of a harp.

I started a little, surprised. "Magnificent," I whispered. "Where is the harpist?"

"I'll explain recordings later," Caden said. "For now, let's go over the basics. Do you hear the three-beat rhythm?"

I listened for a couple measures, then nodded. The tune was slow and simple, though beautiful and soothing. "Does this piece have a name?" I asked Miles.

"'Gymnopedie,' by Erik Satie," he said.

"I love it," I said, closing my eyes and swaying to the rhythm.

"Good," Caden said, "you feel the beats. One, two, three; one, two, three. This is the foundation for the waltz."

I watched as he stepped forward and to the side, then back and to the side to return to the same spot he started.

"This," he explained, "is the simplest form of the waltz. The women mirror the men, so as I step forward with my left leg—"

"I step back with my right. Yes, yes," I said. It all looked boringly simple to me. Where was the hand movement? The hops, kicks, and claps? He continued to show me the footing and ways they could transition into more complicated steps. Still, I became bored with the simplicity.

"Alright, I think I have this one ready," I said. "Do you have anything else?"

"Hold on," Caden said, and gestured for me to step closer. "Now that you know the footing, will you honor me with a dance?"

"Were we not already dancing?"

"Not as partners. The waltz has a specific position."

I took his offered hand and wished to feel his warmth. His other hand…slid around my waist.

Goddesses above, what—

He pulled me closer. Very close.

"Caden!" I hissed. "What sort of ball is this?"

"A modern one." He smirked. "I know the waltz was scandalous when first introduced, but I assure you, this is our most proper dance these days. Your free hand goes on my shoulder. Just feel the motion and follow my lead."

I muttered, "You know that I cannot feel you."

He paused. "Er, right. That will make this harder. Try to follow the motion of the music. I'll guide you through the rest."

He stepped forward, and I matched him with a step back. I watched for the pressure he put on my waist and hands, willing my mind to relay the pressure (woolen as it was) to my body. I stumbled a couple times, but Caden's arms kept me from falling.

"Keep your eyes on me," he said. "Feel the motion of the music."

I raised my eyes to his. By the goddesses, he was close! We were almost embracing, like we danced with danger, halfway between taking each other into our arms and pushing each other apart. My mind and feet stumbled on the paradox. His foot landed on mine and we tittered with our apologies.

"Perhaps," I said, "it would help if I demonstrated the styles I know. Somnus and Ormio have a few dances that do not require touch to lead."

Caden raised a curious smirk. "Oh? You want to do a solo?"

"If it would help. Could you play something with a similar tempo, but a little more bounce to it?"

Miles searched through the strange musical machine until the music stopped abruptly. The next sound I heard was difficult to describe. It began with vocals that sounded warped by water. The instruments were light and quick, in and out with strange rhythms. Within a couple measures, synchronized clapping joined, and the instruments crescendoed into deep drums. The rhythm overwhelmed all else. Even as I stood shocked by the cacophony and strangeness of the noises, my muscles desired to move with the beat.

"What hypnotism is this?" I gasped. "What a complicated piece to play."

"I bet I could play it," Caden teased, "on my phone. Miles," he called, "a little less bounce. Emer, give us an idea of the music from Somnus."

The sounds that claimed to be music stopped.

Somnus. The sounds of Somnus. They were all too easy to remember, even if they were less clear. I closed my eyes and stepped aside for more room. I pretended my partner stood to my left and began to move with the melodies in my head.

The first song that came to my mind was a slow one. My arms waved gracefully in wide arcs over my head and across my body. Every measure had three strong beats followed by two half beats. At first, I hummed the tune. When I became lost in the memories, I sang the words.

"When I contemplate
On our sorry state
You will demonstrate
Your love's heavy weight.
Do not complicate
Or commiserate
Stay, don't separate
Say 'tis not too late."

I opened my eyes again to find myself only a step away from the wall. Blushing, I spun back to Caden. He wore his usual expression of wide-eyed wonder.

"Where did you learn to sing so well?" he asked.

I shrugged to subdue the fairies in my stomach from his compliment. "I grew up singing along with the melodies of life."

Miles stared at me with knitted eyebrows. "That was…an interesting tango."

"Tango?" Caden laughed. "Miles, play 'Don't Fall in Love.'"

"Yes, m'lord."

A new piece began that almost reminded me of the sounds of Somnus. I stepped in time, taking a few simple steps from my homeland's dance. Caden mirrored me.

"You can fall in quicksand or down a canyon,
Just don't fall in love.
You can fall like rain on a land of famine,
Just don't fall in love."

Caden followed my movements one step behind. I stepped closer so our hands met in the center for the turns. By the third repetition, he began to remember the steps and focused on my face instead of the motions. We locked gazes. My cheeks heated from the piercing of his blue irises. I focused on the song's lyrics to distract me from his stare.

"You can fall on concrete, dust off and stand,
Because what goes down, can still rise again,
But falling in love
Is a fall that breaks or will never land."

With the close of the song, our hands met in the center and we faced each other, hearts beating heavily. I could only blame the dance for half of my throbbing heart.

Chapter 10

"My lord," Miles said, breaking the moment as he stepped away from another servant at the door. "Dinner is ready to be served."

"Right," Caden said, then returned to me. "May I escort you to the dining hall, my lady?"

"How chivalrous of you."

He extended his arm and I looped my hand around his elbow. I allowed myself to appreciate his gentlemanly manner as he escorted me. Every second that I wished to feel his arm under my hand, I reminded myself to remain aloof. Those reminders became more feeble and faint with each memory made with Caden. The dancing had not helped.

"I've been thinking," he said as we walked down the hallways, "of places to take you in London. It's not particularly magical, but I'd like to show you Kew Gardens."

"Kew Gardens?" I repeated.

He shrugged like an adorable sheep. "I know you're worried about returning to Somnus, but there's so much to do and see in London. If we go to the gardens in the morning, you can stay for this week-end's ball. Perhaps we may include an appropriate dance for you."

Unable to bite back my smile, I said, "I would appreciate that."

He wanted to prolong my time in England. He wanted me to stay and dance with him again.

"I'll have Jessabelle help you prepare in any way necessary. Has she served you well?"

"Oh, yes. She is marvelous. She even showed me the loft and shared some glimpses of your childhood."

"Nothing too embarrassing, I hope?" He rubbed the back of his neck.

I laughed. "You may never know."

We stepped into the dining hall. An older man and woman were already seated at the head and right side of a wooden dining table, set for five.

"Father, Mother," Caden said, greeting the two people at the table. "May I introduce Lady Emerald Reo from New Zealand."

Caden was a perfect blend of his parents from the analyzing eyes of the man and the angular facial structure of the woman.

"Ah, yes." Lord Seaver stood and smiled with a touch of amusement. "We hope our boy presented our family well, despite his adventuring soul."

I curtsied. "He and the Honorable Wright were perfect gentlemen, my lord."

Lord Seaver's smile broadened, and he gestured for me to sit two seats away. That would put me beside him.

Lady Seaver cleared her throat with a mouse-like cough. "I believe that seat was saved for Lady Elmsworth."

If his parents noticed Caden's little groan and slumped shoulders, they ignored them. Lord Seaver's smile faltered for only a flash before he passed the speaking role to his wife.

Lady Seaver grinned at me, though her smile faded before reaching her eyes. "You must forgive my husband. His mind is preoccupied with legislatures, not table placements. Lady Reo, please, take a seat beside me."

While her words sounded friendly, I knew better. Sitting next to her set me farthest from Caden.

Still, I was a guest at their table. As a stranger, I counted my blessings. Pretending it was all inconsequential, I took my seat.

Caden remained standing as the door opened again to reveal a beautiful woman. She was not beautiful like my younger sister, Pearl, whose innocence radiated from her even if she was covered in muck. This woman was beautiful in a methodical way that testified to hours of practiced styling and years of disciplined posturing. She was maybe a year older than I was and wore a slim red dress that cropped above her knees and accentuated her lovely features.

Her silvery blonde hair was pulled away from her face in an intricate braid. Either her skin was truly unblemished or she used face paints that perfectly blended into her pearly skin. Her nose was as straight and sharp as an arrow, and whatever she did to her eyebrows made them perfect without a hair out of place.

Lady Elmsworth greeted us with a cunning smile to show off the whitest teeth I had ever seen. She crossed the room to Caden with open arms.

"You've returned!"

Caden met the lady's approaching embrace by reaching for her hand. Lady Elmsworth ignored it and slipped her thin arms around his shoulders. Caden's father made a small coughing sound while his mother smiled like a sly fox.

Lady Elmsworth held onto Caden longer than appropriate, then turned victorious eyes on me.

"And who is this? Are you going to introduce yourself?"

I stood and dipped myself into the smallest curtsy. "Lady Emerald Reo, from New Zealand."

"Another lady?" she asked, raising one of those perfectly manicured eyebrows. "Come for the festivities? How sporting."

She narrowed her scrutinizing eyes at me while smiling like she already considered herself a victor over me. I may have challenged her back without

Caden's apologetic grimace behind her periphery. Instead, I smiled.

Lady Elmsworth took the seat beside Caden, and my smile dampened. Would this whole evening be a sea of little ups and dashing downs? How much of this could my heart take?

Lady Seaver spared me no more than a glance. So much for her friendly invitation to sit beside her. Instead, she gestured with her eyes between Caden and Elmsworth. Caden was either blind to his mother's promptings, or he ignored them.

Servants placed a small plate of leafy vegetables before each of us, and Lady Seaver gave up on subtleties.

"Lady Elmsworth has been most helpful in arranging the preparations for your party. You should demonstrate your gratitude by offering her the first dance."

My insides squirmed at her implications. If his mother's words agitated Caden, his only reveal was an irritated wiggle of his fork. Otherwise, his expression was cool as a stone.

"Of course, Mother. Charlotte, will you accept our small token of gratitude by honoring me with a dance during the ball?"

"Oh," she said, glancing at me victoriously. "The honor would be all mine."

Lord Seaver did another one of his small throat-clearing coughs.

"Lady Reo," he said in a voice that was mildly rougher than Caden's, "Caden says you hail from New Zealand. What brings you all the way to London?"

"University," Caden answered. "Isn't that right, Emer? You were traveling the country before the term started. You'll be studying agriculture, right?"

Struggling to keep up with his fabrications, I simply nodded. Our salad plates were removed and replaced with plates of some juicy meat and baked pastry. Both were seasoned with flavors that occupied our attention for a few glorious bites.

"Agriculture?" Lady Seaver asked. "What do your lands produce?"

Caden took a bite, leaving me alone to answer.

I shrugged. "A little bit of everything. Our largest market is fishing, but I find joy in plant cultivation."

Lady Elmsworth piped up. "Gardening is tedious, but I do love the smell of flowers." Touching Caden's arm, she asked, "Could you take me to Kensington Gardens again? I hear the palace has a new exhibit."

I struggled to suppress my fury at her casual contact. How dare she be so friendly with him? How dare she enjoy the sensation of touch—the simple capability to feel something, anything, especially Caden, without the intrusion of wool blankets? Except her infuriating tactics continued. She lightly stroked his forearm and cooed, "Do you remember when I was in the hospital after that dreadful accident? You filled my hospital room with more roses than I could count."

Because she was too dim-witted to count higher than a dozen? I literally bit back my snide remark.

Unfortunately, Lord Seaver noticed. "Lady Reo, as a botanist, do you have a favorite plant or flower?"

My initial thought was of the unbreakable vines that grew kilometers long and were strong enough to use as fishing lines. I doubted that they existed in this world. I scrambled to remember the types of plants of England.

"The dandelion," I said.

Caden choked on his food, Lord Seaver stifled a laugh, and Lady Seaver blinked.

Lady Elmsworth sneered. "The pokey little weed?"

"A weed is no more than a plant in an unwanted spot," I said. "The dandelion is one of the first flowers I encountered in England and gives me fond memories. I consider its bright yellow colors and white balls of cotton to be friendly and cheerful. Even its 'pokey' leaves show a sense of self-preservation that inspires natural defense." I had even done a little research on Google while working on Mrs. Priddy's garden to discover more. "They are also entirely edible—roots and all, replenish soil, and provide nectar for bees and butterflies. Then you have the custom of making wishes by blowing away the seeds, which I find positively delightful."

The table was silent for a couple of seconds after I finished. Finally, Lord Seaver smirked to his wife.

"How about we save some money next Valentine's Day and I grab you a bushel of dandelions instead of roses?"

She replied with a downward stare of disapproval, and Lord Seaver laughed. Caden joined in the laughter, his eyes meeting mine. My stomach became a flurry of dandelion seeds. Lady Elmsworth added her jittering sounds, as if the whole conversation was a joke.

After a small serving of pudding cake, I thanked Lord and Lady Seaver for the meal, then excused myself with a curtsy.

"Would you like me to escort you?" Caden asked.

"Caden," his mother rushed in. "We have matters to discuss regarding preparations for your party and news of London during your absence. Jessabelle is fully capable of directing our guest back to her quarters."

Caden clenched his jaw, but nodded.

Sleeping was difficult again. My thoughts crowded with Caden, his parents, Lady Elmsworth, this home, this lifestyle, and how I fit in none of it. I closed my eyes and concentrated on the true feeling of lying in my bed at home between wool blankets…

I must have fallen asleep somewhere in there, as the next moment had me waking with the sun shining through the lightwell windows. The low murmur of vehicles driving by echoed through the well. I expected the city to be noisy, but these sounds were different from Somnus.

Only then did I realize that I had not dreamt of Somnus. I remembered no dreams at all. I closed my eyes and tried to picture my sisters. Garnet helping Father with some tricky situation, Marin at the docks with her husband, Pearl complimenting my work in the gardens, and Tanzi tagging along for all of it.

I tried to expand the scenes beyond my sisters, but the vision blurred at the edges. Which people were Garnet and Father trying to help? Where were the dock workers beside Marin? What flowers did Pearl admire? I could picture my sisters in our bedchamber, but where were their morning whispers? Where were the cling-clangs of kitchen pots as the chefs prepared breakfast? Where were the dock workers shouting to each other?

A knock on my flat door shook away my confused thoughts. I went to the door and opened it for Jessabelle.

"Good morning, m'lady," she said with a little curtsy. "How may I assist you this morning?"

Strange, how much relief a handmaid offered. Despite the early hour, I smiled.

"Come in. How much time do I have before breakfast is served?"

"The cooks are working on some omelets and oatmeal. Do you have any requests?"

I waved a hand. "Whatever they make will be fine. It all sounds delicious. Will you help me with my hair?"

"Yes, m'lady. The young master said you didn't have much for a wardrobe, so he had me fetch you a couple dresses. I hope one of these will be to your liking."

She laid various outfits across my bed, most of them involving trousers. I chose a tan skirt that hugged my hips with a matching jacket that Jessabelle called a blazer, and a pink blouse for underneath.

Jessabelle made a couple suggestions for my hygiene, then prepared some accessories in the living area while I showered. Dressed in a provided robe, Jessabelle sat me down. She stylized my blonde hair with the skills of a professional, taming it with hot irons to perfectly frame my face.

"The young master mentioned Kew Gardens," she said, "so you'll want your hair up and a hat to keep it from blowing around. We want to show off this beautiful hair of yours, though. My daughters would call this princess hair."

"What?" I looked up, startled.

"Your hair. It's like a Disney princess. Long, blonde, thick, and naturally wavy. It's enviable. I know it's a lot to work with, but I hope you consider yourself truly blessed."

"I do. Thank you." I smiled to think of her reaction to Pearl's hair.

142

Jessabelle wove my hair into a large and flowering bun that rested against the back of my neck, then pinned a funny little pink hat at a harsh angle over my right eye. What an odd fashion statement.

The sun was fully up when a knock came at my door, and Jessabelle answered. "One moment, m'lord. She isn't quite ready yet."

I smiled at Jessabelle's definition of "ready." Finally, someone I could agree with. My face and hair were fancier than most days in Somnus, but I still wore only the robe. Jessabelle helped me into the clothes, then allowed Caden inside my living room. Since my bedroom was closed off from the rest of the flat, the living area was considered public enough with Jessabelle accompanying us.

He stopped short at the sight of me. "Wow—er, you look lovely. Are your accommodations suitable?"

"More than suitable," I said. Leaning in, I whispered, "Though, to be honest, the kitchen area confuses me."

He chuckled, then stepped over to explain the appliances.

"Mini fridge, keeps food cold. There's a freezer section on top for anything that needs the extra preservation, like ice cream or gelato. You're familiar with ovens, right?"

"Is that an oven?" I asked, pointing at the boxy appliance.

"And this is a stove top. It's outdated, but should still work. I believe you burned yourself on something similar at Boscastle? You probably won't need to use any of these since the staff prepares breakfast, lunch, tea, and dinner, but in case you want something on your own, you have the option. If you have any questions, Jessabelle should be able to assist you."

"This is all very kind. Thank you."

"Of course," he said.

I smiled, unsure what else to say. My mind was filled with his generosity and kindness, and how attractive it made him.

He shuffled in the silence. "I'm sorry about Lady Elmsworth. I forgot she'd be here."

I waved my hand with no consequence. If an irritating lady was too much for me to handle, I hardly deserved to be a princess.

"No matter what she says," Caden said, "I'm glad you're here."

"Thank you," I said, "though she said nothing to suggest otherwise."

"Good." He then raised a questioning smile. "You want a tour of the city?"

I grinned. "Show me everything."

Caden called Mica to meet us outside five minutes later. Hopping into the black vehicle with Miles driving, I felt like we were about to embark on another adventure.

"Where are we going first?" I asked.

"Kew Gardens," Caden said. "It's not particularly magical, but I think you'll like it."

We drove through the city for a few minutes before coming to an enclosed park. As soon as Mica handed me a map, I agreed with Caden. The place was magnificent and entirely dedicated to cultivating plants from various climates. I wished Marin could be with me. She would praise their fascinating greenhouses filled with plants that expanded my imagination.

"Are you gaining any inspiration?" I asked Caden. We stopped on a wide walkway lined with shrunken trees that Caden called bonsai trees. Whatever they were, they looked like fully-grown, magnificent trees, yet stood fewer than fifty centimeters tall.

"I'll admit," Caden said as he escorted me, "it's more fun to watch you interact with the plants than to watch the plants themselves."

I blushed and tried to busy myself with the shrunken oak tree labeled "Eastern Leaf." Caden's slow but long strides came to a stop behind me.

"I can't figure you out, Emer."

I straightened my spine to face him directly. At least, as much as I could for one as tall as he was. "What is there to figure?"

He rubbed the back of his head. "What were you like in your homeland? You're a princess, but you weren't the heir. You wanted to lead, but you didn't want to take your sister's place. What was the point of leading then?"

"My goal was never to become the leader. I wanted to prove myself capable of leading to support my sister. A leader cannot do everything alone and needs supporters. Without supporters, a leader cannot know what to do, and they will follow the whims of the people. If a leader only follows the people, then everyone goes in circles."

"Why do you want to take on that responsibility?" Caden asked. "I've seen my father in Parliament, and it looks exhausting. All the responsibilities, all the politicking, all the hoop jumping to pass small laws that will only satisfy a small group of people at best. Where's the satisfaction?"

"The satisfaction is in those people—however few—who benefit from my help. It is *because* I know that leading is difficult that I want to do it. I trust Father and Garnet to lead well, but I see how it taxes them. I want to aid them, but first, I must prove myself useful."

"Why?"

"What do you mean, 'why?'"

"Why do you need to prove yourself?"

Irritating man. Did he understand nothing? I burst, "Because what else am I good for? Garnet takes care of the laws and the throne. Marin takes care of the environment and trades with other kingdoms. Pearl takes care of the social wellbeing of the people,
146

and Tanzi…she still has time to determine where she fits. I am just the middle child with no prospects other than to marry well."

"Is that what you think?" He paused, sorting through my words. "So, if I'm understanding this right, you want to be valued?"

His words struck my core. Yes. I wanted more than to be seen or acknowledged. I wanted to be worth something. Valued.

He answered my silence with a little smile. "Doesn't everyone?"

We continued our walk, lost in thought while wandering between varieties of deciduous trees.

"What about you?" I asked. "How do you want to be valued? You have the opportunity to rise to lord under your father's tutelage, yet you traversed the country to find inspiration for your fictional stories. You have a convenient arrangement with Lady Elmsworth, yet you spend your time with a woman who belongs in another world. Why do you run away from the value others have given you?"

After a slow exhale, he said, "I'm a paradox, it's true. My heart is a Lake District Romantic who wants to live in the country and write fantasies from my mind. Yet my mind is entirely realistic and knows magic isn't real. One can't survive on dreams alone, and my heritage leaves me with certain expectations."

I frowned. "You do not believe in magic? Even my influence over plants? And I have survived on this dream for weeks. My very existence is a solid argument for magic and dreams."

"Sure." He shrugged. "You're an argument for chasing my dreams, yet your dream is to lead, which argues for me to rise to my father's legacy. So you're a paradox too."

"Perhaps I am. What are you going to do about it?"

"Not sure," he said. "But being with you inspires my dreams."

"How fitting for a person within my dream."

He laughed. "You really need to stop thinking that this whole world revolves around you."

"Oh, it definitely does not," I said. "I have absolutely no control over this dream. If I did, I would be home already, and you would be—" I cut myself off before blurting my honest thoughts. Instead, I finished with "—an actual gentleman."

He laughed again. How I loved the sound of his joy. "Come on, I'm escorting you, aren't I? This is only the beginning of your tour around London."

He was right. After Kew Gardens, we had gelato and crepes for lunch, then went to the Natural History Museum, including their butterfly exhibit. Mica sufficiently hid himself behind his camera within the exhibit, taking pictures of everything that moved, especially if it landed on me or a flower.

We ended the evening at a theater called The Globe. Caden rattled off a fanatical number of facts

148

concerning the theater house and some man named Shakespeare. I had to admit, the presentation of *A Winter's Tale* was highly entertaining.

If I was in charge of the sun and moon, I would have stopped them in their places to make the day last forever.

Despite our many adventures, sleep evaded me that night. Alone in my room, my mind returned to the dooming thoughts regarding my dreaming state and blurring memories of Somnus. I crept to the kitchen for a midnight snack, but a voice from behind a closed door stopped me in the hallway.

Caden.

I schooled my desire to eavesdrop until I heard the topic that kept me awake.

"—all she wants is to leave us forever."

"Forever?" a second voice asked. Mica. "Is that why you picked a bunch of non-magical places to visit today?"

"The Globe Theater's production of *A Winter's Tale* is magical enough, the way they make you believe the story's happening before your very eyes."

"The point is," Mica said, "you're prolonging Emer's stay. You distracted her with science and entertainment instead of researching how to actually help her."

Silence.

Then, a relenting grunt from Caden. "When she leaves, it'll all be over. She'll probably disappear with a show of twinkling lights and never look back."

"Will she?"

Caden's voice lowered, and I needed to press my ear to the door to hear. "She needs to. She'll never leave my thoughts, but it doesn't matter how crazy she drives me. Either she's certifiably insane, or she's a princess in another world. I'm already reaching above my station by entertaining ladies. I'm a man who's in over his head, even with my head in the clouds."

"Maybe you can go with her," Mica suggested.

Caden scoffed. "How? I'm not asleep like she is. That's assuming she even wants me. She's been distant lately, like she knew this was coming. Like she knew the only thing that would ever happen between us was a heartbroken goodbye."

Mica chuckled. "Have you been writing poetry again?"

"Shove off."

They said nothing for a few long seconds, and I forced myself to step away. As much as I wanted to barge into the room and declare my true feelings, Caden spoke the truth. We were worlds apart. Even if I wanted him to come with me when I woke up… how could he? It was better for us to deny our feelings and prepare for goodbye.

If only my heart could agree. The pain in my chest weighed heavily like an anvil. I was a fool, falling for a dream.

Chapter 11

"Does m'lady have any requests for tomorrow's ball gown?" Jessabelle asked while fixing my hair the next morning. "There isn't enough time to make a custom order, but anything from Harrods should be acceptable for the event."

I smoothed my hands down the lightweight dress Caden had bought me in Penzance. "My particular tastes might not be available or in fashion."

"You can browse their gowns on their website. I'll need to grab my phone from my locker if you want to look through it."

I nodded in thanks. "Yes, please."

My handmaid curtsied, then left the room. I complimented my little potted dandelions while waiting for her return. She came back with her phone and typed away to bring up a selection of dresses. The gowns were extravagant in the most incredible ways. The dresses flowed to the floor and covered the entire legs and ankles (save for a few that had slits all the way up the thigh). At least the modesty was closer to what

I was used to, but the fashions were beyond anything I knew from home.

Many were entirely sleeveless, some with almost no backs, and I wondered how they were supported. I picked out a few with sleeves. "Something like these will do. I am…unaccustomed to showing more skin than this."

"Of course, m'lady. We'll find something elegant."

"This one is lovely," I said, pointing to a dress with cap-style sleeves.

"That would be more appropriate for a horse race. What about this one?" Jessabelle pointed at a slim dress with lots of ruffles.

"The price is rather high," I said.

Jessabelle laughed. "Darling, they're all more expensive than my entire wardrobe, but that's the point of these fancy parties. If you don't spend more than a thousand quid on a dress that you'll only ever wear once, then you're not rich enough for these folks. The Honorable said he'll pay all your expenses, so if I were you, I'd pick the prettiest one."

I blinked in astonishment. "I thought that balls were meant to support and celebrate the craftspeople in their talents?"

"That's a novel idea," Jessabelle scoffed. "Now, what about this one?"

After a few more minutes of discussion and debate, I chose a green dress with tones of brown, thinking of the gown I had worn on my birthday.

Jessabelle took my measurements, glancing out the window between each notation.

"Is something the matter?" I asked.

She pointed at my plants. "Are those potted dandelions?"

I grinned. "Yes. I brought them with me from Boscastle."

Traveling with them had been easier than I thought, since Caden's vehicle had plenty of "cup holders" to keep them upright. The hardest part had been ignoring everyone's funny looks. Regardless, I adored them and placed them on the window sill of the lightwell. It was little light, though I encouraged them to grow with compliments every couple of hours.

"Are they special or something?" Jessabelle asked.

I said, "Yes. They were the first plants I gardened in England. They are my favorite, and I mean to keep them."

"Huh." My handmaid eyed them. "It's only that in the short time I've been here taking your measurements, I could swear they're blooming. See that one that's all big and yellow? I could have sworn it was just a bud when I came in."

I bit my lip, wondering how much to tell her. She seemed trustworthy enough, but I did not want to worry her.

"Jessabelle, I have two questions for you. First, can you keep a secret?"

She gave me a sideways glance. "I'm great at keeping secrets. It's the people I tell who have problems."

I laughed. It was the wrong answer, but I decided to move forward anyway. "Alright, second question: what if I told you that it was magic?"

She shoved her hand down the front of her dress to pull out a necklace with a five-pointed star, a crescent moon, and an eye in a triangle.

"What does that mean?"

She laughed. "It means I'm five steps ahead of you. What's magical about the plant then?"

"The plant is not magical, but I am. I can make plants grow by talking to them."

"Ah." Understanding lit her eyes. "That's why the young master speaks so highly of you."

Caden spoke highly of me? Except Jessabelle now believed that my magic was the only reason Caden had any interest in me. Was she wrong?

Pushing that thought away, I said, "Caden asked me not to say anything. Please, tell no one else in the household."

She made a sign of sealing her lips shut. "Just the household? Can I tell my psychic?"

"Psychic?" I asked, unfamiliar with the term.

"She's brilliant. She predicted which of my moles were cancerous. Saved my life, she did."

"Is she a seer?" I asked. There were magicians in this world after all? "Could I meet with her?"

"Normally, I'd say she's a busy woman, but I bet she'd make time to meet an enchantress like you. A lady from New Zealand, to boot. I should've known there'd be more magic there. I'll make an order for your dress, then stop by her shop to ask if she can meet you."

"Thanks," I said. "I was unaware of any other magics in this—area." I caught myself from saying "world." Admitting that I could perform mysterious feats of magic was one thing. Claiming to be asleep and from another world was another. The more I learned about this world and its different expectations, the more amazed I was that Caden and Mica believed me.

A knock on the door announced lunch time. Jessabelle opened the door to welcome a servant with a platter of food.

"Room service?" she asked.

The servant bowed. "The Seavers send their apologies to Lady Reo. They'll be unable to attend you for lunch as they're entertaining Lady Elmsworth at Kensington Gardens today."

"Oh," I said, annoyed at how much those words pierced me. Caden and his parents left me here alone, but took Lady Elmsworth? They toured gardens without me? Not that I had any claim on Caden, but he knew I liked gardens. His mother probably had a hand in the matter, but I still felt left out.

Pretending not to be bothered, I shrugged and accepted the platter. "Their apologies are accepted. I had preparations to make for the ball anyway."

Lunch was a quiet affair as Jessabelle became a servant in waiting, standing off to the side to refill my water and remove my dirty plates. I wanted to continue our conversations from before, but thoughts of Caden escorting Lady Elmsworth down garden pathways bogged my mind.

After lunch, Jessabelle left on her errands, and I wandered the townhome. Having nothing to do gave me too much time to think. I clenched my jaw, frustrated at myself for allowing Caden into my heart. Why should I care if Lady Elmsworth won his affections? He belonged in this world where I was no more than a false Lady from New Zealand. I found myself wandering up the stairs to the loft. I hoped to be alone, but found someone in the window sill.

"Caden?"

He sat with his back to the window, using the daylight to illuminate a small book in his hands. He wore grey trousers and a matching buttoned and sleeveless tunic of sorts over a long white shirt. His eyes snapped to mine, then his shoulders relaxed with relief.

"Emer?"

"I thought you went to the gardens with Lady Elmsworth," I said.

He answered with a sheepish shrug. "Miles might have mentioned that Charlotte was looking for me. I might have forgotten to come downstairs. I suppose they left without me."

"Why, Caden," I chided, stepping between the forgotten furniture to stand beside his bay window. "Did you come up here to hide?"

He ruffled the back of his hair. "Maybe," he said, squirming with sudden nerves. "I'm curious. From an outsider's perspective—particularly a woman's—what do you think of Charlotte?"

"Charlotte?" I asked. "You speak on a first name basis."

"So do you and I," he retorted. Point taken.

I sucked in my lips to keep my cheeks from reddening. He asked for my opinion as an outsider and as a woman. Not as a possible contender. Swallowing my jealousy, I said, "She is a smart match for a lord's son."

"A smart match," he repeated, studying me. "Sure, any lady of status would solidify mine, and I suppose Charlotte is socially affluent."

"To say the least," I agreed. "And handsome, is she not?"

Caden shrugged. "She's not hard on the eyes, if I'm honest."

"If you are honest?" I repeated. "Does that mean you lied to me other times?"

"No," he said. "Not exactly. I'm not a liar, but my father's having me read this book that argues true honesty is a myth."

"A myth?" I frowned. "In the same way that you think that my world is mythical? Then you have lied to me?"

He reached for my arm, as if worried that I might leave him. "Princess, is it possible to know every little thing about someone? The book explains true honesty gives full disclosure without censorship. I haven't lied to you. But everyone withholds truths that aren't important for the moment. Consider everything you've learned these past few weeks. Would you have asked me to explain every single detail about myself in that first moment when we found you on the path outside Boscastle?"

I grumbled rather than admit the sense in his reasoning. "What really matters is the fact that you avoided the truth right now. What do you think of Lady Elmsworth? Your mother obviously considers her a fine match for you. Do you agree?"

Caden's eyes met mine for a long second. "No. She's as shallow as a puddle over a sewage drain, wittingly sharp as a rubber ball, and as politically delicate as a brick through a window."

I laughed and my heart lightened. She had a long road before winning his affections.

"However," he added, and my heart sank. "My opinion doesn't matter. So long as I skirt my responsibilities, my father skirts my opinion. Without the will to follow my father's legacy and lead our political faction, I haven't the will to lead my own heart—so thinks my father."

"That is false," I said. To emphasize the honesty of my next words, I sat next to him in the bay window and took his hand. "You can lead, and you do have the will to lead your own heart, which proves that you can lead the fac—"

"Emer," he said, placing his free hand on top of mine. "Please. My failings are not your concern. Even if I played myself to my father's standards, he'd say my heart shouldn't have opinions in politics."

"And if your heart had an opinion?" I asked carefully, meeting his blue eyes as they wavered between decisions.

"As a writer," he said, "they say to show, not tell." His eyes softened and sank to my lips. He leaned towards me.

My heart leapt to my throat with both elation and fear.

"That would be a mistake," I said. As much as I wished for his kiss, the image of his death—of his betrayed eyes—haunted me. "I dreamt that we—that I shared a kiss with someone, and the poison that put me to sleep was spread to him. He died."

"He died?" Caden rocked back in surprise. "From a kiss?"

"Anything as much as a kiss will kill them," I said, my voice drifting as I echoed my sister's warning.

Caden frowned. "But that was only a dream, right? That doesn't mean it would happen in real life."

I tilted my head. "This is also only a dream to me."

Caden's hands pulled back a little from mine. I wanted to hold him tighter to me, but that desire was the very reason I needed to let him go. And now he knew why. He pursed his lips in thought.

"So it's a good thing we didn't try the fairytale princess method and line up a bunch of men to try kissing you awake."

I squished my face with disgust. "Goddesses above, did you truly consider that?"

He laughed. "Not enough to advertise. Can you imagine the headlines? 'Sleeping Princess Kissing Spree.' My father would be ashamed if word got out that I was involved."

I smirked back. "The more status we have, the more responsibilities we have for our people. As my father would frequently remind my sisters and me, we were chosen from birth for these rights. It is our duty, privilege, and curse."

"Curse, indeed." Caden nodded.

"Speaking of responsibilities," I said, "we should probably part. Sitting alone in this bay window might create its own gossip."

His smirk almost challenged the gossip to do its worst. As much as my heart wanted to agree, my mind argued. I stood and stepped back to the door.

"Thank you," Caden said, "for your confidence in me, and for explaining your concerns."

"Of course, Honorable Seaver." I departed with a little curtsy.

I caught the return of Lady Elmsworth and Caden's parents while on my walk back to my room.

Lady Elmsworth called out to me with all the fondness and excitement of a long-lost friend. "Lady Reo! There you are! How unfortunate you couldn't join us for Kensington Palace. Come—" she linked her arm around mine "—I have some things to discuss with you."

Too confused to say no, I let her lead me to her flat across the landing from mine.

Lady Elmsworth's flat was, in brief, more open than mine. While mine welcomed its occupants with a narrow hallway between the water closet, living space, and bedroom, Lady Elmsworth's opened directly to the living area, brightly lit with two windows facing the front street. I considered my kitchen area shiny, yet hers was blinding. Everything from the sleek window cupboards to the flat stovetop looked impressive and futuristic. I was actually glad Caden had assigned me the other room. I would have fumbled with such appliances.

There was also the matter of the bed location.

No walls or panels hid its whereabouts as it occupied the left side of the room. There was absolutely no privacy. I blushed to think of Caden explaining my kitchen appliances with this layout.

As soon as we stepped over her threshold, all charm disappeared. Lady Charlotte Elmsworth sat like a woman of power on her couch. Only her eyes and mouth moved as she directed me to "Sit."

My natural annoyance wanted to glare at her orders. I was a princess. She would not dare to command me if this world acknowledged my royal status.

I sat in the armchair beside her couch and waited for her to state her mind. She had brought me here. Asking her why would bow to her whims. Instead, I waited in silence, scrutinizing the woman who refused to feel intimidated by me.

Unfortunately, she knew the game of quiet scrutiny and played it well. We sat in silence, analyzing each other for weaknesses, for more than ten minutes.

Finally, Lady Elmsworth huffed. "You might have nothing else to do other than to sit here and bask in my presence, but I have tasks to perform."

"Perfect," I said with a gracious smile. "Since you forced my detour, I thought you simply wanted to bask in *my* presence."

I might have missed her wince without my previous scrutinization. Shifting her expression to a challenge accepted, she smiled back. "Caden really is a tease, isn't he?"

Unsure how to respond, I said nothing.

"You probably didn't notice, but he came to my flat last night. I'll leave it to your imagination why. But I will point out the fact that I was assigned this room. Not because it's more updated, but because it's a more welcoming and open layout. It feels so much more intimate, don't you agree?"

No matter how stoic I kept my expression, my blood rushed to my cheeks. I refused to give in to her jests. She was testing me, pushing to see how I would break. Garnet would hold strong. Marin would hold strong. Pearl would probably misunderstand her implications. Tanzi—if she understood—would have thrown a tantrum. Me? I pushed back.

"Are you sure you want to leave it to my imagination?" I asked. "I recently discovered just how wild my imagination can be. For instance, have you ever wondered what unicorn meat might taste like? I imagine it would taste a lot like your personality: too gamey and tough, bitter and salty, and overall most unpleasant."

Her eyes flared.

Without waiting for her permission, I stood. "If you will pardon me, people actually rely on me, so I had best be going."

"Yes, you had best," she snapped. "What was that definition that you gave for weeds at dinner?" She paused thoughtfully. "Oh, yes. A plant where it isn't wanted. In that case, little weed" —she sneered at me— "stay out of my way, or I'll have you sprayed."

"Sprayed?" I asked. I never heard of spraying plants before, unless— "Does that make you a skunk? How appropriate."

I gave her a courtesy curtsy with a side of sarcasm before making my way out.

Jessabelle greeted me in my bedchambers with the most beautiful gown. It was a deep green with thin designs of golden vines climbing from the bottom hem until they connected and interwove around the waist. The neckline was lower than my usual, giving the gown a hint of rebellion. The sheer sleeves draped to my knees like wings, transforming any rebellious thoughts to birds and angels. Jessabelle helped me into it, tsking over a snagged thread around my bottom hemline.

"I can tighten it with a little threadwork, and that should fix it just right. Don't you worry; it'll be ready before tomorrow evening. How about we find some shoes and jewelry to complete your look?"

Chapter 12

I tiptoed from my room and felt transported back to Somnus, sneaking out of the castle with my sisters. Jessabelle had thoroughly distracted me all day with shopping online and at various places around the city. London truly was a marvel. I stepped from my room in the gown, shoes, and jewelry Jessabelle had ordered from Harrods. It was much slimmer and more form-fitting than the gowns of Somnus, but beautiful and elegant in its own way. I wore deep green emerald earrings rimmed with gold to match the tones of the ivy gown. My new shoes hid beneath the gown, but I loved the way that they supported my arches and wrapped around my ankles with glittering straps and little jewels.

Jessabelle was a master of hairstyles and managed to pin my hair up with curls and a braid. A golden barrette in the shape of a vine held back the braided portion from my face. She also sat me down for a makeover, adding creams to smoothen my face and highlight my cheeks. She added golden colors and dark browns to my eyelids to make my eyes pop almost as much as my lips with their musty red lipstick.

For the first time in my life, I considered challenging Pearl to a beauty contest. If only she was there with me. Her presence might have calmed my nerves.

Quiet as a church mouse, I followed the music to the west wing. Unlike the music that Caden introduced to me the other day, this music was orchestrated and proper. It reminded me of the slow swaying music from the Ormio kingdom.

A few guests chatted on the stairs or in the hallway serving as overflow from the ballroom, where the majority of voices emitted. As requested, I refrained from calling attention to myself among the guests. I walked among them, staring straight ahead to avoid eye contact. My periphery still noticed a few eyes following me as I stepped through the doorway.

I spotted Caden and Mica talking by the empty fireplace with someone who wore several metals pinned to his chest. Mica noticed me first. His eyebrows and the corners of his mouth went high. He nudged Caden and gestured towards me. Caden was in the middle of speaking, but his words faltered when his blinking eyes recognized me. I had to suppress a smile at his awe-struck response. He kept his eyes on me even as he said some apology to the stranger. The other man followed Caden's gaze to me, then accepted Caden's excuse with a knowing smirk.

A couple of guests tried to grab Caden's attention as he crossed the room, but he side-stepped all their remarks. He refused to stop until he stood before me.

"Why, Emer," he said, "why didn't you tell me you were a princess?" He took my hand and bowed over it.

"I believe I did," I said. "I hope my attire is appropriate for the occasion. My handmaid suggested it."

Caden grinned. "I need to give her a raise. You look…radiant."

"Thank you. And thank you for allowing me to come. This feels almost ordinary for me."

"You mean you always look this way in Somnus?"

I laughed. "No. I mean that dressing up and coming to a ball feels ordinary…like home. Thank you."

He gave my hand a squeeze. "Someone once said that 'once in a while, right in the middle of an ordinary life, love gives us a fairy tale.'"

Love? My breath caught. For a moment, I thought he would sweep me off my feet and carry me to a secret place. My mind ran wild to Caden and me alone in some tall hedge gardens…or a gazebo.

Someone called his name, distracting his attention. The spell was broken, and my mind returned to reality. At least, the reality of this dream.

He released my hand, but escorted me to Mica.

168

"Unfortunately," Caden said, "being host means that I need to welcome and entertain everyone. Please accept the company of my surly friend on my behalf."

Mica laughed, and I teased, "When did Mica become the surly one?"

Mica bowed over my hand. "Please accompany me for the next dance? I've always wanted to dance with a princess."

"It would be my pleasure, Honorable Wright."

Mica led me to the center of the room where we danced as Caden had taught me. Mica moved with a little bounce, contrasting with Caden's fluid steps.

"I'm glad Caden brought you straight to me," he said. "I might have never caught a dance with you otherwise. You're turning heads, Emer."

"Oh," I gasped. "Caden asked me not to make a spectacle. Have I done something wrong?"

Mica laughed. "No, but that dress on a fresh face would spike interest anywhere. You've just outshined every other lady in the room. It's easy to believe you're a princess as you are now."

I blushed, then focused on the dance and its variations. He turned me outward for one measure, then rotated to do the same in another direction. I added my own bounce to follow his steps more closely. My mimicry of his movements seemed to encourage him to take more challenging steps. Perfect.

"You're a natural," he said. "Are you open to some harder maneuvers?"

"Teach me everything you know," I said. I grinned at the thrill of dancing, learning something new, and spending time with a friend.

We gallivanted across the room, then back before the piece ended. I wanted to applaud the musicians, but everyone else was preoccupied with honoring their partners. I curtsied to Mica as his bow was interrupted with a hand on his shoulder.

Mica stepped aside. "Lord Westfield, may I introduce you to Lady Reo?"

"Charmed," Lord Westfield said with a bow. He was maybe a year younger than I was and stumbled a little in his footing. I smiled and complimented his bravery in asking me to dance, then asked him for advice for my first dance in London.

We chatted amiably until the next piece, when another lord approached me. Two more dances passed, but I was barely winded. I could do this all night.

On my sixth dance, another lord cut in for my attention. This one was possibly twice my age and placed his hand closer to my hips than my waist. That was when I began to hear the whispers.

"Men are fools for a pretty face," a particularly snide voice said. I recognized the speaker without looking. Lady Elmsworth. "She's playing them all like fiddles. Especially Honorable Seaver. Promise to help me sway him from her enchantments?"

Turning away with the dance, I missed whether her listeners agreed. I hoped that would be the last of the whispers, but caught more during the next dance.

"No one has heard of her," Lady Elmsworth said. "Maybe that's why she came here."

The other woman gasped. "Do you think she left New Zealand to escape her reputation?"

"Either that or she's a fraud."

My blood boiled, and I struggled not to step on my companion's toes. I was one thread away from breaking from my partner and into their conversation when—

"Ladies! Might I interest one of you in a dance?" Caden's voice spoke over the gossip.

"Why, Caden," Lady Elmsworth swooned.

"Ah-ah, you already had your turn. Lady Fairweather, may I?"

I only assumed Lady Fairweather responded kindly as my partner turned us down the ballroom.

The song finished after only a minute more, though it was plenty long enough for me. I was not surprised that little Lady Fairweather asked to continue the next dance with Caden. I was surprised, however, when my older partner asked the same.

"Sir Lakewood," I said, "forgive me if the one dance was unsatisfactory. Unfortunately, as I am new to this scene, I must give every man a chance before limiting myself. You will forgive me?"

"Of course, my lady," he said, still holding my hand in his, "after this next dance."

"Sir Lakewood," I protested, failing to pull my hand away.

"Sir Lakewood!" A hand appeared on the older man's shoulder. Caden's face slipped into view. "Mind if I cut in?"

The older man glanced around at the other guests, a few of whom whispered with gossiping undertones. "Don't you have the event to host?"

"My parents can cover for me for one dance." Caden grinned like a schoolboy skipping lessons.

Reluctant, Sir Lakewood stepped back and departed with a bow. Caden reached for my hand.

The next piece began and we danced the way he had taught me, with his left hand in my right and his right hand on my waist, my left hand resting on his shoulder. He stepped forward and I stepped back. He stepped to the side and I followed. We spun around the ballroom this way. I relaxed in Caden's arms. I trusted him to lead me.

"How are you enjoying your first London ball?" he asked.

"It feels like my first midnight masquerade again, surrounded by unfamiliar faces, dances, and music. I dare not tell you how that first ball ended, or you might have me removed."

"Now you must tell me." He grinned and leaned close for the secret. Goodness, he smelled like a victorious knight.

"Keep in mind, it was my first ball, and my sisters knew little what to expect of the midnight dances on Noz Isle. We had no idea how lively the dancing would be, or that it literally went all night until sunrise. Also, I had never danced with potential suitors before. Naturally, I grew nervous, tripped, and ripped my gown all the way to my hips."

"Oh," Caden moaned. "Please tell me there was a gentleman who offered to help cover your embarrassment?"

"Oh, yes. I had at least five offers."

"Should I be jealous?" Caden asked, pulling me closer.

I flushed and found myself in a rare speechless state. My lack of a response turned my focus to our dancing. Caden held me closer than when we had practiced. I felt the warmth and comfort of something wrapped around me. Blankets. Not Caden's arms.

"This," I said, "is only a dream?"

He leaned away. "Maybe not. You say you're still dreaming, and you're like a dream to me. Yet my feelings for you feel very real."

"What do you mean?" I asked. "How can your feelings be real if our realities are false?"

"Our realities aren't false. I'm real in this world, you're real in yours. As long as our feelings are real, maybe we can build a bridge between."

I shook my head. "How?"

"I'm not sure," he said, "but could you trust me and take the leap?"

I wanted to trust Caden—I wanted to trust him with the most fragile part of my heart—but it was illogical.

"The peak of the song is coming," he said. "Do you want to finish with a bang?"

Unsure, but curious, I nodded.

Caden pulled me in closer to dip me backward. A small yelp escaped me from the sudden drop. His hand on my waist had curled around to my back, holding me as if to ask me again to trust him.

Unable to feel the grip of my feet, they slipped. Good thing I was already in Caden's arms for him to catch me.

"Testing gravity?" He smirked. "Hey look, it still works. Go figure, because I think I'm falling too."

Maybe it was just the position, but my breathing quickened.

He pulled me up after the song ended. He bent over in a bow over my hand and hesitated before letting go.

The other dancers kept us from lingering. Another lord asked for my attention as a man pulled Caden away with the intention of introducing a sister.

We danced away the evening until it turned to night. Fewer guests arrived, and more strayed to other rooms for politicking. That was the main difference I loved about the midnight masquerades on Noz Isle. Whenever Father or another royal held a ball, the event was mostly to sort allies from foes, schmoozing dignitaries, and persuading partners—less dancing on the floor and more dancing with words. It was less about making friendships and more about impressing others through etiquette and smooth talk. It was exhausting.

I had hoped to replicate the freedom of Noz Isle's midnight masquerades during my sixteenth birthday ball. Frustrated and sad as I was that I had likely slept through my own party, this dance at Caden's home was close enough. No one knew me, and I knew no one. The best part was none of that mattered. At least to most people. Lady Elmsworth glared at me any time she could. I simply smirked back, happy to be in the arms of a dancing partner while she murmured with her little group of cohorts.

I frequently spotted Mica laughing with some friends by the entrance, grabbing a drink or appetizer every time a servant with a platter passed through. I smirked as some servants began to enter from the terrace door. How did the terrace connect to the kitchens? I doubted that the path was direct.

Less frequently, I caught glimpses of Caden politicking with lords and ladies. Sometimes his eyes found mine, and I blushed to be caught staring.

After one such capture, I looked away to hide my blush, but glanced again to see if he noticed. Caden was gone. I may or may not have stumbled while seeking him again.

"Is something wrong?" my partner asked.

"No, sorry." I fumbled. "I thought that I recognized someone. Silly me. Who else would be here from New Zealand?"

My partner chuckled. "Not tonight anyway."

I spotted Caden again as he came towards us from the direction of the orchestra. The current piece finished, and we bowed our respects.

"If you'll excuse me," Caden said to the next man who approached me, "I requested this next piece specifically for Lady Reo. May I have this dance?"

Several eyebrows raised other than my own. Instead of taking my hand in his for the waltz, Caden put one hand on his chest and extended his other in my direction. The music began with a familiar rhythm, and I grinned. I mirrored his position, then began a dance from Somnus. Caden struggled with the footing for the first round, but followed closely enough for the second. Other dancers paused, unsure about the change of rhythms, then to watch our style. Soon Caden and I were the only dancers on the floor.

Caden missed the change after the third rotation, but we laughed together as he rushed to catch up. While Lady Elmsworth scoffed and tried to belittle my "folk dancing," another couple dared to follow our repeating movements on the floor. Finishing a third rotation, the dance changed again, but smiles grew as they learned the pattern.

"Last one," I called, as the fifth set of rotations began. A couple that joined us on the floor actually complained.

"But I was just getting the hang of it."

"It's over already?" Caden asked, then gestured to the musicians to wrap up their piece. "Maybe we should repeat it for our students." He added a wink, and my heart fluttered. We finished with extended arms as our audience clapped. Caden pulled me close. "Again?"

"Oh my," I said, heart pounding for more than one reason. "Three dances in one night with two consecutively? People will talk."

"Ah, that last one was too short to count."

"I doubt others will see it that way."

"They'll see what they want to see."

He had half convinced me, except, "I told Lord Lakewood earlier that I sought a variety of dancing partners tonight. If you ask me for a third, he will surely ask for a second."

He pursed his lips in an adorable and teasing pout. "You'll make me wait until the very last dance before I can steal you away again?"

I laughed. "If you persist enough, it is yours."

"Until then." He took my hand and bowed over it again. This time, he kissed my hand.

Instead of feeling the pleasure of his lips or even familiar wool on my skin, a sharp pain stabbed my index finger then shot up my arm.

I gasped and pulled back my hand to cradle it against my chest. "Caden! Are you—"

Caden's wide eyes worried only for me. "Emer? I'm sorry, did I offend you?"

"No, no. I—" The tingling sensation of a stabbing needle continued to throb through my index finger. "Are you all right?" I raised my other hand to his cheek, terrified that he might start coughing.

His eyes spoke of confusion, not pain.

The whispers grew around us. He asked me not to create a spectacle, yet there I stood in the middle of the ballroom with my hand on his cheek.

I stepped back into a little curtsy. "Sorry, I pricked myself. Please excuse me."

Without another word, I turned and stepped as quickly as possible from the ballroom without causing more of a stir among the guests. As soon as I was alone, I ran to my bedchamber, trembling. What was wrong with me? Was it a side effect of Caden's dance? Unlikely. It stung like that condemned spindle. Inside
178

my chambers, I sat on the sofa and tried to massage my index finger back into feeling.

A soft knock on the door announced my hand-maid.

"M'lady." She entered with a little curtsy. "Master Caden asked me to check on you. Are you unwell?"

Caden. What did he think of me for running away like that? As much as I wanted to apologize and run back into his arms, I remembered my need to stay aloof from attachments. Too late.

"I am well enough," I said. "I pricked myself on a needle a while back." I shook my right arm and flexed my fingers. My index finger continued to throb from the inside.

Jessabelle came to sit beside me. "I used to do manicures before the Seavers took me on. I can do a mean hand massage, if you'd like." Before I could stop her, she took my hand in hers. She rubbed her palms across mine, squeezing my fingers between hers. I only felt a mild pressing of wool.

She looked ready to say something else, but I huffed with frustration. "Nothing works! I cannot feel it. I feel nothing. All I feel is wool."

Jessabelle frowned. "I don't understand."

"Everything I touch feels like wool," I said, removing my hand from hers. "I have—oh, I forgot what Mica called it. It is a side effect of being asleep."

Still confused, my handmaid repeated, "Being asleep?"

I groaned. It was all too confusing. How could I explain? "I look awake, but this world treats me like a dream. My body is somewhere in my father's kingdom of Somnus while I sleepwalk here. I cannot feel the misty rain, the heat of a burner, nor the tender touch of a gentleman."

Jessabelle's mouth dropped open. "I must take you to Madame Gazelle! She's the psychic I told you about. I saw her and told her about you and your gift for growing plants. She wants to meet you. She believes you're special and marked for destiny. She also does herbal medicines. Maybe she can help you wake up too."

"Truly?" I asked. "I had the intuition that a magical place would wake me. Caden and Mica already tried lots of places, such as St. Michael's Mount and Stonehenge."

Jessabelle laughed. "Not a bad guess, but those boys don't have the third eye like Madame Gazelle. She's a medium and might be able to reconnect you to your world."

"Could she?" Hope burst through my heart.

Jessabelle nodded. "She has a shop in Camden every weekend. She's closed right now, but we'll see her first thing tomorrow morning if you'd like."

My finger still tingled from the strange surge of pain. "First thing in the morning."

Chapter 13

I lay on the mattress, unable to sleep despite my tired legs from dancing and my tired mind from thinking of Caden, Mica, Lady Elmsworth, Caden, Jessabelle, the mysterious Madame Gazelle, and more Caden…

I rolled over, taking more space than necessary on the large bed. It was big enough to fit Tanzi and Pearl with me. The emptiness beside me stretched into my heart.

What could I do? I was no leader in this world. I was hardly a leader in Somnus. What was the point? Did anyone miss me? Did my sisters worry about me? How much time had passed in Somnus? How long had I been sleeping? I knew dreams skewed time for reality, but at least two weeks had passed since I arrived in England.

Eventually sleep took me. I hoped the numbness of my right hand would go away as I slept, as if it was a headache with sleep as the cure. Silly me. I was already sleeping.

When I awoke, every finger of my right hand refused to move.

I panicked and called for Jessabelle. "Why does it persist?" I cried. "It is worse than before. How soon is your healer available for visitors?"

"In a half hour. I can have you ready by then."

Jessabelle deserved a raise for her considerate care for me. She gave me some pointers for a quick scrub and cleanser, then helped me into a new pink maxi dress, and framed it with a thick brown belt around my waist. No matter that I felt like death, she made sure that I looked fabulous before stepping foot outside of my flat.

Jessabelle hailed a black cab and instructed our driver to head to Camden market.

We exited on the side of the street, in the middle of various shops with large colorful signs.

"If you don't mind, m'lady, it's best if we stay close here."

She gestured for me to follow as she headed for a trinkets shopping area covered with an awning. With no walkway between, we were suddenly in another shop for shirts with various sayings. A couple steps farther, we were surrounded by leather booklets with another vendor calling for our attention. Every direction were more vendors with a variety of crafts, clothing, trinkets, flowers, food... How did we get there, and where did it end?

Jessabelle took my hand to keep me beside her, but I followed her more by sight than the non-existent tug on my arm.

We passed an odd shop with two tall horse statues, then followed a ramp to a lower level of even more shops. Madame Gazelle's shop was squished between one that sold colorful woven rugs and smelled heavily of incense, and another shop that sold the exact same leather booklets and handbags as another shop on the upper level.

Jessabelle walked into the shop that was draped with symbols like those on Jessabelle's necklace. A variety of mirrors hung on one fabricated wall, and pictures of strange people or haunted places covered the opposite side.

Madame Gazelle looked up when we entered. She was a woman who averaged around middle age, but with wrinkles and stretch marks of someone older and the bright grey eyes of someone younger. She wore a long dress with various designs and a multi-layered blouse with patches and lace.

"Miss Johnson," she said. "I wasn't expecting you until tea time."

"It's an emergency," Jessabelle pulled me forward. "This is Lady Reo from New Zealand. She's the one I told you about, with powers of plant growth."

"Ah, yes!" Madame Gazelle waved us in. "Come in, come in! I'm humbled to meet you, Lady—no. I sense that you are more than a lady." She curtsied all to the way to the cobblestone ground. "Princess."

Jessabelle gasped.

After days of going about as a common laborer, then as a lady, it actually unnerved me a little to be truthfully titled and honored.

"How did you know?" I asked.

Madame Gazelle remained with her knees almost to the ground. "Your aura speaks of royalty."

"Please stand," I said. "That cannot be healthy for your joints. Unfortunately, others disbelieve my birthright since my kingdom is not of this world."

Jessabelle nodded to back my story. "She says she's dreaming and she can't wake up."

"Fascinating," Madame Gazelle said. "Yes, very fascinating. Please forgive my ignorance. Yes, I see it now. Your aura is a little dim, like one who is unconscious. But you walk and talk like a waking person. What's the true name of your kingdom?"

"My father is King of Somnus. Jessabelle said that you may be able to wake me?"

"I may," she said. "You said it was an emergency?"

I extended my right hand. "The fingers of my right hand are numb. All I have ever felt of this world is wool. Whether the softest of flower petals or the cobblestone streets, it is all wool to me. Last night, however, a painful prick entered my fingers and spread through my palm."

184

"How curious," she said, rubbing her hands across my palm. "Very curious. Please, tell me more about your world. Also, it'll help me to reconnect you if I have a visual demonstration of your magic."

Madame Gazelle grabbed a little succulent that already looked well cared for.

"You care for your plants." I smiled.

"Of course. They're kinder to me than most humans. Far kinder."

I grinned. The more I learned about this Madame Gazelle, the more I liked her. "Does it have a name?" I asked.

"Lily," she said. "Yes, I know it's not a lily. I just like the name, and it responds well to it. Don't you, Lily?"

"How about it, Lily?" I asked the succulent. "Will you grow for me to show your appreciation for how well Madame Gazelle has cared for you? She waters you the right amount and keeps you out of direct sunlight. I can tell that you like it that way. Your leaves are so strong and thick. My, I think you might be one of the most beautiful and healthy succulents I know."

As I complimented the plant, it stretched slowly. Madame Gazelle and Jessabelle gasped and grabbed each other with excitement as a new leaf grew from the tip of the stem, budded, then blossomed.

"Wicked!" Madame Gazelle said.

"Based on your smile, I gather that was meant as a compliment?"

Jessabelle laughed. "Yes, m'lady—er, Your Highness."

As we stood in the middle of the market, casual shoppers walked by with curious glances, but only a couple stepped under Madame Gazelle's canopy. A male shopper came closer, but Madame Gazelle ushered him out.

"We're having a private session. If you want to shop or ask questions, come back in an hour."

He huffed and muttered something unintelligible, tossing one of Madame Gazelle's pictures to the ground.

Madame Gazelle replaced the picture, then pulled a large drapery from her roof to effectively close her shop. Hidden from public view, she went to a small treasure box to retrieve a large uncut crystal. Jessabelle's gasp was enough to say that this was no ordinary crystal.

Madame Gazelle set it on a small circular table. "Now, please, take a seat. Both of you, take my hand to form a triangle."

"The strongest of shapes," Jessabelle explained.

"Yes. Now, Your Highness, close your eyes and describe your homeland to me. I will use the crystal to connect to your world. I want you to picture your home. Picture it very clearly. The more details, the better the connection."

186

I closed my eyes and looked back on my memories that felt more like dreams these days. Somnus.

"There are mountains, so far away, but always on the horizon. Imazhin Lake makes our city smell like sealeaves on windy days."

"Yes, yes," Madame Gazelle encouraged. "Very good. The smells, the tastes—what does the seafood taste like? Did you have a favorite place along the lake? Tell me."

"The fish are our biggest trade. My favorite is the horned fish, and Marin refuses to eat any of it. Tanzi would take juicy bites to mock her. Garnet is understanding, but encourages the fishing trade. I miss them. I miss my sisters more than anything else. I miss the mountains, taller than your glass buildings. I miss the Imazhin Lake, so blue and clean, unlike this river."

"The Thames isn't our model for cleanliness," Jessabelle muttered. Madame Gazelle hushed my handmaid and I continued.

"I miss the plants and trees. Somnus is filled with them. The Ormio forest goes bare during the winter, but not the forest of Somnus. Our trees would stay green all year with their thin—" I cut off. Their needles.

Suddenly, their spiky branches filled my mind. Each tree was a hundred little green needles. Maybe thousands. Their points beckoned me to come closer, taunted me that they were untouchable, that of all my lovely plants, they did not need my care. They did not want me. I was expendable. I could fall at their feet, fall to the ground with their discarded needles. Falling, falling, falling—

"Princess?" Madame Gazelle called. How did she sound so far away when I could feel her woolen hand in my left? "I started to see something, but it went dark. Very dark. Wherever you're going, come back. Don't get lost. Let's go to another place. What was your home like? Did you have a favorite room? Go back to your sisters."

My sisters broke through the falling needles. My home. The castle where I lived with my sisters, and the room we shared...

"My bedchamber," I said. "I shared it with my younger sisters, Pearl and Tanzi. They were both too scared to sleep alone. I think that my physical body is there, lying in bed, between my wool blankets. The window to my left should have woken me from the sunlight. I could never sleep through the sunrise before."

"Yes," Madame Gazelle encouraged. "I see you on your bed. You're wearing a beautiful brown gown. Very beautiful."

I gasped. How had she known that my sixteenth birthday gown was brown? "Do you see anyone else?" I asked.

"Not yet. Tell me more about your surroundings, and they might come into view."

"The room was always so bright," I said. "The windows faced east and west, lighting the room throughout the day. At night, we always had the fireplace running, even on the hottest of nights, and several candles burning."

"I..." Madame Gazelle's voice faltered. "Your room is dark. Very dark. There's a lot of green around you though. Did you have a green carpet or rugs?"

I frowned. "No. Our floor was wooden in our bedchamber, colors of pale yellow against the blue stones of my father's castle."

"How odd. Very odd. Try concentrating on your body. Can you feel it?"

I squeezed my eyes shut and tried to concentrate. "I feel the wool. I am lying down. I almost feel weightless, like floating in water, but my hand stings. It refuses to move." I focused on my right hand. Pain zipped from my fingers, up my arm, down to my heart, then out to my toes and other hand.

Jessabelle and Madame Gazette yelped and released my hands. Opening my eyes, I found them massaging their hands and wrists.

"You felt that?" I asked.

"Oh, we felt that," Jessabelle said. She looked both spooked and awed, like we had communed with the dead.

Madame Gazelle reached for my hand again. "May I?" She took my right hand and analyzed my fingers, bending them, turning my hands over, and stroking my nerves. I felt none of it, not even wool. The poison had spread to numb all nerves below my wrist.

"There's something different about your home," Madame Gazelle said. "I believe the reason my vision was blurry is because it's not the same Somnus you once knew. Your numb hand and your lifeline say that your time's running out. Your physical body is dying."

"What?" Apparently, my panic had been understated. My physical body, my sleeping body, *me*. "How am I dying?"

"You were poisoned, right? The poison was slowed by your sleeping spell, but it's starting to take root. Quickly, very quickly. I'm afraid I can't stop it. You'll lose the ability to use your fingers, hands, toes, and feet. Since your magic's verbal and of the mind, it'll probably be the last thing you'll lose."

"Are you serious?" I gaped. This was how I would die? I would slowly lose control of my limbs until I became bedridden? "How much time do I have?"

Madame Gazelle frowned. "I haven't seen this effect before, though considering its current state and acceleration, I would suppose a couple of days. Three days at most."

Chapter 14

"Three days?"

I wished that I could take pleasure in Caden's wide blue eyes, full of worry for me. They meant that he was concerned about me and cared for me. Except they confirmed the seriousness of my situation. I had three days to wake up and be cured from my poison before it slowly killed me one numb limb at a time. What if I went completely numb? Who knew what would happen to me after that? I already spent the last couple weeks trying and failing to find a cure to wake myself. How would I find it in three days without the use of my dominant hand?

An anxious tapping sound directed me to Mica, who sat on the armchair of Caden's home lounge. Jessabelle and Miles stood silently at the entryway. I sat on the couch, proper as always, keeping my demeanor calm while my insides raged with storms of confusion and fear. When first summoning Caden and Mica to divulge our discovery, I had warned them that I had "difficult news." Caden had sat beside me on the couch until my announcement, when he stood to pace behind the couch.

"How credible is this Madame Gazelle?" he asked. "She could have said that just to encourage a sale."

I frowned. "She knew that I was a princess and even the color of my gown from my birthday masquerade."

"She might have called you a princess because every girl secretly wishes to be one. And anyone could guess a color."

"Oh?" I challenged. "What color do you say my gown was?"

"I'm not a charlatan who tells lies for a living."

"Your father bred you as a politician. You are close enough."

"Ouch," Mica hooted.

"You're no different as a princess," Caden retorted.

I huffed. "Fair point. Though I cannot guess the color of my dress since I already know the answer. What is yours?"

"I don't know," Caden said. "Girls like to wear colors that bring out the colors in their eyes, right? So, green?"

"No. It was brown for that reason."

"Oh, then that would have been my second guess," he said. "It's safe to assume this Madame Gazelle knows more about fashion than I do. Not that it matters. You don't need a dress to make your eyes captivating."

Was that a flirtation? No, his face was completely stoic. He simply said it as he saw it. Apparently, he saw my green eyes as "captivating."

Fool of a man and the things he did to my heart without even trying.

"Regardless," I said, "she was the closest to returning me to my waking state. She saw my sleeping body in Somnus. And there was something else, something wrong." I thought of the green floor she saw. What could have happened?

Jessabelle spoke up, "Madame Gazelle said that your highness should return to the place she began the dream. That there was some significance to how her dream started."

I nodded. That had been a conversation after the proclaimed deadline. I barely listened, too distracted by the thought of dying in three days. Regardless if I woke or died, I only had three days left in this dream world…with Caden.

"We found you on the Coast Path," Caden said. "Is there something special in that area that we missed?"

Mica slapped his forehead. "Of course! Why didn't I think of it before!"

"What?" Caden and I asked.

"Merlin's Cave!"

Caden took a turn for an epiphany as his eyes went wide. "Of course! That was on our agenda, wasn't it? But we upended our plans when we found Emer. You think we need to go to Tintagel Castle?"

"We have no time to second guess," I said.

"We also don't have time to be wrong," Caden said. "Tintagel's on the west coast. If we're wrong and we're supposed to be in London, that's a whole day wasted by driving."

Jessabelle coughed with a suppressed retort. She fidgeted with her necklace, and I understood her concern. Madame Gazelle said that a magical place was only one component for waking me. She also suggested an undeniable truth was part of the key.

"A truth?" I had asked.

"Yes," Madame Gazelle had explained. "Your magic's created by your words and feelings. When I connected you to your sleeping body, I became a conduit. I sensed the connections you'd need and the barriers that kept you. Princess, a large lie surrounds your heart. A very deep lie. I don't know what it is, but you must face it before you can return home."

A lie surrounded my heart. What ever could that mean? Would I find the truth in London or traversing the countryside again?

To Caden and Mica, I said, "London has more opportunities to explore. We should expend every possible solution before leaving it behind."

"There's no need," a snide voice said from the doorway. Lady Elmsworth. She wore a purple blazer with matching trousers—a look that I came to understand as professional attire. Her expression was that of victory, hatred for me, and eagerness to squish me.

"Charlotte?" Caden asked.

"Your missing peoples report was answered," she said, walking into the room like a champion fighter. "You left messages with the police departments, right? Asking if there were any missing people fitting the description of a young girl with blonde hair and green eyes?"

I answered her with only glares. What was she talking about? Caden mutely nodded with surprised eyes.

Lady Elmsworth grinned back at me with a wicked glint in her eyes. "The game is up, Amber. I know who you are. Are you going to tell these gentlemen the truth, or will I?"

"Amber?" Mica echoed.

I frowned. "My name is Emerald."

Lady Elmsworth's grin only grew. "But you go by Emer, right? Probably because it's easier to respond to names closer to your real name, Amber."

"Excuse me? My name is Emerald Reo from—"

"Of Somnus," Lady Elmsworth said. That caught our attention. How did she know that? I claimed to be from New Zealand ever since coming to London. Why did her grin only grow more victorious?

"I found this in the dining room," Lady Elmsworth said, handing Caden his phone. "It was ringing, and I didn't want you to miss an important call. It was the police from Tintagel, saying they found someone who matched your missing persons report. Her real name is Amber Princeton. She's an actress from Tintagel who borrowed her costume for a couple days too long."

"An actress?" Caden asked.

Lady Elmsworth continued, her smile growing more smug. "She's in a play based on the Twelve Dancing Princesses, set in the fictional kingdom of Somnus. It's not uncommon for actors and actresses to get caught up in their work. You hold true to your act," she said to me. "I'll give you that, but fooling Caden and little Mica isn't the hardest trick in the world."

"I am not acting!" But even as I said it, something else in her words struck me. How did Lady Elmsworth know there were twelve princesses of Rezhina? And how did she know about our dancing? Not even my parents knew about that.

Caden's shoulders and expression sank. "Looks like she's remembering. Amber?"

I glared at him. "You believe her? How can you trust anything she says? She has belittled me and tried to discredit me from the moment—"

196

Lady Elmsworth laughed. "I wasn't the one who filed the report, stupid girl."

Caden grimaced.

"Caden?" I asked. What was he thinking to cause such anger and disgust?

"Go on, Caden, dearest," Lady Elmsworth cooed. "You know this isn't something I made up. I just happened to pick up the phone when they called with information. They sent an email too, but I guess you haven't checked your phone yet."

Even as she spoke, Caden thumbed away at his phone. His eyes raced quickly back and forth, and his frown deepened.

"Caden?" I repeated, my voice weaker.

To my surprise, Mica explained with a hollow voice, "After leaving you at Boscastle, we called around the area. We needed to make sure you weren't needed somewhere, that anyone looking for you could find you. We left messages with the police departments, asking if there were any missing people reports about you."

Why? I knew no one in Boscastle other than Mrs. Priddy. Who would be looking for me?

Another thought struck me: Caden and Mica had not believed me. All this time, they smiled at my face, pretending to help me on my search. All the while, behind my back, they waited for reports to tell them lies about me.

"Inconceivable. I actually thought I could trust you."

"Wait," Caden said, sounding pained. "There must be some mistake. What about your—" he paused for an uncomfortable glance at Lady Elmsworth "—plants?"

"Her what?" she pressed.

"That's right!" Mica said. "Not even the most talented actress could fake magic!"

"Magic?" Lady Elmsworth guffawed.

Caden moaned, "Mica."

"Sorry." He shrunk sheepishly. "But how else are we supposed to convince Lady Spiteful?"

"Excuse me?" Lady Elmsworth snapped. "If you think to convince me with something as ridiculous as 'magic,' you are sorely misunderstood."

"Show her," Mica urged. "Make a plant grow, Emer."

Lady Elmsworth laughed, dubious. "Yes, please. Show me." She grabbed the nearest plant—a succulent—and set it on the stand a meter away.

I frowned. The last thing I wanted to do was reveal my power to Lady Elmsworth, but how else could I convince her of my claims?

I spoke to the plant. "Little succulent, this mean woman calls me a fraud. Please, grow for me and prove her wrong."

We all watched and waited. Nothing.

"Please," I whispered, "grow for me."

Another painful three seconds passed. Caden's face and shoulders sank with each one.

Swallowing hard, I wondered what could possibly be wrong. "Succulents are slow to grow. Perhaps this one is shy."

Lady Elmsworth scoffed. "Of course. That's what a charlatan would say."

"Come on," Mica muttered. "We've seen your power before. The tree at Boscastle Cottage, the vine at St. Michael's Mount, even the grass at Stonehen—"

"Did you actually see what happened at Stonehenge?" Caden asked, void of emotion. "Because I didn't. Emer had her back to us, crouched on the ground."

"Alright, so that could have been faked, but the vine—"

"Could have been a plant—I mean a fake, a setup, a trick." With each option, Caden's indignation grew. "That vine was unlike anything I'd seen before, like something out of a fantasy. She could have plotted it. I don't know how, but…" He frowned at the succulent. "Why won't this one grow? And why's there a report for Amber, an actress in a play with your exact story—the story I wanted to—" He ground his teeth and avoided my eyes.

My heart cracked. "Is that all I am to you? A fantasy? *You* filed the report. From the beginning, you never believed me."

Caden muttered, "At least the betrayal's mutual."

I was such a fool. I never should have trusted them. It was only fair. They never trusted me.

Lady Elmsworth had smirked through the whole exchange. Of course, she had to rub salt in my wound. "It's time you went home, Amber."

"My name," I spat, "is Princess Emerald R—"

"Stop." Caden refused to look at me. His fingers curled tightly into fists. "We know who you are now, so stop lying to us. Here, I thought I had an original story to write. Turns out I've been writing fan fiction from someone else's script."

"What? This is absurd!"

"Actually," Mica said, "it makes a lot of sense."

"No! No, I am a Princess of Somnus, and this is just a dream!"

Lady Elmsworth gave me a false frown and tapped Caden on the shoulder. "Oh, dear. Caden, I think she actually believes her own act."

"She was unstable when we found her." Caden's frustration softened, but mine grew.

"This is ridiculous! How could I make up an entire kingdom? Of my sisters—"

"The other actresses," Lady Elmsworth explained. "You didn't make anything up. You were just fol-lowing the script."

Caden scoffed. "My mother was right. This is what I get for chasing a dream. Maybe you were right too," he said to me. Before any hopes could rise, he dashed them by saying, "I've been avoiding my

200

obligations to honor my family name the way my parents want. My dreams to write something inspiring and adventurous were just that: dreams. Thank you for making that clear, Amber."

Without another word, he spun on his heel and left. Lady Elmsworth shot me one last victorious grin before chasing after him.

"Caden?" I asked, my voice too weak to reach him.

Mica shook his head, frowning. "It was fun while it lasted. I believe you didn't mean to lie to us. Keep my phone number. If you're this passionate about your acting, I'd love to see what you can do on a stage. Maybe when Caden's cooled off, we can come watch your play."

His words muddled in my mind. I heard them, but nothing made sense. Did I truly belong in this world? All my memories of Somnus felt so far away. Were they actually memories, or only my imagination?

A tear crawled down my cheek. I wiped it away with my arm as my numb hand refused to respond.

"Wait," I said. "What about my sense of touch? What about my numbness?"

Mica gave it all of two seconds to think about it. "Hypoesthesia isn't proof. Maybe you need to see a doctor. Or it's part of your stage character. It might all be a product of your mind. The brain is a complicated organ that can trick itself into believing anything."

I sagged into my chair, wishing to fall through to the floor. Even Mica thought I was a straw short of the coocoo's nest.

Were they right?

If I was not Princess Emerald of Somnus…who was I? Amber Princeton? Who was she?

Chapter 15

"I can't believe this!" Jessabelle shouted. "I've never been angry with the young master before, but I sure am now."

I quietly packed my limited belongings as she ranted. None of my possessions were truly mine. The shoes from Mrs. Priddy, the pictures from Mica, the dress Caden gave me in Penzance… I left the dress and jewelry from the ball. Each item in my bag from Jessabelle was a reminder of how temporary everything was and how generous Caden had been. Despite my fury at his disbelief, he had helped me and provided for me in more ways than I could repay him…especially if I was a lowly actress from Tintagel.

"You tell them you're dying in a few days and they call you a fraud? How can you stand for this? Aren't you a princess of Somnus? They should be helping you, not casting you out!"

"I cannot prove anything."

"But Somnus—your kingdom!"

"Is a figment of my imagination, according to your all-knowing Google."

"And your numbness—"

"Might be an ailment of my mind."

"Madame Gazelle—"

"Could have been playing off my emotions and the facts you gave her. Look, Jessabelle, you are marvelous, and more supportive than a friend. I count you as a sister in my heart, but…there were people searching for me. I cannot remember them, but they say that they know me. I need to meet them and learn what they know of me."

"What about your magic?"

I had no answer for that. Caden had accused me of trickery. It was no trick, but… "I could not make a succulent grow. I cannot say what my magic is, but it took me no closer to home."

"You're giving up?" My handmaid slouched. "You're turning your back on everything you know based on a claim someone else made for you?"

"I am not giving up," I said, facing her directly. "I will find my truth—whatever it is. I will meet these people who claim to be my family. If they can help me to regain my past and my sense of feeling, then I will take it. Either way, I have been away from home for too long."

"And if they don't?" Jessabelle asked. "If you don't remember them and the numbness spreads?"

I swallowed. "Then I am still lost."

My handmaid's groan said that answer was unacceptable. "If that's the case, hold your bags for a half hour more. I need to pack."

"Pardon?"

"I'm going with you. Besides, if you don't have any memories of England, you'll need someone to guide you through the tube and trains."

"Do you have responsibilities here?"

"I'm no princess," she laughed. "You were my last responsibility for the week, so I have a couple of days off. Besides, I've always wanted to see Tintagel, and I'm sure Madame Gazelle will want to know what becomes of you."

I laughed a little, grateful for her faith in me and her assurance to see me safely home…wherever that was.

Jessabelle's packing took a little longer than a half hour, as she packed everything she thought we could need. She also looked up directions and instructions on how to reach Tintagel on her phone, explaining it would take all day. She left instructions with Lady Seaver about her sudden trip, but made a show in front of Lady Elmsworth. Jessabelle played on Lady Elmsworth's desires to be rid of me and to feign charity in front of Lady Seaver. The snooty young lady blessed our safe travels with a stack of paper money.

And she called me the actress?

Jessabelle rushed me out the door. "We need to hurry to make it to the 11:04 train."

I took a longing glance back through the town-house, wishing to stay, wishing to say goodbye to Caden or Mica…wishing they still valued me.

Jessabelle and I walked to a strange station filled with people either loitering or rushing. There was no in-between. She spent a few minutes standing at a machine in the wall, feeding it the papers given to us by Lady Elmsworth. Tapping a couple of cards to the odd paper-eating machine, Jessabelle finished and let the next person in line have a turn.

"Here," Jessabelle handed me some cards. "Don't lose these. They're my husband's Orca and rail cards. I loaded them with the money from Lady Elmsworth, but there's only enough to get us both to Tintagel."

Understanding only half of what she said, I asked, "Your husband? You never mentioned you were married."

Jessabelle shrugged with a natural smile. "Not much to say. He's just the love of my life. He's used to me taking random day trips with the Seavers, so he won't expect me home for a day or two."

As much as I wanted to ask her more, my attention was stolen by the massive and sleek machinery Jessabelle called the tube. Then the train. The insides of these long vehicles were similar to Caden's automobile, except tall enough to stand in and long enough that we walked past seats for dozens of passengers before choosing our own.

"Get comfy," Jessabelle said. "It'll take us all afternoon to get to Exeter St. Davids."

"I thought we were going to Tintagel?" I asked.

"We are, but we need to stop at St. Davids to take a bus to The Strand tomorrow morning, then another to Tintagel. We'll arrive in Tintagel tomorrow around noon."

"Why?" I asked. "Why can we not use the same method as the time I came with Caden and Mica?"

"Because they had their own driver and took direct routes. Welcome to public transit. It takes twice as long, but it's economical and caters to the common folk."

I thought on that, relating to the shipments between Somnus and…the other places across the lake. What were they called?

A part of me considered how Marin would appreciate the public transit for its economic reasons, then another sister would appreciate its easy access for the peasantry classes…but was it Garnet or Pearl?

I shook my head, frustrated by my dimming memory, yet irritated by my desire to remember things that may or may not be real.

I took twice as many naps as my trip to London, but all were restless. No more dreams of Somnus, despite my hopes otherwise. I wanted to remember the life I used to have—that I used to believe in. The dreams had abandoned me. They left me to believe the claims that I was from Tintagel.

When Jessabelle slept, I cried. Everything had gone wrong, and nothing made sense. Lady Elmsworth claimed my real name was Amber Princeton, but I felt no emotional ties to that name—no memories or connections at all.

The train took us across the country all day and into the evening. Jessabelle found a hostel for us in St. Davids. She said that we still had several hours ahead of us on buses. Despite my many naps during the trip, my head ached from crying and exhaustion drained me. I fell asleep right away, hardly taking the time to put my bed together. Jessabelle ended up putting my duvet together and throwing it over me. Not that it made any difference to my woolen senses.

I had seen plenty of buses in London, but these cross-country buses were less crowded. We found seats near the back and made ourselves comfortable for the long trip going from the southern end of England's west peninsula to the northern. One more bus exchange, and we found ourselves in Tintagel.

I hoped to feel an inkling of a memory when we arrived. Nothing. Either I was Princess Emerald of Somnus, or a forgotten mind. Either way, I was as lost as ever.

We hopped off the bus at the visitor's center. Was I supposed to walk inside and ask who had reported my absence? The idea repulsed me. Would I remember the people who reported my absence? What if I did not? It might have been wrong, but I hoped

208

not to remember them. Remembering would confirm that Somnus was no more than a story, that I was mentally broken with the wrong memories.

Sensing my hesitation, Jessabelle took my hand in hers, then gave it a squeeze.

"Thank you," I said and squeezed back.

I barely had the chance to step into the octangular building before someone called out.

"Amber!" A young woman about my age ran up to me, spouting several unfamiliar words that made Jessabelle wince. "Where've you been? I knew that hiking trip to Boscastle was a bad idea! You should have taken someone with you! You'll have to tell me all about everything that happened." She swore again. "But you're back! We're so glad you're home!"

She pulled me into a hug. My left arm went as stiff as my right. I really hoped to feel more than wool when she hugged me. Nothing changed.

The young woman pulled away and frowned at me. "You okay, Amber? You're acting kinda odd."

"Forgive me," I said. "I apparently forgot the definition of 'normal.'"

Her lips went thin as she held back a snorting laugh. "I'll say."

"Are you the one who reported my disappearance?" I asked.

"No, that was your mum." An epiphany lit her eyes and she swore again. "Has she seen you yet? Let me phone her."

Without giving me another option, the young woman pulled out her phone and made a call. She clearly seemed to know me somehow. A group of tourists came in, and she was pulled away by their questions. Ten minutes later, the door opened.

A crying woman ran over and hugged me. Again, I missed the sensation of warm love cradling me in embracing arms. She looked like my mother, with her blonde hair and green eyes, but wore plain clothes of simple jeans and a blouse. The queen of Somnus would accept death before wearing such a simple outfit.

"Amber! You're alright! Thank heavens you're home! Where've you been? Why didn't you come home? I've been worried sick about you!"

"I am unwell," I said, downplaying how I really felt.

"Oh, I know. The police told me everything."

"Everything?" I asked. "How could they know everything when I hardly know the half of it?"

"Oh, well, not everything." She flustered—something the queen never did. "They said you have amnesia."

"Am—what now?"

"You forgot everything and think you're that princess character you were playing. What was her name?"

"Princess Emerald of Somnus," I whispered.

"Yeah, but you're home now, and we'll get it all sorted out."

She pulled on my hand to lead me out of the station.

Jessabelle watched our conversation, eyes worried and unsure.

What could I tell her? I shook my head. "I hoped that seeing you would strike a memory if this was my life...but I do not remember. Forgive me."

The woman who resembled my mum turned her attention to Jessabelle. "Who's this? Did you bring my Amber home?"

"This is Jessabelle," I introduced. "She was my handmaid in London and a dear friend to me."

My mum's twin gaped. "What were you doing in London? With a handmaid? My dear," she said, returning to Jessabelle, "I'm so sorry if she promised to pay you. We really don't have a lot, but I'll compensate—"

"I'm employed by Lord Seaver. Any expenses in Emer's behalf were paid by him and his kin."

The mouth of Mum's twin only dropped lower. "Lord Seaver? Amber, what did you do?"

"Please," I said, raising my left hand to my head. "It was a long journey, and I am quite tired. May I lay down?"

The woman laughed with curious disbelief. "Yeah, yeah. I have your bedroom all set up still. Let's go home and we can talk."

"Alright. May I say goodbye first?" I gestured to Jessabelle, and my mum consented.

My handmaid might have only expected a proper handshake, but I pulled her into a hug.

"Thank you," I whispered in her ear. "Please do not forget me."

She chuckled. "Dear, I don't think even my hereditary Alzheimer's will let me forget about you. If ever you need a listening ear, you give me a ring."

Sniffling, I nodded and pulled back. "I cannot remember this life at all, but Somnus might be lost to me. Tell Caden—" I stopped, then shook my head. "Never mind."

"Ah, luv," Jessabelle smiled. "Never suppress a good heart. What should I tell the young master?"

I shrugged. "I was going to say that I wished things were different, but if they were, I doubt we ever would have met and shared the experiences we had. In that case, if he ever happens to think on me, tell him 'thank you.'"

"I'll do that, luv. I'll do that."

I left Jessabelle to follow my mum's twin outside. We walked across the visitor's center parking lot to cut into a neighborhood. We passed individual houses with shingled rooftops and brick walls.

"Sorry," she said. "I wasn't able to keep your room just as you left it. After you'd been gone a whole week, well, you have to understand. I thought you'd abandoned me, so I was angry—"

212

"What happened?"

"I sold your telly."

"Oh," I said. I was still awed and frankly confused by the technology of television. "No matter."

She pulled up straight to stare at me. "What? 'No matter.' That's all you have to say? You're not angry?"

"Should I be angry?" I asked.

"No, but—" The rest of her words sputtered. "I understand if these last few weeks changed you, Amber, but I didn't expect you to be fine with losing your telly."

"Was there sentimental value to it?" I asked.

"No."

"Did I purchase it from my own funds?'

"No."

"Then it was not mine to decide its fate. I only hope that selling it helped you with your finances."

She stared at me with worried eyes. As if I was a stranger sitting beside her. For all we both knew, I was.

She pointed out landmarks and asked if I remembered them. No. She then told stories with each landmark, hoping that would trigger a memory. No, again.

We eventually stopped at a little house with a steeped roof and blue trim. The side garage looked like it had been added later and was in ill repair.

"Welcome home," she said with a big grin. "Remember the O'Malleys across the street? And the Smiths live on the left. Do you remember—"

"No," I said, and marched ahead, tired of answering that question.

We stepped inside and she gave me a brief tour of the family room, kitchen, water closet, and two bedrooms. She loitered at the doorway of my bedroom, waiting for me to have some epiphany. Nothing was familiar, from the black skulls and roses bedspread to the posters of people who wore black facepaint over their eyes and lips. This was my room? I had a hard time imagining a peaceful sleep with such frightening people staring over me.

"I wish to rest," I said, "but this room makes me uncomfortable."

Mum's twin widened her eyes. "I thought you'd never outgrow your goth bands. Do you want me to fix you some dinner?"

I shook my head. "I am not hungry. Only tired."

"Alright," she said with a ghost of a confused frown. "I'll set out some blankets for you on the couch. Let me know if there's anything you need. I'm glad you're home."

"Thanks…Mum," I said, forcing out the word. She laid out some blankets on the couch in the front room, then situated herself across the room with a book. I crawled between the blankets that smelled like cats but felt like wool.

214

Dreams continued to evade me.

Waking in the strange home that was supposedly mine might have helped if I could feel my arm again. But my subconscious attempt to sit up halted me. Tears sprang to my eyes as I realized my entire arm was numb. The poison, whether it was in Somnus or in my head, had not healed by coming to this home. It was worse.

# Chapter 16

"Mother!" I called. She was gone from the room. I called again, then footsteps sounded in the hallway.

The woman who looked like the queen I knew came into my view. "Amber? Are you alright?"

As if my tears said otherwise. I cried, "I cannot feel my arm! The numbness only grew! What is wrong with me?"

"Oh, Amber." She came and sat next to me on the bed. She picked up my arm and pressed different pressure points. The scene disjointed my mind, like watching her massage someone else's arm that was somehow attached to me. The whole life of Amber Princeton felt that way. "We can go to the doctors if you think—"

"Where are my sisters?"

"Your who?"

"My sisters. Where are Garnet, Marin, Pearl, and Tanzi?"

She shook her head. "You're my only daughter."

My turn to shake my head. While my mum's twin shook her head to deny having other children, my denial was of never being without them. I knew I had sisters. They were my best friends. We did everything together. Even if I forgot their voices, I could picture their faces, how we each looked like bits of Mother and Father.

"Forgive me," I said. "This feels wrong."

The woman bit on her lips as her eyes glistened. "Please," she whispered. "You look just like her. Can't you be my Amber?"

"What do you mean?" I asked.

The glistening in her eyes dropped down her cheeks, and she sniffled. "You're not my Amber, are you." Her words were more of a statement than a question.

I simply stared and blinked. She sniffled again.

"My Amber disappeared a couple of weeks ago. I only hope she ran away to be an actress. When the police saw your report, they said they had found you. I thought…I hoped…" She rubbed her hand across her face and blinked back more tears. "You're not my Amber, but you look so much like her. Can't you stay with me until my Amber comes back?"

She took my hand, but I was too numb to return the gesture.

I gulped. The woman was broken and desperate. But if Amber and I were truly different people, then I could never satisfy my mum's twin. I could not stay. "My mum needs me too."

I stood and gave the woman the courtesy of seeing my face as I stepped backward to the front door.

"Where will you go?" she asked. "What if you get lost again?"

"Then maybe I will finally wake up," I muttered, confused as ever.

I left the house and wandered down the street. Following the pathway, I was unsure of where it led, but knew my direction was towards the great expanse of water.

The ocean. I had never known oceans in Somnus. I had to see it again.

A strong wind pulled my hair in wild directions and forced me to keep my depressed face down. There were no people in the streets due to the strong winds. I reached an intersection and the corner of the neighborhood. On the other side of the street, a mere hedge of random plants, probably weeds to the locals, separated me from the grassy fields before the rocky edge of the ocean.

I turned right to follow the road until it bent right again, taking me into town. Vehicles drove by. Some of them honked at me. Their blaring noises blurred with the constant commotion in London, but here, in this smaller town with only the wind to occupy my ears, their sounds startled me. I continued walking, quickening my pace despite the stronger winds. I walked straight through town, continuing up the road until a walkway broke with a sign for Tintagel Castle. It was in the same direction as the ocean, so I took it.

The pathway to the castle was wide and flat, though unpaved. Dirt and small rocks flicked into my face as I stubbornly walked on. Surrounded by hills covered with long grass on both sides, the ocean remained blocked from my view. The wind tunneled between the hills on either side of me, pushing me backwards. I pushed harder. After several minutes, I came to some signs and buildings labeled for toilets, gifts, and a cafe. The ocean was close, but I wanted more than a little alcove. I wanted to see it all from a hilltop. The sign stated that the area was closed, but no one else braved the storm to stop me from following the sign that pointed up towards the castle. I walked alone, unsure if the roaring in my ears was the crashing waves or the building wind.

The rocky, narrow path gradually took me up the hill, winding back and forth until I reached another sign and a small shack. I stood behind its wooden walls for a moment to catch my breath and hide from the unrelenting wind. The salt in the air urged me onward.

Whatever I expected of the Tintagel Castle—a tall fortress like St. Michael's or a wide settlement like my dreamy memory of Somnus' castle—I did not expect ruins. As if St. Michael's mount had met the fate of Stonehenge, all that remained were vague impressions of walls built from stacked stones, narrow as bricks, and broken as my heart. Not one wall remained tall enough for a window.

Even if Somnus was real, was this its fate?

I walked across what might have once been a courtyard until I looked over a low wall to the roaring ocean. My viewpoint was still blocked on the sides by the rocky cliffsides. A large mound—similar to the one at St. Michael's—blocked my view ahead. A long metal bridge stretched to the mound. Despite this world's advancements in technology, the new bridge still creaked in the high winds. I tested a foot on its oddly layered surface. Regardless of the ocean mist, my shoes held on the gripping surface, as if smart people designed it for stupid people like me who would try to cross the bridge during a storm.

Assured, I set to cross the bridge, then stopped halfway. The mound still blocked my view forward, but to its sides I had windows to the great waves.

The scene was absolutely stunning. Below me, the water foamed with blue-green waves in the alcoves. Farther away, the water turned gray like the storm clouds above. Like seeing it for the first time, its endless horizon took my breath away. Caden believed I was a native resident of Tintagel. If so, how did I forget such a sight? Instead, I remembered a fading dream of mountains all around and a great lake.

Rain fell in fat droplets. They splattered to the ground with little taps until they came too quickly to discern one from the other. Water dripped down my cheeks, undefined between my tears. Despite my numbing senses, the rain chilled my bones.

A sharp pain seized my right arm. The numbness throbbed, weighing my entire arm like a stone. I shouted out my surprise and agony, stumbling to the side of the walkway, leaning against the bridge railing for support.

"Emer?"

My head snapped up. Hope sprang through my chest at the sound of Caden's distant voice. How dare he have such an effect on me after his betrayal?

"Emer!" he called again.

I spotted him with Mica, standing at a lower lookout, turning about, searching for me. Their black vehicle sat with its lights on behind them. Miles stepped from the driver's door with an umbrella. Caden gave no notice to his valet's attempts to keep him dry.

Seeing Caden, my heart leapt with joy. Traitorous thing. I was supposed to ignore his calls, right? I could easily excuse my temporary hearing loss over the rushing waves below and rain above. Speaking of hearing loss, did he call for Emer or Amber?

"Emer!" he called again, searching without guidance, his voice laced with worry.

"Caden?" I called back. "Why are you here?"

His face jolted towards me on the bridge. "Emer!" he shouted. His laced worry turned into full panic. "What are you doing up there?"

At least, I thought he asked that. Who knew between the roaring wind and waves?

Mica gestured wildly at me to come down, then to stay, then come back. Caden made no such communication attempts. He simply ran towards me. I leaned against the bridge railing to keep him in my sights.

A great crack sounded through the air. At first, I feared lightning and my own safety on the open metal bridge. Then I saw the wooden fence below. It grew branches with thorns to block Caden's path.

Caden stopped in shock, and his confused eyes met mine.

I had not done that. Even if I had, I never made dead wood grow. The branches continued to reach out with long spikes…like needles.

"No! Stop!" I shouted. To my surprise, the thorns listened to me. I reached towards them and called them back. I was so tired: physically from the long walk, mentally from my debate about Somnus, and emotionally from Caden. Despite their fast growth from the wood, my efforts to shrink them came as slowly as my usual influence.

Caden wedged his way through as soon as there was a gap large enough. Some of the thorns caught him. Caden shouted but scraped through.

I released my concentration over the thorns, and they immediately shot back across the pathway, blocking Mica and Miles from following Caden.

He took the stairs two at a time, fumbling for the wooden railing as he slipped more than once. He spared a few glances at me to make sure I stayed, but continued running until he reached the edge of the bridge.

For one second, he stood there, drenched by the rain, the wind tossing his short hair. Red stripes bloodied his left arm and leg from the thorn scratches. He braced himself against the railing, then ran.

As soon as he reached me, Caden took me into his arms. He embraced me as if he had collected all my broken pieces and now held them in place. Oh, how I wished to feel his warm arms around me instead of wool.

"Are you alright?" he asked. "Are you hurt?"

How could I answer that? *Yes, you stabbed my heart, and Lady Elmsworth attacked my mind. Amber Princeton is someone else, and I am as lost as ever.*

Instead, I said, "My entire arm is numb. What about you? Those wayward thorns cut you badly."

"Just a flesh wound." He smirked with some inside joke.

"What are you doing here?"

"Charlotte's plant—the succulent in the living room—was fake! That's why it didn't grow! You *do* have magic. Then Jessabelle saw you walking down the street towards the castle. She called us right as we drove into town. I had to find you again. Whether you're truly a princess or truly insane, you're an adventure I don't want to miss."

"Is that all I am to you? An adventure?" I asked.

Caden groaned. "Do I have to say it out loud?"

"Say what?" I demanded.

"Whether you're a con artist, an amnesiac, or a lost princess, I fell for you, Emer. I need you in my life."

Fell for me? Like I was a joke? Or…in love?

I gasped as his warm eyes suggested the second option. "I thought you decided to give up your fantasies?"

"Can we ever truly give up our dreams? Regardless, I realized I was a prick—"

"Yes," I quipped.

"—and a true gentleman would ensure your safe return home."

I wiped the rain from dripping into my eyes and frowned. "Where? To Amber Princeton's home in Tintagel, or my home in Somnus?"

"Either," Caden said. "Will you forgive me? I was a real dolt yesterday—"

"Only yesterday?" I asked. "I thought that was just your personality."

"Please, Emer," he moaned. "I'm trying to say sorry."

I chewed on my lip to keep my smile from breaking free. I failed.

Caden's shoulders relaxed, and he released his own smile. "Does that mean you forgive me?"

"It means that I will think about it," I said.

"Good enough," he said. "May I escort you to Merlin's Cave?"

"I suppose." Allowing him to accompany me would give him more time to prove his change of heart. "We should probably seek shelter first."

"Of course, in Merlin's Cave," he said over the growing wind. "Wait, you didn't know?"

"Know what?"

"Merlin's Cave is right below us." He pointed down to the small rocky beach far below. How convenient. And inconvenient in the storm. Or, maybe it was more than convenience. Maybe the call to the ocean had come from the cave. I smiled and took his hand with my left, since the numbness reached up to my shoulder on my right.

We crossed the bridge, then began down the worn and slippery stone steps that zigzagged to the shore below. The wind buffeted us. My limp right arm flopped heavily, useless to grab the wooden railing. Caden used the railing and placed a hand on my back every couple steps. Whether for my support or his own, I knew not. Four steps away from a landing with a small shack, pain raced to my core, then zapped down my right side like lightning. I cried out and fell the last few steps like a drunken sailor.

"Emer!" Caden shouted over the storm and failed to grab me.

My body took a beating as my legs tumbled over each other until my skull hit the wooden railing. If my nerves still worked, I might have cried from the pain. Blood dripped from my forehead and down the side of my face.

Caden swore. "Are you alright?"

"Well enough," I said. "I feel nothing. My body might be severely injured, but I feel no pain. I can carry on. I must carry on."

Looking to the right, we had almost reached the path with the wild growth of thorns. Caden called, "Mica! Call an ambulance! Get help!"

We heard no response between the roaring water and rushing wind. My eyes registered Caden holding my right arm. The bizarre scene cracked my senses again. Like watching him help a stranger, I saw him raise my arm and gently pull me upward, but felt nothing. Only the stinging pain that throbbed through my right arm and leg.

"Can you stand?" he asked.

"Not without your help. I cannot control my right side," I said. Wrapping my strong arm around his neck, Caden helped me to stand. My right foot dragged.

"Are you sure you want to go on?" he asked. "We might be able to scrape by those thorns to grab a doctor."

I gritted my teeth and shook my head. "Those thorns are under someone else's control." A terrifying thought. Who else had that power? Or was it a symptom of my poisoned dream? Either way, "That pathway is blocked."

"Then forward we go," Caden urged over the storm. "The cave is rumored to be a sanctuary of the world's most legendary wizard. Maybe it can be ours too."

He led me to another turn down the steps. I really hoped this worked. If not, I dreaded the thought of going up all those stairs in the middle of the storm.

At last, we made it to the rocky beach. There was no path, only large rocks and boulders to carefully step around. The area probably would have been quite beautiful under different weather. On the left, a narrow waterfall splashed down the cliff and across the sand to join the ocean. On the right side was the cave.

From our position on the beach, we could see Mica on the lower outlook, stuck behind the wild thorns. He waved at us and shouted words that were lost in the storm.

Caden threw him a gesture to hold on, then limped me around some boulders to the cave. It was deep enough that the end was swallowed by darkness. As soon as we stepped through its wide opening, we found relief from the wind. Caden walked me to the side to lean against the rocky wall.

"You're alright?" Caden asked. "I'll need to leave to tell Mica to call an ambulance."

"Why not use your phone?"

Caden pulled his phone from his pocket. The black screen had a spiderweb of cracks across it.

"It broke during one of my stumbles to reach you on the bridge."

"Oh," I said. "How tragic."

He shrugged. "It was about time for an upgrade anyway. All I care about is your safety."

"Then stay, please?"

He graced me with a kiss on my forehead. Fear and elation clenched my heart at his kiss. A wayward draft sent rain into the cave. Caden's arms shuddered around mine, and he shuffled us deeper into the cave. Tripping on my right foot, I fell. The numbness pricked my core, and I screamed.

"Emer!" Caden knelt to the ground beside me.

The numbness creeped down my remaining limbs. No strength remained in my body, not to stand up or even crawl forward. The storm's angry fingers only reached so far into the cave, but something shuffled in the darkness. Someone watched us.

A woman stepped from the shallow shadows. She stood tall and proper with her raven black hair tied back, but frayed. My eldest sister stood before me in a dark red gown. Her mouth and eyes weighed heavily downward.

Caden gasped. "Who—"

"Garnet?" I asked. "What are you doing here? How did you get here?"

"Emer," she sighed. "You can be such a stubborn fool sometimes. Your body is dying, Emer, and nothing can fix it. Anything accomplished in a dream must be done again in reality."

"I know," I said. "I need to wake up! Help me to wake up!"

"I cannot do that, silly," Garnet chided. "I was the one to put you to sleep. You would have died much faster without this preservation. I still need to find the cure."

"What do you mean?" Caden asked. This place was supposed to have all the answers. All I had were more questions.

"She poisoned you all. One by one. It was the least I could do to put each of you to sleep."

"Who?" I asked. "Who poisoned us? Who else is asleep?"

"I tried to be so careful," Garnet whispered. "I tried to keep the others safe, but she grew in power as her poison spread…until everyone…" She choked on her words. "After everything I did…everyone…"

"Everyone? Who else is asleep?" I repeated. Both of my legs were fully numb.

"They called us the twelve dancing princesses," Garnet whispered. "We danced while everyone else slept. Now, only one of us continues to dance."

My heart plummeted. My worst fears suspected all of my sisters or my family. Not all of my sisters plus the sisters of Ormio and Huiess. Only one remained? Which one? What happened to all the others? Amy? Marin? Dia? Please not Pearl or Ruby. What about Dot or Sapphire? Surely not Opal or Toto. Tanzi?

The thought of any one of them betraying the rest of us was absurd. We were all the best of friends.

Caden asked Garnet questions, demanding explanations. If she could hear him, she ignored him.

The numbness spread down my legs and arms. It crept faster and gained speed every minute. My arms refused to obey my desires to move. My legs did too. I could not move. I was trapped.

No. I refused to die in my sleep, trapped in a dream. This was my dream, but I had no control over it because it—this land, these people—were *real*.

The hardness in my limbs inched towards my heart. Even if I could control my dream, my physical body was still dying.

My vision shifted as arms lifted me into a sitting position.

Caden.

The storm broke for a shining sun ray to beam into the little cove.

"Why are you here?" I asked.

"I told you," he said with a wavering smile. "I'll never leave your side again so long as you let me stay."

"Stay," I said, feeling weak. How could I be tired after so much sleep? The hardness crept up my neck and into my heart. My body would be dead soon, and this dream would finally end.

"Emer," Caden whispered, "don't leave me. I can feel you slipping away. Will you stay if I kiss you?"

My breathing stuttered, half from Caden's words, half from the pain reaching my heart.

"I know you're scared your poison will spread," he said. "But I think you're worth the risk."

Worth. He valued me. Whether I was a princess or an actress. He cared not if I could organize an entire birthday celebration by myself. He saw me as more than a pawn for politics. He saw me for the authentic individual that I was.

The lie that I needed to prove my worth broke around my heart. I was worth loving.

"All the more reason I cannot lose you," I said.

"Please, Emer. I can't lose you either. Telling you doesn't seem to work, so let me show you my true feelings."

True feelings. An honest kiss was a truth that promised love. Caden had called love a magic of its own.

My breath caught in my throat again, but I welcomed him as he leaned in. I closed my eyes and *felt* his lips against mine. Not wool. Not even cloth or fabric. A warm and smooth mouth pressed over mine, timid and nervous while also jubilant and triumphant.

I still faded. My consciousness slipped, and my world went black.

Chapter 17

My eyelids weighed as heavy as stones. My limbs were stiff as bags of flour. My mouth was dry like the Sesso desert, and my body moved like dead weight. A slight tingling remained on my lips.

"Princess Emerald?" a voice hesitated.

I forced my eyes open. Caden leaned over me, his expression openly surprised.

"Yes, Caden?" My throat rasped with neglect.

He gaped. "Whoa! You're awake! You know my name?"

"Of course I know your—" I broke off as I realized that Tintagel was gone and night had come. With a few blinks and a little wiping, I cleared my eyes. A single torch lit the room of blue-grey stones with vines and moss intertwining the cracks.

The bed, the windows to the right and left, and the door to the front… This was my bedchamber?

Just as Madame Gazelle had described it, I was surrounded by green. Moss stretched across the floor, vines hung from the walls and ceiling, and various ferns and flowers poked between the stones.

What happened to my possessions? How did all these plants grow here? And all the moss…

"How long have I been sleeping?" I asked Caden. He looked no different than in Tintagel, but he wore a green and white tabard of dragon crests and a cape with golden silk embroidery. His clothes may have once been fine enough for a prince, but they were smudged with dirt and ripped to ribbons along his left shoulder and leg. The longsword at his side needed cleaning too.

Despite his tattered state, he took my hand to help me sit up from my resting place. I was too weak to grasp back, but soaked in his touch. His calluses, his tenderness. It was all real.

"Legend says," he said, "you've been asleep for a hundred years."

"What? How?" I asked, and studied myself. My hands were stiff, though still youthful. I wore the brown gown that Elisa had mended for my birthday celebration.

"Caden!" a voice called from within the castle. Mica?

"Up here!" Caden called back. "Mica, come here! I found her! She's awake!"

"She's…what? Hold on, I'm coming!"

I studied Caden as he waited for Mica to fumble his way to us. How was he in Somnus? With Mica too. Peculiar as it was to see Caden in a tabard, the formal tunic was shorter than those from Somnus. It

234

cut at his hips instead of thighs—like the shirts of England.

Mica arrived at the doorway, wearing a padded joupon of coated arms over his suit of armor. He also carried a longsword and fire torch.

Caden acknowledged him with a nod. "You made it through the thorns?"

"Thorns?" I asked.

Mica shook his head and spoke to Caden, though his eyes bounced between his friend and me. "The thorns disappeared. Suddenly, the entire forest of thorns sank into the ground and was replaced by mild trees and shrubs. And flowers. Lots of flowers."

"Flowers?" Caden asked. He stepped over to the room's window and scoffed. "Would you look at that? Flowers. No wonder you came through without a scratch."

Mica joined Caden's side to confirm the view, though his eyes kept glancing at me. Caden nudged Mica. The familiar expression of friendship warmed my heart.

"I came as soon as the thorns disappeared." Mica gestured to me. "If she's awake and the thorns are gone, that must mean the curse was broken."

"Hello, Mica," I said, slowly pushing myself from my bed. My feet wobbled, but I could feel them. "Yes, it seems that my poison is cured. What do you know of the curse?"

"Princess." He bowed. "The legends say you were cursed to sleep like the dead for…well, it must not be important if you've woken now."

I frowned. "The poison was my curse, not the sleep. My sister put me to sleep to slow the poison."

"Interesting," Caden said. He opened a small pouch to retrieve a piece of parchment and drawing charcoal. "You say your sister put you to sleep to slow the poison?"

He leaned against my bed post to prop his leg, using his knee as a writing tablet.

I laughed. "Always taking notes. Are you writing a book about your adventures?"

Caden looked up from his notes, confused. "Yes. How did you know that?"

"I know you, Caden." I grinned, and reached for him. Taking his hand, hard with calluses. "We danced once upon a dream."

Chapter 18

"Beshrews," Caden cursed and visibly trembled. "Charlotte's going to kill me."

"Charlotte?" I asked. "Lady Elmsworth is here too?"

Mica scoffed. "She'll react the same way to everything you do. She'll shout and threaten to eat you."

"Eat you?" I cried. Apparently, Charlotte was not the same lady I met in my dream. "Why would Charlotte threaten to eat you?"

Caden's discomfort deepened. "She's an ogress."

I tried to hold it in, but failed. I laughed. It was too perfectly fitting.

Mica cleared his throat, then clarified, "She's his intended wife."

My laughter cut off, and my jaw dropped. "Your what?"

Caden's mouth shifted as if he wanted to spit out something disgusting. "My kingdom needs peace with the ogres. After years of war, they've surrounded us with our backs against the mountains. Our only options were to submit to the ogres or seek help from

Rezhina's queen. I never enjoyed the prospect of marrying Charlotte for the treaty. Hence my adventuring through Rezhina." He gestured to himself and our surroundings.

As he spoke, other parts of the conversation registered through my mind. Charlotte was here, but she was different. Caden and Mica were here, but they were also different. Caden and Mica had not come to life from my dream. They had their own lives, with their own pasts and obligations.

A piece of my newly healed heart broke at the thought of losing England's Caden, but the two men were similar enough to hope…

Mica mumbled, "It also means Charlotte won't be the only one upset by this turn of events. If you mess up the treaty, our people will suffer the consequences."

"Yeah." Caden rubbed the back of his head and shrugged to me. "But now we have an audience with a Rezhina princess. Maybe we don't need to go all the way to Noz Isle anymore, supposing you still have influence after a hundred years of sleeping. Er, maybe this plan wasn't as ideal as I thought. You couldn't have woken up sooner, could you?"

I frowned and folded my arms. "Oh? Now it is my fault that I was poisoned and put to sleep for a hundred years? I would have woken up sooner if possible, believe me. Enough time has passed that my father's castle is abandoned and overgrown with moss."

Mica blinked and stepped closer to study me. "It's really been a hundred years? You don't look a day over sixteen."

"Yes," I said. "How is that possible?"

Caden shrugged. "Sleep is healthy for the soul, I guess. That or immortality runs in your family. The other princesses are said to be only sleeping, and your queen looks hardly a day over twenty."

"My queen?" I asked. My mother?

"Long live Queen Tanzanite," Caden said, with a small bow.

Tanzanite? My youngest sister was queen? How? Wait, did that make her the traitor? Little Tanzi? Did my adventurous little twelve-year-old sister poison us all to become queen?

"Caden, Mica," I said, slowly testing my strength by standing without leaning against my bed, "tell me the honest affairs of my kingdom. How did my sister become queen?"

Caden flipped through some pages of his writing until he found the right notes. "Every heir was poisoned in their own way within about a month. Then each of the kings and queens of Somnus, Huiess, and Ormio were killed in battles or stepped down when Queen Tanzanite united the valley."

I gaped. She united the valley? Such an accomplishment was praiseworthy, but what was the cost? Poisoning every other heir? Then what Garnet said was true about all of the other princesses. They were all asleep. What had happened to my parents?

"The king and queen of Somnus?" I asked.

Caden flipped to another page of his notes. "Died in imprisonment."

The worry in my stomach ripped open. I leaned against a wall for support. Not enough. I sank to the floor.

Mica punched his friend in the arm. "Tact?"

Caden winced, then found me on the floor. "Er, right. Sorry. The purest records we have are the prophecies claiming Tanzanite would rise to the throne after the royal heirs were poisoned."

Prophesies? From whom? If someone had magic, I knew nothing of it, just as I knew nothing of a prophecy that forewarned my poisoning. A warning would have been nice.

Caden ruffled the back of his head again. "Official documents are unfortunately less trustworthy, as they say that you tried to poison Tanzanite during your birthday celebrations. She cursed you for your betrayal and others who wanted her dead by putting you all to sleep. So you say that you were put to sleep to *slow* the poison you put on the Rezhina Queen? Does that mean that Queen Tanzanite is still poisoned by you? What about now that you're awake? You said your curse was broken?"

Mica glanced out the window again. "The air towards the lake doesn't look any clearer than when

240

the castle was surrounded by thorns instead of flowers."

"Hold on, back up," I said, raising my hands. "I never poisoned Tanzi. I loved my youngest sister. I was the one who was poisoned. That was why Garnet put me to sleep—to slow my poisoning until a cure could be found."

Mica frowned with confusion, and Caden—beshrew his doubtful nature—raised a curious eyebrow and scribbled away at his parchment.

"No, Caden," I demanded. "Now is not the time to take notes for your stories. I need answers. What exactly do those 'official documents' say?"

Caden shuffled and reluctantly set aside his charcoal. "One hundred years ago, the prophetess claimed that Queen Tanzanite was the true heir to the entire valley. You and every other royal got offended and tried to kill her with poison. She was only twelve, but she was warned of the coup and had friends in high places. Queen Tanzanite cursed you all with nightmares until death took you."

"That is false! Every word!" I fumed. History was always told by the victors, but my youngest sister had made it a lie. "It was my sixteenth birthday. I planned a great ball, but needed mending on my gown. I pricked myself on a spinning wheel and was poisoned."

Caden, doubtful as ever, folded his arms. "So you confirm the prophecy came true. You were poisoned

241

by a spinning wheel? Forgive me, princess, but that sounds a bit contrived."

"It was contrived!" I argued. "I saw Garnet in my dream, and she said that my numbness was Tanzi's doing. If Tanzi knew about the prophecy—that I would grab the spindle—then she could have poisoned it. Come to think of it, she was the one to damage my dress and leave the weaving room before I entered."

"You saw Princess Garnet in your dream?" Caden asked. Why did he repeat my words, like I was un-clear? "Even as you saw Mica and me in your dream?"

My bottom lip quivered. He disbelieved me. Again. I was awake and back in Somnus, but everything was still wrong. If this Caden did not know and value me, then why…

"Why did you kiss me?" I demanded.

"Er—" Caden fumbled with my sudden accusation.

Mica turned surprised eyes to his friend, unaware of Caden's actions before he arrived.

"I came to know you," I said, "or a version of you, in my dreams. If you are not he, why did you assume to know me?"

"I—er…" He fumbled with his notes. "Dreams? I, er, feel like I know you. I mean, I researched you. I'm writing a book about the sleeping princesses."

"You were a writer in my dream as well. However, you wrote fantasies, not historical studies."

Caden shuffled. "The legends about the sleeping princesses almost feel fictional. I read all of the legends and histories, but people scoffed at me when I planned to see you for myself. I never guessed I'd be present when you woke."

I frowned. "You did not know that I would wake?"

"No. Not that I'm complaining," he added in a rush.

"Then," I asked again, "why did you kiss me?"

"Errr." He squirmed. "After all my research, our travels and struggles to find you, then, I saw you…I mean, you were really pretty, just lying there and… er, you didn't look dead at all."

My jaw dropped. "Is this your way of flattering me? You kissed me because I did not look dead?"

"Considering how old you are, yeah, I'd say it's a compliment."

Mica moaned and ducked his face into his palm.

"Beshrew you!" I threw my hands in the air at Caden. "You are just as infuriating as I dreamt you were! Except you *earned* your kiss in my dream!"

"Was I a good kisser?"

"I died with it! Then I woke up to…gagh!" Anger welled up until it spilled out with a word I learned from England. "You prick!"

"Wha—"

"Go!" I shouted and pointed at the door. "Between my parents' deaths, my best friends poisoned, my youngest sister calling me a traitor, and my kingdom in ruins, I have enough already without the fact that the man I fell in love with became an insufferable dolt. Again!"

Caden and Mica stared in shock. Mica scampered out while Caden raised his palms and slowly backed to the doorway. As soon as he stepped out of sight, I released my angry glare. I wanted to march them outside and search my father's castle for clues of the past, but I had absolutely no energy. Instead, I collapsed back onto my bed and cried.

Chapter 19

I cried until my tears ran out. Depressing thoughts stole away any desire to leave the comfort and familiarity of my bed.

A hundred years had passed. Everyone I had known was gone, except my sisters and closest friends who were cursed with poison and sleep. My youngest sister had betrayed us all and spread lies to turn *us* into traitors.

Still, I found it difficult to believe that my little sister had planned and overthrown all of us by herself. Was there another traitor involved? Who was the prophetess who only revealed her secrets to Tanzi?

Then Caden. He was different from the Caden of my dreams. He was similar in so many ways, but he distrusted me. He did not value me.

I had accepted Caden and the people of England as real people, but wondered what happened to them. Was my Caden still a world away?

When I eventually pulled my face away from my pillow and blankets, it was actually a surprise to find myself still in Somnus. The odd growth of moss and vines throughout my bedchamber aided my struggle to ground my consciousness.

I lay in bed, muscles still sore and tired from sleeping and crying. The light from the window slowly brightened the room, confirming a new dawn. The sound of Caden's laughter echoed from outside. Apparently, he and Mica had not left me completely alone. While a small part of me was annoyed at their presence, I was also grateful they had stayed. I felt as lost in this new Somnus as I had in England.

I forced myself to sit up and shuffle out of bed. I tripped on my brown gown to land on my hands and knees.

"Ow!" I cried, then grinned. Strange that even pain gave me joy simply because I felt it. I crawled forward, soaking in the textures of the wood flooring and the moss crawling between the cracks. Crawling was easier anyway. Mrs. Priddy would have spouted odd phrases about lemons and squash as her way to tell me that I looked dirty and needed to bathe. I smirked at the thought.

I crawled my way out of my bedchamber, to the stairs. I slowly gained some height and strength as I lowered my feet to one step, then the next. The vines stretching along the walls served as helpful railings down the steep stone steps. By the time I reached the bottom, I stood tall—at least, for one leaning against the wall.

I stood in the corridors of my childhood home, somehow feeling lost. Despite the vines, moss, and ferns covering the worn stone, the castle was empty. No servants tended to the fireplaces, no king paced the courtyard, no queen scrutinized the cleanliness, and no sisters teased me for sleeping in too late.

Whoops and hollers from men came from outside, near the gardens—or what used to be the gardens.

I spied from an upstairs window to my beloved gardens. Despite the rising sun, the morning mist lingered and obscured my view beyond an acre.

Where servants once carefully plotted and planted flowers of every color in strategic rows, now grass and wildflowers overran the gardens. In a way, it reminded me of England's countryside, and I smiled.

Two unknown men stood at the edge of the trees. They pointed and clapped one another on their backs as a large dog returned with a pheasant, speared with an arrow.

Caden and Mica stood to the side, close enough that I could just make out their words.

"Do you think Princess Emerald will eat with us?" Caden asked.

Mica shrugged. "Best way to know is to ask."

"You say that like it's easy."

"It is easy," Mica said. "Just go up and ask, 'Would you like to join us for breakfast?' Or we could set it all up that Thachuma plays the lute while you two drink our last bottle of—"

"Beshrew you." Caden shoved Mica's arm. "We don't need two of us messing things up. How am I supposed to go up there and explain what I hardly understand myself? What am I supposed to say?"

Mica laughed, then went into a dramatic grovel. "Oh, Princess. Please join me for breakfast and make all my dreams come true."

Caden grumbled something too quietly and shoved Mica again.

Mica stopped. "Wait, you're serious?"

His friend groaned and rubbed his forehead, then slid his hands to the back of his hair.

"Shrooms." Mica's substitute curse made me smirk. "You are serious. Last night?"

I frowned and leaned closer. Somewhere in Caden's grumbles, I lost the topic.

The handsome devil of my dreams and his minion spoke in the unintelligible language of man grunts, leaving me to only wonder what they discussed. And men said women were hard to understand?

I continued to explore my own home. Every room was as I remembered it, except wild plants had replaced the tapestries, vases, and books. I wandered through the castle to refresh my memories and hope for some clue as to what happened these last hundred years. The sun rose to midday before I could no longer ignore my stomach's demands. I made my way to the kitchen, finding four men and a woman in various activities. One stranger cleaned the dead pheasant on the butcher board as Mica loitered nearby with a piece of parchment and drawing charcoal. Caden sat on a stool with his own writing scroll and utensil. The other strangers looked busy with meal preparations, drawing water and starting a fire.

Mica noticed my presence first. "Ah, I hope you don't mind that we're borrowing your kitchen. Will you join us?"

Caden checked on me before ducking his face back down to his parchment. His neck burned red.

I cleared my throat and suppressed my anger from building again. "I did not poison my youngest sister—I hardly know how to do such a thing. I loved Tanzi and had no idea that she aspired to the throne."

Mica's shoulders sagged and Caden winced. The others in the room stood silent and watched with nervous eyes.

"We don't believe you're a traitor," Caden said.

"Oh?" I asked. "Do you not?"

He shuffled to his feet and stepped slowly to me, reading from a page of notes. "If you'll forgive me for writing a script, I'm a writer, not a speaker. I never believed that you poisoned Queen Tanzanite. The histories didn't make sense. That's why I wanted to write your story. I had a feeling that if I traveled through your land—researched your people—and saw you for myself, I'd learn the truth. Then you woke up and confirmed my every theory. It seemed too good to be true." His blue eyes glanced from his parchment to me as he approached. Reaching me, he set his notes aside, met my eyes, and took a knee. "Will you forgive me?"

This Caden seemed humbler than the Honorable Caden, though the Caden of my dreams had felt more betrayed by the misunderstandings. I stewed on his explanation long enough to make him squirm with unease. Unfortunately, my smile threatened to leak free. I bit it back.

"I will think about it," I echoed from my dream. "You should know, this is the second time you offended me with your distrust. I warn you not to test me with a third."

"Please," Caden said, standing. "Do not insult me with the assumption that I will. Jesse," he called to the woman at the soup pot. "Prepare a plate for her highness."

"Jesse?" I asked. Jessabelle? The woman turned around. I had not recognized her with her long black ringlets free from her English bun. I grinned, then pinched it back again at her confused response. I told the room, "Please, call me Emer."

"Emer?"

Hearing my nickname in Caden's voice broke loose my smile. He matched my grin and returned to his seat. Mica breathed with relief, and the others returned to their activities.

Jesse handed me a bowl of soup with a little curtsy. I sat at the preparation table to enjoy the first few bites. The food was immensely more fulfilling than my dream food. The pastries, tasty as they were, had never satisfied my stomach. The soup, simple as it was, tested my taste buds and filled me to the brim.

"Please clarify for me," I asked, "you came from beyond the northern mountains?"

Caden nodded. "My father's King Seaver of Uldra, the last kingdom of the great northern grass-lands. The ogres have overtaken all else."

"You are a prince?" I asked. "In my dream, you were only a lord's son."

"We are princes," Caden said, gesturing to himself, Mica, and a third man.

"We *were*," Mica said quietly. "What remains of our kingdoms has been absorbed into Uldra. The only way we could fend off the ogres was to combine forces…as we hope to do again with Rezhina."

Caden scoffed. "You'll get your lands back as soon as we eliminate the ogres. That was the deal, so you're still princes." Back to me, he asked, "Did you dream of Prince Leo too?"

Caden prodded the arm of the largest stranger, with shoulders wider than my elbow-span. I analyzed his long brown hair, light brown eyes, and full beard. Perhaps I had seen him at Caden's ball.

He bowed, but kept his eyes on me as I curtsied. He spoke with a deep rumbling voice. "Prince Leo Bahr of the lost kingdom of Braeder. We were one of the first to enter the war with the ogres, but the last to fall."

"Technically," Caden said, "Uldra hasn't fallen yet, so we're the last." Leo scowled at him, but Caden laughed. "Prince Leo's a master with any bow you give him. He's hard of hearing, so be sure to enunciate and speak directly to him."

I nodded and gave him my friendliest of smiles. "What of the talented cook?"

The stocky man at the soup pot turned around with a little bow. His narrow eyes looked like they were made for laughing. "Name's Thachuma—" His surname was a jumble of consonants.

"Thachuma…forgive me, how do you say your surname again?" I asked.

He laughed. "My parents came from the fallen dwarven kingdom of Chafan. Just use my given name."

"Thachuma it is then," I said. "Where does Jesse fit into the mix?"

"The beautiful Jesse is my wife," Thachuma said. "I'm blessed to have her company as we serve our traveling princes."

"*Somebody* needs to mother you all," Jesse said with a dramatic eye roll, then pointedly accused Leo. "You'd all suffer from lice and worms without me."

Leo scoffed. "Minor inconveniences are part of the traveling experience."

Mica smirked. "We wouldn't have lasted a week without her."

I smiled, remembering Jessabelle's irreplaceable aid as she helped me through London society life and the public transportation.

"I wonder," I said, "do any of your kingdoms have hand-held communication devices or horseless vehicles?"

Caden raised startled eyebrows. "What?"

"The world in my dream was highly technological. They had no magic, but everyone—including the common folk—had access to these light boxes. They were small enough to hold in their hands, yet powerful enough to send conversations, carry maps, contain libraries-worth of information, and even show theatre productions."

The men shook their heads.

"Sounds bizarre," Mica said.

Caden frowned. "And you met us in this strange dream world?"

"Indeed." The dream world that seemed realistic, and had somehow predicted this time with Caden, Mica, and Jessabelle without my sisters.

Setting down my empty bowl, I asked, "Where are my sisters?"

No one spoke at first. Mica cleared his throat. "Caden, that question's for you."

"Oh." Caden took a deep breath and his eyes shifted upward as if sifting through mental files.

"Queen Tanzanite is obviously on Noz Isle in the middle of the Imazhin Lake."

"Obviously." I smirked. Obvious to everyone except me. Though, if she ruled over all of Rezhina Valley, I supposed it made sense for her to be in its central location.

"No one really knows where Princess Garnet is," Caden continued. "As for Princesses Aquamarine and Pearl, they're said to be somewhere in the Sophor Forest, near the lakeshore."

I let out a long exhale. They were as good as lost. While I looked up to Marin, my senior by a year, I cared greatly for my younger sister, Pearl. I hated the thought of her in any harm.

"I would like to find my sisters. Perhaps now that I have woken, the others may wake too. I want to welcome them appropriately into this new Somnus."

Mica grinned and nudged Caden. "Caden— Caden."

"I know! Stop!"

Caden brushed Mica's eager tapping away. I smirked, remembering a similar scene from my dream.

"You wanted to find history and allies," Mica said. "We were present when Princess Emerald awoke. She wants us to help her find her sisters. What more could you ask for?"

"I suppose we could help you to search for them," Caden said, sliding his hand through his hair and

254

daring his nervous eyes to meet mine. "Except I need to return to Uldra first. Charlotte sent a letter yesterday. If I don't return soon, she might follow me here, and I think we can all agree that's a bad idea. Let me convince my father to make rearrangements for me, or at least to give me more time. Perhaps Charlotte will lose interest in me if I'm gone long enough."

"Doubtful," Mica muttered.

Caden grunted with agreement, then turned back to me. "Would you mind if we spent one more day preparing? Your lands are incredibly fertile and alive now that your curse is broken. We could hunt for enough food for the duration of our absence. Also, the ogres believe I've been hunting this whole time—for food, not for alliances, I mean. Returning with meat will solidify my alibi."

Mica scoffed. "You'll want to sharpen your razor of wit before confronting Charlotte again. It was getting a little dull."

"I just switched out the blade." Caden shrugged.

Mica laughed. "I think you were shaving in the wrong direction."

I tilted my head, remembering a similar conversation in England. Was it possible…?

Unable to answer my own questions, I asked, "How long will you be gone?"

Mica answered, "We traveled for a fortnight to find your castle. The return trip should only take half of that since we know where we're going."

"Only one week?" I asked, surprised. "Travels through the Rezhina Mountains used to take three weeks."

Caden grunted. "That was before the droves of refugees. Hundreds fled Rezhina when your sister came into power. Now the path is worn by our people fleeing *into* Rezhina from the ogres. We can return here in a fortnight if we ride quickly, which I'd like to do."

His quick glance at me suggested his reasons why. Beshrews, I had wanted to stay angry at him longer.

Chapter 20

We spent the rest of the afternoon and evening becoming reacquainted. Caden indeed knew a great deal about my sisters and me from his research. He knew all of our hobbies, talents, and how we each contributed to my father's kingdom.

Likewise, I came to know Caden and Mica for the second time. As if we were childhood friends who grew apart and reunited, they were the same, yet different.

The men retired to the study hall, where they had set up camp atop the thick grass that blanketed the decayed wood flooring. I returned to my chambers up the stairs, despite the struggle to lift my stiff feet to each steep step.

The spring night brought a chill, but I had enough of wool to last me a lifetime. I lined my bedding with linen and topped it with furs to keep me warm. I remembered England in my dreams, but nothing was the same. Plants climbed over the great structures of London and Caden kept changing clothes every time I looked away. One moment he was the lord's son, then the prince, then a stable boy, then a priest. I woke, grateful to return to my father's plant-filled castle.

The men's voices filtered up to me, encouraging me down the stairs. I found them saddling their horses in the front courtyard.

Caden spotted me first, immediately dropping his pack to join my side. "Emer, I'm glad you woke before we left for the hunt. I preferred to speak with you than to leave a note. To, er, save parchment."

Mica whispered loudly from behind his horse, "He wanted to see you."

Caden's neck burned red. "I didn't want you to think we left you, especially if you preferred to join us. I know hunting isn't exactly a duty for a princess, but we expect our hunt to take—"

"I need to find my sisters," I said.

Caden stumbled on his words before rerouting. "Er, I understand you might have trusted Queen Tanzanite before you were put to sleep, but are you sure you want to see the one who—"

"I meant Garnet," I said. As much as I wanted Tanzi to welcome me with open arms, Caden's explanations about the current state of Somnus made me hesitate to see my youngest sister. However, if any of my sisters could sort out this mess, it was Garnet.

Caden shuffled. "No one knows where she is. All my research only gave me vague directions for you and Princesses Aquamarine and Pearl."

258

"Then we find them first," I said.

Leo frowned as he watched our conversation. "There's no time," he growled. "You asked for three weeks to postpone your wedding. The ogres only agreed because they believe you're on your last hunt as a bachelor. We had enough time to go straight to Noz Isle, beg Queen Tanzanite for aid, and return. But you—" he accused Caden "—took us on a detour to chase legends. We might have an alliance with a princess, but you didn't tell me she was mislabeled as a traitor. She has no power in this kingdom, no resources to accept our people, and no authority to command an army to aid us. The best option we have is to return to Uldra with the pretense that we hunted as promised. We're already pressing our luck by staying an extra day to hunt."

Caden opened his mouth to argue, but I interrupted again.

"He has a point, Caden," I said. "I schooled myself to become a leader beside Garnet, but that was a hundred years ago. The economics and politics of Rezhina Valley have changed. I cannot command these people when I hardly know them. They have no idea I have returned. Trying to command them without Tanzi's permission will be nothing short of a revolution. Also, from what you told me, official documents claim I betrayed Queen Tanzanite. If I return to their lives now, claiming power over them, that would only solidify their false opinions that I am a traitor."

Caden frowned in thought. "I suppose that wouldn't look good. But if you woke your sisters, and they stood beside you—"

"That would take too long," Leo said. "We don't have half a year to chase legends when the treaty with the ogres was supposed to be signed weeks ago."

My mind raced for a solution. I needed to find my sisters and save them from the poison that almost killed me. I needed Caden's help to find them, but he needed a kingdom to ally against the ogres.

"We do not need to wake everyone to influence Somnus," I said. "Only Garnet and Pearl."

"Princess Pearl?" Mica asked.

Caden's thoughtful frown deepened. "I understand the need for waking Princess Garnet—the eldest of all the sleeping princesses and true heir to Somnus—but why Princess Pearl?"

"Pearl," I explained, "is the key to winning the people over. Garnet may win their loyalty, but Pearl will win their hearts. People cannot help but love her because of her genuine kindness. Also, you may not know where Garnet is, but Pearl might."

Leo grumbled. "That doesn't fix our need to hunt and return to Uldra to satisfy the ogres this week."

I pointed at the writing set that poked free from Caden's saddle pack. "I gather you and Mica will be more preoccupied with your writing and drawings while Prince Leo does the actual hunting."

Leo smirked, and Mica laughed. "She's not wrong."

"Perhaps," I began, "while Leo hunts, Caden and Mica may join me as we search for clues regarding my sisters."

Caden glanced among his friends for approval.

Leo grunted. "I work better alone anyway."

"I'll stay behind," Thachuma said. "Jesse and I will prepare a feast for your return tonight. With you gone, I can make all the dreamy faces I want at my wife without the rest of you rolling your eyes."

Leo laughed and pulled a disgusted face while Mica moaned with anticipation of food. "I won't argue with a feast."

With that, Caden helped me to saddle one of their horses. We rode through the abandoned courtyards. Tall trees with young leaves lined our pathway while wildflowers surrounded us.

"Incredible," Caden shook his head. "We spent an entire day trying to find a way into your castle, but it was blocked on every side with the thickest of thorn bushes. There was no way past them, and cutting through them proved fruitless. The next morning, I girded myself with my best armor and began to push my way through. Then, as if magic intervened, the thorns pulled back and created a path for me to enter. I stepped in, but the thorns closed the way again before Mica or Leo could follow. I ran the rest of the way, barely scraping through as they caught my left side."

"Interesting," I said. "Something similar happened in my dream."

We crossed the threshold beyond the castle and into thick fog. Leo rode off to the north while Caden pointed us west, perpendicular to the Imazhin Lake, where the fog remained thick despite the rising sun.

The great city of Somnus was small compared to London, but had once been the central location for tradesmen and leaders. From what little that I could see through the fog, the desolate city was now ruled by wild plants. Vines grew up the criss-crossing wall supports, trees poked through the rooftops, and mushrooms broke between the cobblestones.

"What happened?" I asked.

Caden nodded at our surroundings as if all was normal. "The records say that within a week of your sleep, thorns began to sprout around the castle. Of course, they also say it was your own poison on Queen Tanzanite that caused the thorns to grow. Queen Tanzanite hunted your sisters for their 'betrayal,' chasing them from town to town. Princess Aquamarine was caught somewhere in the outskirts of Somnus City, and Princess Pearl is said to be somewhere in the Midnight Forest."

"Midnight Forest?" I asked. "Where is that?"

Caden rubbed the back of his head in thought. "Right, I think it was renamed after your sister's curse caused the entire area to go dark. It's somewhere off west, close to the Ezuthithe Caves."

"That far?" I asked, my heart sinking. There was no way that we could travel to the caves before Caden needed to return to Uldra.

Seeing my disappointment, Caden pulled his horse close to mine and reached to touch my shoulder.

"I'm sorry," he said. "Let's start on the outskirts of Somnus today and search for Princess Aquamarine or clues."

I nodded, determined. Even if my sisters were poisoned a month after I was, I hoped to save them before they suffered more.

"My father had a favorite inn that he liked to visit for their pub. If my family fled from our home, they probably went there."

Caden gestured for me to lead the way.

Thinking of my sisters and the timeline of their poisoning, I wondered, "Why was I poisoned first?"

"What?" Caden asked.

"If Tanzi was after the throne, why poison me first? Why not Garnet or my parents?"

Caden blinked. "You weren't poisoned first. After some deep research, I found records that suggested assassination attempts on Garnet and Pearl."

"Pearl?" I asked, worry clenching my heart. As if my sister's past changed her perilous present. I raked my memories for a time when Pearl's life was threatened. Was there ever any animosity shown towards her kindness? Perhaps…

Caden shrugged. "You said it yourself. She's influential. Maybe Queen Tanzanite saw her as a threat."

"Also," Mica added, "isn't she said to be the most beautiful of all the sleeping princesses? Maybe Queen Tanzanite was jealous."

Both options were possible, but nothing was sure until we found her.

We arrived at my father's favorite inn—at least, what remained of it. The door and windows were broken, and half of the roof planks were gone. The entire building was burnt black.

Fresh tears welled in my eyes. My mind flashed with memories of joining my father inside for puppet shows and entertainers. It was the place that my elder sisters snuck into before we discovered our midnight masquerades. My mother would sing a line every time we passed.

"You are gone," I sang quietly, "but not forgotten."

My parents were gone, never to return, just like the inn.

I dismounted my horse and stepped carefully into the charcoal inn. Dust covered what little was left behind. The chairs, tables, and bar counters were burnt almost beyond recognition. No paintings of the past entertainers remained. The stairs leading to the upper rooms had collapsed.

Beyond my blurry vision, Caden shuffled uncomfortably. Mica nudged his friend and made a gesture. Whatever it meant, the men left me alone to wander through the ruins. My parents were lost, but maybe my sisters could be found.

I nudged away some of the pieces of furniture, looking for clues. Had my sisters stayed here before the fire? Were there any secret doors or hideaways they could have used?

After scavenging through the main floor, Mica managed to climb a tree from the outside to drop into the upper level. Caden and I remained below, listening for his commentary.

"Emer?"

"Yes, Caden?"

He rubbed the back of his head. "What were your dreams like?"

"Dreams?" I asked.

Caden shuffled again, obviously nervous. "I've had these dreams the past two nights, about a place without magic, but with incredible technology like plastic and phones. Forgive me for being such a prick."

My eyes widened and my hands went to his face. "Caden? Is it truly you?"

"I'm Prince Caden of Uldra, but," he paused to sort through his words, "I enjoy dreaming of you, even if the man I inhabit is a dolt."

I laughed, but kept my hands on his cheeks, *feeling* his short beard. "He turned out to be a good man."

He raised one of his hands to wrap around mine. He stared back at me with tender eyes that spoke of mysteries unfolding. "Will you give me the chance to be the same?"

I swallowed, overwhelmed and unsure of the feelings rising in my chest.

Mica shouted from above, "I'm coming back down. I don't think there's anything worth salvaging up here."

Caden cleared his throat and stepped away from me. "Alright. We should probably return to the castle for the night. Be careful on your way down."

I bit my lips to hold back my flustering. Caden was still a different man than the one from England, but what could it mean if he shared the same dreams?

Mica returned to the safety of the ground floor and we mounted our horses. We had maybe an hour before sunset. On the way back to the castle, I rode ahead of the group.

"Do you know where you're going?" Caden asked from behind.

"Of course, I do," I said. "This is my father's kingdom."

"Technically," he said, "it's your sister's. You should know there's a reason the cities around the lakeshore are abandoned."

I pulled my horse short. "Around the lakeshore? Where else are the people living?"

Caden said, "They all live pressed up against the mountains now. Several hundred have fled as refugees to my kingdom."

Mica nodded to validate Caden's story. "Jesse's grandparents came from Huiess."

"I do not understand," I said. "Why would they flee? Tanzi united the three kingdoms, did she not? Are they not at peace?"

"It's not other kingdoms they fear," Mica said. "It's the poison."

"Pardon?"

"The plants, creatures, even the water is poisoned. You don't sense it? Or was Somnus foggy before you were put to sleep?"

I looked around myself, truly analyzing the overgrowth of plants and hazy air for the first time. "I thought the plants were simply from the wilderness taking over as humanity withdrew. And the haze is more than a morning fog?"

"Much," Caden laughed. "The legends say it's Queen Tanzanite's magic, creating the thick mist, feeds the plants and water, and affects the animals. The closer you go to the lake, the stronger it becomes."

"The plants?" I asked, wondering about the strange plants I had encountered in my dreams and the stranger way that I affected them.

"Yes," Caden said. "Stay away from them. They have minds of their own. That's why it was so tricky for Mica and me to find you."

"I wonder…"

I looked for a test subject and found one in a small vine climbing a nearby tree. I hopped off of the horse and knelt before the little sprig.

"Er, Princess?" Caden asked.

"Look at you," I said to the plant. "Strong and stubborn, growing right in the middle of the tree roots. You refuse to let anyone stop you, finding any crack you can to push your way through. Can you show me that strength? Can you grow for me?"

The vine wiggled with my compliments. Before I could celebrate at the demonstration of my dream-like magic, the vine expanded. The little sprig slowly grew taller and thicker.

My companions shouted and jumped back.

"What the devil?" Caden swore. He pulled out his large glittering sword and angled it against the vine.

"Wait! Stop!" I shouted.

Whether I directed my command at Caden or the vine, to my amazement, both listened.

Mica gaped. "Incredible."

"Indeed." I smirked. "Caden actually listened to me."

Mica laughed and Caden scowled.

"You didn't care to mention," he growled, "that you can control the demon plants?"

"They are not demonic." I put a hand on my hip. "They are the most beautiful creations of this planet, and I consider their overgrowth as an improvement to the city."

The vine, trees, shrubs, and grasses around us quivered with excitement.

Mica laughed nervously and Caden stared in horror at the greenery around them.

"Still," he said, "you could have mentioned it."

"I was unsure if it would work. I had no such magic before I was put to sleep. I had it in my dream, but it was less effective. I could only influence one at a time, and they never responded this eagerly."

"Devils of the southern hills," Caden swore. "Are you a witch like Queen Tanzanite, Princess Garnet, and the prophetess?"

I frowned. "I work no evil with my powers. Princess Garnet only used her power over sleep for harmless pranks or to slow my poison. As for the prophetess, I do not know enough about her to make any comparisons."

"No one does." Caden grunted and stepped around the enlarged vine with a critical eye. Mica also stepped cautiously around the vine, studying it, then sketching quick marks on his parchment for notes.

I giggled to myself. Caden and Mica were two peas in a pod—or maybe, two scrolls to the same parchment roll.

"Emer," Mica asked, "does Princess Pearl have magic?"

I shook my head. "Only Garnet showed any signs of magic. After all these years though, who knows?"

We returned to the castle without any other incident. As much as I wanted to practice more with my dream-like magic, I did not want to frighten the men any more than I already had. Jesse and Thachuma had a feast of pastries filled with fruit and nuts to accompany the last of the beef soup. I was most delighted at their request to remain with me when the princes returned to Uldra. Yes, please.

Leo had caught several rabbits, a fox, and a buck. The princes cleaned and wrapped their game, preparing all except their sleeping packs to depart in the morning. We chatted lightly as the stars emerged.

Staring up at the stars, I remembered a night in Penzance, looking over that vast ocean.

Caden approached me with a timid step, and an idea struck me. Grinning, I grabbed his hand.

"Come," I said. "I want to show you something."

"Wha—"

I pulled him from the kitchen, down the corridor, up the stairs, and to the watchtower. The night stars lit the expansive sky. No moon dominated the night. Only thousands upon thousands of stars.

270

"Look how beautiful they are," I said.

"What?"

"The stars! I never realized how much I could miss them. When the rain stopped, it was cloudy, or the great buildings as tall as mountains blocked the sky. The one night I saw the stars in all their glory, they were different stars. The constellations were different. They were beautiful, but…not mine. Does that make any sense?"

"I suppose," Caden said, rubbing the back of his hair.

My excitement sank. This Caden did not live every day in the rainy city of smog. He did not appreciate the rare beauty of stars the same way.

At the sight of my disappointment, he tightened his hold on my hand and stepped closer. His nervous smile spoke of a victorious catch far greater than Leo's buck.

"Forgive me," he said. "I'm still grasping the situation. My wildest dreams hoped you'd be awake and show an interest in me. I've been, er, fascinated with you and your story for years, and I feel like I'm living a dream."

"I did that for a few weeks," I said. "You get used to it."

He chuckled and dared to brush my hair behind my ear. "Do you have any idea how marvelous you are? I wish I didn't need to return to Uldra."

My heart leapt and cracked at the same time. For a moment, all time and space blurred as my world focused on Caden standing before me. Whether we were in England or Somnus, he valued me. But he was leaving me again.

"Must you leave? I feel like a stranger in my own home. Having you and everyone else here has helped it to feel less empty."

"Jesse and Thachuma volunteered to stay with you," he said, "I wish you could come with us, but it'll be safer for you here. If Charlotte learns of you, she'll kill you, without doubt. I know my father would graciously take you in, but…he'll need time to accept your true history and our new plans for Uldra's safety."

"Oh, I understand," I lied. He seemed earnest, but could I trust this Caden as wholly as the first? Even the first betrayed me, and this one already doubted me once. Would he truly return as he said? Or would he leave me alone in my forsaken kingdom and marry Charlotte? My heart ached at the thought.

"I promise," he said, "to return as soon as possible. We'll find your sisters, wake them, and declare the truth of what happened. We'll save our kingdoms."

Chapter 21

I woke the next morning to the sound of horses clomping across the courtyard. I sprang from my bed and stumbled, ripping my brown dress. Again. My knee burned and scraped, but I gave it little thought as I scrambled for the window. Lifting myself above the awning, I spied four horses galloping away from the castle. I recognized Caden's colors on the horse in front and watched until they were engulfed by the forest. He never looked back.

A heavy gulp failed to swallow my emotions. He told me this would happen. He promised to come back…as if the word of a man was unfailing. Even if he returned in good time with good news, his departure meant postponing my search for my sisters. I shuffled back to my bed and sobbed. I needed my sisters more than ever to ask them what to do with my silly heart.

I tried to fall back to sleep, to forget Caden and how he left without saying goodbye. Instead, I focused on my sisters and where to search for hints to their whereabouts, how to save them from the poison, and how to welcome them to this broken Somnus.

Maybe I fell asleep somewhere in there, as a smell invited me back to consciousness. I sniffed again.

Cooked meat? Right. Jesse and Thachuma had remained behind.

I shuffled out of bed, taking more care this time, and down the stairs. My legs and feet had enough strength to hold me straight, but I still used the wall vines for support. I followed the scent to the kitchens, catching a soft whistling tune.

Thachuma stood at the fireplace, stirring a stew in the great cauldron.

"Thachuma?"

He jumped, splattering a couple drops of stew. "Oh, Your Highness. I thought you might be hungry for breakfast."

"Yes, thank you," I said. "Thank you, also, for remaining here with me."

"Of course, Your Highness." He cleaned his hands on his apron, then grabbed a bowl to serve the stew. "Prince Seaver didn't want to leave you all alone in these strange forests. Jesse and I were the obvious solution. The princes will travel faster without us anyway."

Logic edged into my heart. Even if Caden left me forever, he needed to send someone to retrieve Jesse and Thachuma, allowing me at least another chance to contact him. "Still, thank you for your sacrifice in accompanying me so far from your home."

Jesse walked in, carrying a bucket of water.

"It's no sacrifice," she said, sharing a quick smile with her husband. "I practically volunteered. I wouldn't have dared to speak out of turn, but I've been meaning to offer my assistance regarding your dress."

I frowned at my brown bliaut, its dirt smudges and tears. "Yes, it needs some mending and a wash."

"For starters," Jesse chuckled. "Does Your Highness have any other garments to wear as I mend it?"

I shook my head. "Also, you may drop the formalities. Emer is fine."

"Yes, Princess Emer." Jesse curtsied. "I'm afraid the only other womanly garments in my possession are my own. I could lend you one while I wash your gown."

"That would be wonderful." After living with dresses provided by others in England, accepting Jesse's dress was like accepting her friendship. Besides, all these layers had felt stuffy lately.

We continued to chat while I ate my stew, discussing washing instructions and mending options for my gown. Thachuma left and returned with a load of chopped wood to fuel the fireplaces. The freshly cut logs stirred sorrow in my gut. Odd. I never experienced sadness for lumber before…before I grew a connection to the plants.

"Thachuma?" I asked. "Where did you collect that lumber?"

He pointed left. "From the back side. It's farther from the lake, and the mist is a little less thick."

"You mean the gardens?" I asked.

"Oh." His face blanched. "Are they gardens? Please forgive me, your highness, if they weren't meant to be touched—"

He fell to his knees in humble fear. What severe punishment did he expect from me? What horrible lord had he served to strike such fear in him? Not Caden or Mica, I hoped.

"Please, there is no need to grovel. They were gardens a hundred years ago," I said. "The flowers I once grew are long dead. I merely wondered if I could help replace the fallen tree."

Thachuma blinked. "Every flower about this castle is as new as your wakefulness. Your Highness, the flowers you once grew may have died, but hundreds have sprouted again from your influence."

I shrugged. "If it is as you say, I did it while dreaming."

I knew less about my magic than I did in England. Somehow, it was more powerful in Somnus.

"Thank you for the stew. I will be in the gardens if you need me."

The gardens, as they were, consisted of wild grass and flowers between tall trees with white bark that grew close together. The wild meadow behind my father's castle left no remains of our hedge maze, flower arrangements, or vineyard.

"Alright," I said to my new project. "Shall we start with a pathway?"

I closed my eyes and pictured Kew Gardens, beautifully cultivated, yet not so manicured as to appear unnatural. With my ability to command the plants, I might make the gardens exactly as they once were, but…I wanted them to be different. I was different too.

I walked through the garden meadow, talking to the plants, complimenting their vitality, and asking if they were happy where they were. They answered in no way that I understood. The trees shivered their branches, the grass swayed, and flowers bowed. Clear as mud. Either way, it meant they could hear and respond to me. That had never happened before my sleeping spell.

I asked the grass and flowers to pull back from beneath my feet to create a path where I walked. I did not want to tread on them, and the blades bounced in the surrounding areas. Was that appreciation?

"Your Highness?" Jesse called from the castle's doorway. Oops, I had lost track of the time. The last rays of the day filtered through the mist, scattering the light. A decent little pathway now stretched from the castle to where I stood, several meters away.

"I must bid you goodnight," I said to my mute listeners. "I will return on the morrow."

And I did. An easy promise to keep, since I had little else to do. I explored the castle rooms during the night hours, asking the plants to move when they jammed a door or drawer. I searched my parents' rooms and my sisters' bedchambers. All empty save for the furniture.

Jesse allowed me to dirty her kirtle again as she mended my brown bliaut. After cleaning up breakfast and lunch, she joined me outside, sitting on the castle steps, stitching away at my gown while I walked among the trees. Thachuma joined as well, wrapping an arm around his wife and keeping an eye on our surroundings like a proper guard. The couple returned inside to prepare supper while I continued to roam around my little meadow gardens. I convinced all of the trees to grow beyond the new wide circle path. I also encouraged the grass to bloom stronger within the circle, then the flowers to take priority in the space between the castle and the circle. It had taken me all day, but I was quite proud of the outcome.

The best part was the distraction. I spared no thought for Caden while I talked and walked about my garden.

Wiping sweat from my forehead, I recognized the dimming light as time for supper. I headed inside, but stopped at the door to the kitchen.

Jesse and Thachuma argued within. Despite their debate, they spoke in worried whispers.

"What would you have me do?" Thachuma asked. "You know we can't say no to her. She'd kill us. You've seen her power, but I've seen her anger. I was simply grateful it was directed at Caden, not me."

I held back a gasp, thinking of the argument between Caden and me after returning to Somnus. Had Thachuma heard? Was I truly so frightening that Thachuma thought I would kill the prince? I could not deny my anger at Caden for his terrible explanation for kissing me, but not to the death. I thought that I showed great restraint during the conversation.

I stepped through the doorway, ready to answer their wrongful suspicions. Thachuma and Jesse silenced their argument and failed to look preoccupied.

I swallowed back my emotions from their misunderstanding. "If any of my demands are too taxing, you may say as much. I promise not to be angry."

"No, no," Jesse said in a rush. "We are happy to serve Your Highness."

"Is it too much to ask that you call me Emer?" I asked with a testing smile. "And if not me, whom were you talking about just now?"

Thachuma and Jesse shared a nervous glance and said nothing.

I sighed. Then, I was the topic. I meant no burdens on them, but felt just as helpless as my time in England. The feeling was frustrating…and depressing when I considered why.

Once again, I was stranded in unfamiliar territory, unable to prove my worth. I wanted to find my sisters, but all I knew was that they were somewhere along the lakeshore. Caden knew more about their locations, leaving me to wait until he could guide me…again.

I was a foreigner in my own land. My own kingdom. My own dreams. My own reputation. All twisted by my own sister.

My frustration must have shown as Jesse and Thachuma remained silent during supper. Without light to grow my garden, I retired early to bed.

On the sixth day since my awakening, I rose early with the sun to walk about my meadow garden again. I tested my abilities to command the plants. They easily followed my encouragement to grow in certain areas, grow stronger or smaller, but struggled to grow in ways unnatural to their species. Blades of grass remained as grass, and flowers could not turn into trees. I could, however, talk a yellow daffodil into turning white. That was fun.

I spent the whole morning, coloring the flowers that framed the castle. Jesse made bread from the wheat I grew, complementing her carrot and rabbit stew.

We just finished lunch when a clattering sound reached our ears. Horses approaching? Jesse and Thachuma shared a worried look. I ran up to the watchtower for a better view.

A magnificent coach with four black horses, a driver, and a footman rolled onto the castle grounds. It was too early for Caden to return. My heart jumped when I thought of who else it could be. Had Tanzi discovered my presence and come to arrest me? Or was it some other royal who needed a place to stay?

As the carriage slowed to a stop in front of the main entry, I recognized the crest on the side door. It was the same crest on Caden's tabard.

He had come back! Or maybe he had sent a carriage to bring me to him. Either way, I grinned and skipped down the stairs to meet the carriage.

He had returned to me! After only four days? Four days was hardly enough time to go to Uldra and back. Perhaps, on horseback, Caden and his companions could reach Uldra in five days, but definitely not two.

I opened the great entry doors to have my fears confirmed. Not Caden.

The footman lowered the steps for a large woman to exit. She was easily four times my size and one and a half times my height. She wore a purple gown that emphasized her womanly curves, and bracelets, rings, and a necklace that shone like stars.

Calling her a woman was a misconception though. Her green complexion, frog-like mouth, and sheer size defined her as an ogress.

"May I pronounce," the footman declared, "Lady Charlotte Elmsworth."

Chapter 22

The first words out of Charlotte's mouth were as beautiful as her appearance.

"Where's that measly little cook? I'm hungry."

Answering to her beck and call, Jesse and Thachuma hurried to bow at the ogress's feet.

"Jesse?" I gasped. "Thachuma?"

Jesse whispered back to me, "We're sorry, Princess."

"What's that?" Charlotte snapped.

"We're sorry, Your Highness," Jesse said loudly to the ogress, "that we weren't here sooner to greet you."

"As you should be," Charlotte hissed. "What is this awful place you brought me to?"

I spoke. "This is my father's home, seat of the crown of Somnus, and you are not welcome here."

Charlotte's black eyes zipped to mine with a snarl. "Who are you?"

"Princess Emerald Reo," I said with all the proper bearing of a princess. "This is my home, and you are not—"

"You," Charlotte snapped. "You're the wench who poisoned my intended man's mind?"

I frowned. What was it with everyone thinking that I was some great poison master? Before I could gather my poise to respond, the ogress snorted and spat at my feet. The fist-sized snot wad splattered onto my shoes.

"Harlot," she growled. "Prince Seaver is mine! I will feast on your flesh before giving you the chance to take his kingdom from me."

If I thought the English Charlotte was mean and sickening, this one was cruel and despicable.

I allowed my anger to boil and seethe from my eyes. Behind Charlotte, the vines squirmed to life. "You. Are. Not. Welcome. Here."

Charlotte sneered and glanced left and right. "Who's going to stop me? You're just a weak little princess who slept while her kingdom fell to ruins." Pointing at Thachuma and Jesse, who remained bowed, she said, "These two welcomed me here. I'm the one with loyal servants. All you have is some stone walls."

Beshrews, she was right, but how could she know that? At least she knew nothing about my plant help. "I have unseen forces who await my command. You are not welcome here. I must ask you to leave."

"You must *ask*?" Charlotte scoffed. "Funny, because you cannot demand. Ask all you want, but with no force to command, I think I shall take over."

As if.

"Vines," I called, "block her entrance!"

Sprouts grew around the base of the stairs. Charlotte's eyes widened at their sudden appearance. Her surprise lasted only a second until she commanded, "Gother! Shinópu! Clear the path!"

Two servants leapt into action. Both were large and muscled men, though one was particularly shorter than the other. The taller one unsheathed a two-handed broadsword as the shorter one slipped two curved blades from back scabbards.

The vines snaked upward, faster than any plant I had grown before. But they were still too slow. The two men sliced and diced my vines before they could grow any taller than a few centimeters.

Charlotte grinned a more hideous version of her victorious smile when calling me Amber. "Thachuma wrote all about your powers and lonely little castle. You have no power in your own home—in fact, is this truly your home? I'm fairly certain these lands belong to Queen Tanzanite. I know your sister. I wonder how she would react to hearing about her traitorous elder sister waking from your justified prison?"

Fear clenched my heart like a reminder of the numbing poison that almost killed me in my sleep. Tanzi had gone to great lengths to poison each of us. I doubted she would celebrate to hear that I had escaped her poison.

Charlotte walked right up the stairs and passed my wriggling vines. Her massive body towered over me. She grabbed my arm with one of her fists, the hand the size of my head.

"Let me go!" I cried.

"I think not." Charlotte stomped right over my struggling vines and into my father's castle, dragging me along.

I hit her with my free hand. Smacking, punching, clawing, I bruised myself while Charlotte hardly flinched.

"Thachuma!" she roared. "Where can I lock this wench away until I decide what to do with her?"

Thachuma stood, but kept his eyes on his feet. "Her bedchambers are in the highest tower."

"Good enough," she grumbled. "Show me."

Charlotte's servants filtered in behind her with loads of cases. Jesse finally stood from her bow to follow.

"Stop!" I cried, struggling against her hold on me. "You cannot do this!"

"Why not?" Charlotte laughed. "Yes, let it be known in the history books that *I* conquered these wild thorn lands. After the traitorous Prince Seaver woke the traitorous princess, I restored order under the name of Queen Tanzanite."

Lies. It was all lies.

My mind scrambled for a way to fight back. Anything to make her leave me alone. Except forcing her to leave might lead her to visiting Tanzi. Then Tanzi, with her authority over the people and control of history, would…what would Tanzi do to me? Banish me from Rezhina? Not likely. Poison me again? Possibly.

What could I do to stop the ogress? Garnet would have known what to do, right?

I grabbed at the plants we passed, pleading for their help. They reached for me, but were too slow. Charlotte yanked me from their branches or ordered one of the swordsmen to chop the vines that held me.

The vines wilted like my heart.

Charlotte grumbled to herself, pulling me up the stairs. "The more you struggle, the sooner I might eat you. Is that a wine house down there? Yes, I think I'll be quite comfortable here."

A weaving of vines blocked the doorway to my bedchamber. Swordsmen Gother and Shinópu cut it down within a minute.

Charlotte threw me into the room where I had already spent a hundred years. I turned back to shout, but caught Jesse's sad face between the closing door.

"Sorry," she whispered, so quiet and sorrowful, I almost missed it.

The wooden door slammed shut.

Charlotte ordered someone to keep watch, then footsteps sounded down the staircase. Silence.

I waited ten minutes before cracking open the door.

286

"If you want to kill me," a small voice said, "please, continue."

I paused. Jesse sat at my doorway, her eyes and cheeks speckled red from crying.

She sniffled. "If you escape under my watch, Charlotte will kill me. I almost want to die for betraying you, but I hate to think of what Thachuma would do without me."

Charlotte's cruelty twisted through my mind. My bedchamber had no locks. I could command plants. I knew the secret path that went from the first landing to the base of the castle. My sisters and I used it to sneak away to our midnight masquerades. Overpowering Jesse to escape would be easy. But the evil ogress had gambled I would remain out of compassion for Jesse's life.

"I'm sorry," she said again. "We couldn't risk her wrath."

A small thought of relief and understanding pierced me between my mountains of anger and frustration. I was not the topic of Jesse and Thachuma's heated discussion when I caught them in the kitchen. Charlotte was. Caden was not the master who struck fear in Thachuma's heart. Charlotte was.

Unfortunately, that news only increased the seriousness of my situation. I needed to escape, but I could not allow Jesse to take the fall. I also needed to keep Charlotte from alerting Tanzi to my wakefulness. My word against Tanzi's would fail, but if I managed to find and wake Garnet…

I paced my bedchamber, stepping carefully between the vines and moss. How could I escape, yet keep an eye on Charlotte? How could I force her out of my home, yet keep her from leaking information to Tanzi? Was it possible to keep my wakefulness a secret until I woke my sisters? How could I wake my sisters if I only had vague directions of their locations? Could I search the whole city and forests by myself? I cringed to think of searching and surviving alone in this wild Somnus.

As the afternoon wore on, the plants pulled back a little to give me an easier pacing path. My feet ached for rest, leading me to ponder away the day on my bed. By supper time, a soft hand knocked on my door, but I still had no answers.

"Emer?" Jesse asked.

"Only friends call me Emer," I grumbled. "You have lost that privilege."

"I understand, Your Highness," she said. "I brought you some soup. I thought you might be hungry, and…I hoped to talk."

"Talk?" I sniffed. "As if words mean anything." The potent ham and onions wafted through my door as the soup steamed.

"I wanted to explain why we did what we did. We didn't want to, and I'd take it back if there was any other way."

"There is always another way," I argued.

"I suppose there is," she said softly. "We could have chosen death."

That stirred my attention. I stood and opened my door to her. She extended her bowl of soup as her peace offering. It smelled even better in the open. I stood back as a gesture to welcome her inside. I accepted the soup and led her to sit with me on my bed. My stomach gurgled with want, but I savored the first bite.

After several swallows, I asked, "Charlotte threatened to kill you if you refused to betray me?"

Jesse shuffled in her seat. "It isn't that simple. Thachuma has been trapped by Charlotte's demands for months now. When the Seavers initially invited the ogres over for peace talks, Thachuma added citrus flavors to their dinner, unaware that Charlotte was allergic to citrus. Charlotte knew about the flavors, but excused Thachuma by saying she caught an illness. They were ruthless in the peace talks, though. She claimed Prince Caden, then approached Thachuma in secret. She demanded that he spy on the prince to keep him faithful. Thachuma hoped it would be enough to tell her the truth of Caden's 'bachelor hunt.' But she demanded we join the excursion. Thachuma tried to deny her and feed her false information, except she has more leverage over us now for our spying. She increased her threats every time we fought her demands."

"Jesse, I am sorry," I said. "Have you considered running away?"

She sighed. "Often. We've discussed the exact details of what we'd need to leave Seaver's generous employment and always came to the same roadblock: if we run, Charlotte or her family of ogres would find us, then kill us without question. Also, Charlotte keeps Thachuma's prince as one of her slaves."

"Thachuma's—the prince of Chafan is one of Charlotte's slaves?"

Jesse nodded. "Chafan was the first kingdom to fall to the ogres. They killed King Chushiama and enslaved Prince Shinópu."

"The dual-blade wielder?" I asked.

Jesse nodded again. "Despite his enslavement, Thachuma thinks of Shinópu as his prince. My husband wants to stay close to Charlotte to stay close to Shinópu."

I thought over her words as I ate the soup. My once-empty stomach gurgled with satisfaction, and Jesse chuckled at my unspoken compliments.

"Thank you," I said. "I cannot offer gratitude for you welcoming such a beast into my home, but I understand your difficult situation. One hundred years ago, my father would have tied her feet to the back of a horse, then driven her out to the mountains."

Jesse shuffled uncomfortably. "Yeah, well, a lot has changed in a hundred years. They're a mighty force outside of Rezhina Valley. Uldra is surrounded

290

by tribes of ogres everywhere to the north. Then, to the south, it's the Rezhina Mountains. They have us backed to a wall."

I frowned. "Charlotte says that she's acquainted with my sister Tanzi. Are there many ogres here too?"

Jesse shook her head. "Between the difficult mountain passes and Queen Tanzanite's powers, even the ogres leave Rezhina Valley alone. But if Charlotte creates a stronghold for them here, I doubt it'll stay that way for long."

Yet another reason to banish Charlotte from my home. If only I had the means to remove her.

"Jesse," I said, "how loyal is everyone in her entourage?"

She shrugged. "Hard to say. I know that all of us follow her out of fear, not love, but Charlotte frequently asks us to spy on one another, pitting us against each other before any kind of coup may be staged. Also, there's the matter of Charlotte's family. I know Thachuma and Shinópu are only loyal to Charlotte, but I cannot say the same for the others. They might report to other ogres if any of us go rogue."

"That might be a risk worth taking," I said, concocting a plan. "Cough three times if someone replaces your guard position—someone who might survive Charlotte's wrath. I might be able to escape. If you must remain as my sentinel, ask your husband to bring us food so that we may discuss together. Perhaps the three of us may be enough to convince the others to stage a revolution."

Chapter 23

Jesse left me with an extra roll, and I spent the rest of the night whispering out my windows to the plants that surrounded my father's castle. Considering the ways I asked them to grow, I was actually grateful for the night masking my results. I instructed them until my voice became raw and my eyes drooped. Leaves and moss grew extra soft around me, allowing me to fall asleep by my window.

An angry ogre roar woke me after dawn. I smiled.

A stream of curses ascended the stairs, announcing Charlotte's approach. Apparently, knocking was too gentle for her. She punched down my door and stormed into my room.

"What did you do?" she snarled.

I yawned. "I beg your pardon?"

"Thorns!" she shouted, gesturing outside. "Surrounding the castle! You did this. I know you did!"

"Perhaps," I said, picking at my nails. "Looks like you might be trapped here until you can cut a path. Or, you can learn to play nice and ask me to withdraw them for you."

Charlotte growled. "Gother! Shinópu! Sharpen your swords!"

"Ooh." I cringed. "You might need to help them. See, those thorns were growing all night. I instructed them to be quite thick and to reach into the city. They might be worse than the thorns that surrounded my castle before I woke."

Charlotte roared and slapped me to the ground. I skinned my knee and palms, ripping my dress. Again. Stomping footsteps warned me to shield my face before she kicked my stomach.

I rolled and curled, bracing myself for her next attack.

Beshrews, she was going to kill me.

Her angry footsteps went the opposite direction, marching down the stairs while shouting for Gother and Shinópu.

I sighed, then flinched as my ribs screamed for attention. Even resituating hurt.

"Dear vines," I asked the plants around me, "do you have any healing properties?"

To my surprise, the moss wiggled beneath me. Yes, that could help, but digging it up would kill it.

"Are you sure?" I asked.

The moss wiggled more.

"Thank you. Perhaps you may spread underneath the thorns growing outside. Will that be a fair compensation?"

The moss around me thickened. Was that a yes? I gave the moss time to grow as I struggled to expose my wound. I ended up ripping my once-beautiful gown a couple more times while taking it off. Down to my undergarments, I grabbed a large chunk of nearby moss. Uprooting it from the cracks of the wood flooring, I smeared it across my stomach, knees, and palms until it thickened into a cool paste. It relieved enough of my pain to allow me to prod at my injuries. No broken bones, thank the goddesses. Only scrapes and bruises.

It still hurt too much to climb into my bed. At least the moss was thick enough around me. I lay on my mossy floor, hoping to fall asleep and heal faster. I stared at the wooden ceiling, thinking about how to regain my father's castle without Charlotte killing me or alerting Tanzi.

Charlotte had intimidated and loyal followers, but if Jesse and Thachuma were already on my side, could I sway the others?

Even if I managed to turn them in my favor, I stumbled over the thought of what to do after. Would we chase her all the way back to the mountains? Caden said the foothills were the new homesteads of my people, meaning a chase would not end *at* the mountains, but *through* the mountains. That could take days, during which she could escape, hurt my people, or call for aid. But what was the other option?

Kill her? I had no love for Charlotte or ogres, but death was far from my first choice.

I pondered the issue through the day and night, as Charlotte seemed keen to let me starve without meals. My bedroom door was freed from its hinges, but I hurt too much to escape. Also, a masculine sneeze every couple of hours announced that someone guarded below.

Jesse did not return until the next morning, bearing soup and another roll. Our whole meeting was overseen by Gother and his massive sword. I offered him a smile and bite of my food, but the only change to his static frown was to spit at my feet.

That did not bode well for winning his compassion.

I managed to sit up and do some stretches that day, but no more food was sent to me that evening. My other source of entertainment was to watch Charlotte swing a wooden club at the surrounding thorns. She, Gother, and Shinópu took turns trying to dent the thicket, only to find it regrown in the night. Shinópu was the quietest worker. Gother grunted a lot, and Charlotte cursed with almost every swing.

The next morning was quiet. I went to my windows to check if Shinópu was at work. No. The thorns were as thick as ever.

My bruises were healed enough that I could walk slowly. Maybe it was time to make my escape. As long as Jesse did not keep guard.

I started for my door when footsteps echoed up the stairwell.

Jesse came into view with Thachuma. Either Jesse had hidden filched food in her apron, or she snitched no meal away for me.

"You managed to escape Charlotte's notice?" I asked.

"Hardly," Thachuma said. "She caught Jesse sneaking food today."

Before I could exclaim my dismay and curiosity, Jesse smiled.

"She wants to apologize," Jesse said. "She's willing to play nice if you remove the thorns around the castle."

I frowned. "This sounds like a trap."

Thachuma nodded. "I'll admit, I've never known Charlotte to apologize without ulterior motives, but at least you'll have proper meals each day."

Also, talking to the other servants would be much easier. Even if it was a trap, it was one that brought me closer to my goals.

"Alright," I said. "Thank you for your invitation and escort."

Jesse grinned, and I hated to think of her tricking me with her biggest smile. No, if Charlotte planned to trick me when I came down the stairs, Jesse was ignorant of her plans. I thanked the plants that healed and comforted me, then joined Thachuma and Jesse down the stairs.

Charlotte stood at the bottom and watched us as we approached. Thachuma and Jesse bowed deeply, but I refused to acknowledge Charlotte's position over me. I was a daughter of King Reo of Somnus. We bowed to no usurpers.

Charlotte's jaw twitched with suppressed anger at my defiance. Regardless, she grinned and made a valiant attempt to look pleasant. She failed miserably. Her large smile stretched awkwardly in a half grimace, and her eyes looked more hungry than welcoming.

"Forgive me," she said, "I acted like a brute the other day."

Or like a typical ogre.

"I blame the rough travels," she continued. "But I thought on it and put myself in your shoes—"

As if she could fit her bulbous green toes into my slippers?

"—and I realized how hard it must be for you. That Prince Seaver played with your heart. He never said 'I love you,' did he?"

That froze my snarky thoughts. He had not. Even in my dream, he had only kissed me when it was too late. Then, his kiss in Somnus had been simply because I "didn't look dead."

Charlotte read my face with a knowing smile. "It's because he's bound to me. Whether he loved you or not, it wouldn't matter. He and I are destined to marry. Knowing this, I realized it didn't matter if you were imprisoned or not. You have nothing to threaten me. There's nothing you can do to stop what's written in the stars. Come eat. You must be freezing in those filthy clothes. Jesse, draw her a warm bath. Thachuma, prepare a fresh hot meal."

I stepped down the stairs in a daze. My body moved without thought, like a sleepwalker.

Charlotte wrapped her arm around my shoulders to escort me to the kitchen. I did not shake her off, but I shivered under her touch. Her giant arm felt bumpy and rough. Not wool. This was wakefulness?

Charlotte never left my side as Jesse warmed the water in the large kitchen cauldron. As soon as it began to steam, we carried it in buckets up to my father's lavatory with the largest and smoothest tub. Charlotte walked beside me, rambling about the dull taste of plants and how easily they burned.

I blinked and restudied my surroundings. Where were the vines, ferns, and flowers that had grown during my hundred-year slumber? The kitchens and passageways to the king's room were clear. No—moss still grew in the cracks, but all the vines and ferns had been cut away.

"The vines were particularly stringy," she said as part of her drivel.

A strange sense of loss filled my heart with emptiness. I had eaten plants before. They were a major part of the human diet. Yet her wastefulness, thanklessness, even abuse of these plants that remained as my only company for a hundred years almost hurt like losing a friend.

I bowed my head and sniffled back my emotions.

"Oh, dear," Charlotte said. "I'm sorry, were you…friends with the vines? You are a strange little thing, aren't you. All the better, you don't need them anymore, now that you have me. We'll clean this old place until it gleams. You won't even recognize it soon enough."

I kept my head low, but my periphery caught Charlotte's smile. After three more trips up the stairs with Jesse joining us, the bath was filled with warm water. Charlotte ordered Jesse to crush some flowers to add scents to the bath water. I cringed as Jesse smashed the lilac flowers between two stones. Charlotte grinned wider. When Jesse noticed my reaction to the task, she suggested simply dropping the petals in the warm water, but Charlotte demanded they be crushed.

My old self would have spared no second thought to the abused flower petals. Perhaps my connection to the plants was more curse than boon.

Charlotte remained close as I undressed for the bath. Her black beady eyes followed my every movement. At least our distrust in each other was mutual.

Still clothed in my undergarments, I dipped myself under the warm bath water. Charlotte sneered at my discarded kirtle and bliaut.

"Jesse," she said, "toss these old rags."

A small cry escaped me. "Old?" Give the gown some quick fixes and it would be the top of the line in Somnus.

Charlotte scoffed. "You've worn nothing else for a hundred years now, correct?"

I sank a little lower into the bath.

She laughed. "Have you seen any fashion from the past hundred years? Jesse, I thought you said you mended her dress? If so, why does it have multiple rips? Also, remove the outdated queen's high collar neckline and pocket sleeves."

I sagged. Fashion trends changed with every season, but…changing my clothes was one more change to my memory of the old Somnus.

Charlotte prattled. "Clean yourself quickly before you get all wrinkly. Not that I usually care about a peppering of dirt, but everything about you reminds me of a squealing little pink pig, playing in the forest."

"If Jesse takes my clothes, what am I to wear when I finish?" I dared to ask.

"Jesse," the ogress called, catching the maid on her way out of the door, "fetch my old brown kirtle and surcoat. They should fit her."

Considering Charlotte's massive size, I expected to drown in her clothes. At least I would not be naked or strolling around in my undergarments…as it seemed in England.

The more I thought on England, the more I missed it. I missed the easy plumbing of baths and showers like indoor waterfalls. My dreams of bringing such advancements to Somnus seemed so far away. Worries of surviving the night and removing Charlotte from my life took priority.

If she killed me that night, at least I would die smelling nice. My muscles relaxed in the warm water, and I leisurely scrubbed the dirt from myself.

Charlotte shuffled in the silence. "Did he make you any promises?"

"Who?" I asked.

She scoffed. "Prince Seaver, of course. Who else would I talk about, you silly girl?"

I shrugged in the water. "He promised to come back for me."

"Hah!" She threw her head back with a sharp bark. "The oldest lie in the book! Tell me, you didn't believe him, did you?"

When I said nothing, her face fell into pity.

"Oh, dear. You are too naïve for men."

Jesse returned with Charlotte's change of clothes for me. The off-white kirtle and tanned surcoat were as simple as a peasant's dress, and I was correct in my assumption about their size. Charlotte sliced a vine and told me to use it as a waist tie. I looked like a forest orphan. Considering our surroundings and my lack of family, I could not claim otherwise.

We took our dinner in the great hall. Thachuma served a hot meal of rotisserie duck. Delicious as it was, Charlotte still found points to criticize. I ate my food slowly, hoping that Charlotte would leave me a moment alone with Thachuma and Jesse. No such luck. The ogress insisted on staying beside me and that we sleep in the same room.

Of her many characteristics that annoyed me, her persistence pushed my patience. "I do not understand," I said to her that night, crawling under my covers. "You have a home, family, and betrothed beyond the mountains. Why are you here?"

"You stupid girl," she scoffed. "I came to take care of you, of course."

Her tone suggested a darker definition to "take care" of me.

"I'll admit," she said, "your castle has some charm to it. I can see myself making a home here, close to your sister, and spreading the influence of my family and the Seavers. It's too bad you don't have any servants to fix the place up. I suppose I'll have to take all the credit. What is a queen without her subjects, right? Even a shepherd has some sheep. No wonder Caden preyed upon you, lonely and desperate as you were. But no more. I am here for you, and I'll never leave you alone again."

Chapter 24

Charlotte did not kill me in my sleep that night. I slept as lightly as a feather, half in terror that the moment I lost consciousness, she would sneak over and gut me. Thankfully, her snores helped to keep me awake.

Grateful as I was to still be alive, my sleepless mood took over my attitude in the morning. I struggled to smile for Jesse as she helped me into Charlotte's baggy outfit. There was little for Jesse to do, simple as the clothes were, giving us no time to conspire against the ogress. Charlotte kept a dark and watchful eye on me at all times, regardless.

At breakfast, she reprimanded Thachuma for simply greeting me. With tasty food in my belly, I plotted to steal away from Charlotte. I knew only a couple of the secret passageways, but I knew of at least the one between our bedchambers and the lake exit, and the hidden servant's hall between the kitchen and great hall.

Charlotte made me stand watch as she ordered her servants to pull out the plants from around the castle.

"Please," I said, "do not remove them all. At least spare those in the great hall."

She frowned. "What kind of great hall has you tripping over your feet from roots and vines? A proper great hall needs to be the cleanest of all for entertaining guests around the world. Yes, if those are the plants you're most endeared to, we must rip them out first. Then all the others shouldn't hurt as much. To the great hall, everyone!"

I had planned for her cruelty, but her eagerness to make me suffer still caught me by surprise. I stewed in my anger and pain until Charlotte turned her back. Checking if anyone else watched me, I sneaked to the hidden door. The overgrown vines and moss only hid its position more…and apparently blocked it from opening easily.

Stubborn wood against vines and stone creaked as I pulled on the edge of the hidden door. The sound alerted every person in the room to my escape attempt. Charlotte roared and grabbed me back from the centimeter gap to the pitch-black hallway—my freedom.

She tied my hands together with a vine, then towed me around like a runaway slave for the rest of the day. She kept my hands tied even to eat lunch and dinner. My attempts to loosen my bonds by talking to the vines were fruitless. My magic had no effect on dead plants.

Shamed, sore, and hopeless, I slept deeply that night, despite Charlotte's snores.

My gratitude for waking in the morning was a sad portion of the day before. Almost as sad as the portion of breakfast that Charlotte allowed Thachuma to serve me.

"If we're running low on food," she said, "this little twig of a girl doesn't need as much."

The morning continued the same as the previous, though my heart grew numb from watching the servants cut away and rip out the castle plants.

Before lunch, Charlotte surprised me. "Gother," she called, and her swordsman answered with a quiet approach and deep bow to the ogress's feet. "Watch the fallen princess."

Without further explanation, Charlotte left the room, leaving me alone with her servants for the first time. Hope budded within me.

"Gother?" I asked the swordsman. "Why do you serve the ogress?"

The silent treatment would have been nice. Or a warning.

Instead, Gother slapped me across the face. Hard. I fell to my knees and scratched my wrists as my bonds pulled against my skin.

"We do not speak of the ogress without her present," he said. "Such traitorous talk is punishable. Consider that your warning."

I considered it. After all, I had nothing else to do. Beshrews, I was a fool to plan a revolt with Charlotte's servants. Even if they served Charlotte out of fear as Jesse said, they were too scared to disobey.

Charlotte returned soon after. When her eyes caught mine, they turned hungry. "Come, little hopeless one," she said, taking my bonds. "It's time for lunch."

We stepped into the kitchens, catching Thachuma arguing with Jesse. They silenced and bowed humbly as Charlotte and I entered the room.

Thachuma served me one scoop of broth. My stomach gurgled and Charlotte grinned.

I ate slowly, trying to stretch the meager meal as long as I could. Jesse sniffled with her back turned to us the entire meal. Lost in my own thoughts of despair, I almost missed Charlotte's departure.

"I'll leave you to clean up the mess," she said, leaving the room. Without me. Before I could hope for anything, Thachuma picked up the other end of my vine bond. A full sob escaped Jesse, but she refused to turn away from the counter, beating a bread dough with more force than necessary.

"Princess," Thachuma whispered. There was no hope in his voice. Only sadness and regret. "I may take you on a stroll through the gardens."

I blinked at him. "Yes, please. I would appreciate that."

We were finally given time to plot against Charlotte. Why did Jesse sob?

Thachuma held my leash loosely, like I was a lamb going on a walk. We stepped out to the gardens, which had suffered from my absence. The grass was less lush, the tree limbs drooped, and the flowers wilted. I crouched on the path between the flowerbed and circle of grass.

"I know," I said. "I missed you too, and I know exactly how you feel."

A sob broke out behind me, turning my attention back around.

"Thachuma?"

He stood behind me, breathing heavily, face twisted with anguish. In one hand, he held my vine. In the other, he held a long kitchen knife. Its sharp end was pointed at me.

"I'm sorry," he sobbed. "I don't want to, but Charlotte…she wants to feast on a woman tonight. If I don't kill you, she'll eat Jesse. I can't let her eat Jesse."

Thachuma was ordered to kill me? To save Jesse?

Considering my last few days and my hopeless future, I sympathized with Thachuma's decision. Kill a princess from an era long gone, with no family or home, to save the woman he loved. He had brought me to my favorite place in the castle, to the flowers and gardens.

There were worse ways and places to die.

"Do it," I said, bearing my neck. "Charlotte cannot eat Jesse."

Thachuma's hands shook. He dropped the knife and vine.

"I can't," he sobbed. "I can't kill you, even to save my wife. You don't deserve to die any more than she does."

"Oh, Thachuma." My own tears flowed. Emotionally drained, I leaned into the grass for support. "What are we to do? We cannot allow Jesse to be eaten."

The grass answered. In my mind, I received an image of a possible solution. That was new.

"Thachuma, there is a lamb caught in the thicket," I said. "Would that satisfy Charlotte?"

He sniffled and rubbed his hand across his face. "Maybe. If I use enough sauce, maybe she won't know the difference."

"Do it," I said. "The lamb is stuck and should be easy to catch. Cook a meal like Jesse's life depends on it, because it does. Do not let me down."

A small smile wavered at the edge of his lips. "Yes, Your Highness."

"If I may ask a favor before you leave…" I finished my request by gesturing to the vines wrapped around my wrists.

"Oh, yes, Your Highness." Thachuma picked up the knife again. Instead of using it to kill me, he freed me from my bondage.

I rubbed my sore wrists, then pointed in the direction of the lost lamb. "Hurry."

With a nod, he took off. I did the same in a different direction, running through the overgrown garden to the edge of the thorny thicket. As much as I wanted to flee the castle entirely, I wanted to remain close to make sure Charlotte remained trapped and that Jesse survived dinner.

I found a cluster of trees where the mist and vines grew thick. Dew drooped heavily on the leaves and dripped beside me. I rested against a tree trunk.

"Can you keep me safe and hidden?" I asked the plants around me.

The plants shifted and moved around me. Slow, but steady. I watched, fascinated. Honestly, I had nothing better to do than to watch the grass grow. The trees extended their limbs over my head, inter-locking their branches to create a canopy to keep me dry. The vines draped down the sides as walls to insulate my little spot. The grass and flowers wove together to create a blanket covering. By the time they finished, night had settled, but I was safe and warm in my little hut. Despite all this, and the lack of Char-lotte's snoring, I tossed and turned through the night. Nightmares and worries about Jesse kept me up.

When morning broke, I debated whether or not to go back to the castle to check on her. If Charlotte or another servant spotted me, they would know Thachuma had tricked the ogress. She would probably kill Thachuma and Jesse for their trickery, then hunt me.

No, it was safer for everyone if I remained away. Perhaps I could use the day to search the city for clues about my sisters.

I started whispering to the thorns to create a pathway for me when I sensed…footsteps on the grass. I closed my eyes and held my breath, concentrating on the forest around me. It seemed that spending a night in the woods helped me connect to the plants in new ways. I sensed the weight on the grass, the person's brush against a leaf, and a shadow shading a flower.

"Princess?" a female voice called.

I opened my vine door and smiled. Jesse stood outside with a plate of food. "Thank goodness! You are alive."

She smiled back. "I could say the same to you. I brought you some leftovers."

"Thank you. Come in." I gestured for her to join me inside my hut. The space was tight with both of us, but I appreciated the extra warmth. The meal consisted of a lot of meat with noodles and herbs. I took a bite and almost coughed from the heavy spices.

"I know it is lamb, but is this what human tastes like?" I asked.

Jesse pulled a face. "This is how ogres like human meat to be prepared. It's enough to fool Charlotte, and that's all I care about."

I smiled, agreeing. Beshrews, it was nice to talk with her and joke over a meal. Almost like we were friends in England again.

After Jesse left, I whispered to the thorns again, creating a small and hidden path for me to crawl away and into the city. I had run to the west, allowing me to emerge into the city on the west side—the direction my sisters had fled.

If not my father's favorite inn, where had they gone? Garnet's favorite museum? Pearl's favorite orphanage? No, probably to Marin's favorite dock with her husband. If they could not hide in the inn, then they had run.

I set off with a steady pace southward, toward the docks. The mist thickened with every acre towards the lake. The birds sang less, and the wild trees stilled their leaves. The silence and thick mist were as unnerving as walking into a pitch-black room. I could easily become turned around and lost, especially since many of the buildings were decayed or broken beyond recognition.

Frustrated, I turned back. At the very least, I needed to have a compass to explore the docks safely. I wandered back towards the castle, poking my head into businesses and homes along the way. Every building was picked clean of supplies and functional furniture. Even if the residents had left in a hurry, it seemed that scavengers of human and animal alike had come for the remains.

I surprised a few rodents and birds when opening doors. One door was completely covered with vines until I asked them to move. I hoped the home would be less disturbed than the others. Instead, a large nut tree grew through its backside. I collected some nuts for lunch and dinner and found a berry bush in an alleyway. They tasted sweet as long as I asked the plants for permission to pluck their fruit.

I returned to my hut as night fell. There, I daydreamed of Caden, unsure where the line fell between the Caden from England and the Caden of Uldra. I found a particular sweetness in remembering how both Cadens rubbed the back of his head nervously as he complimented me.

I passed the next day in similar fashion: crawling through my thicket of thorns to search for clues to the past, then sleeping in my little plant hut. The sun fell, the moon rose, then the moon fell and the sun rose. My mind remained in a place between dreams.

The only true marking of time passing was Jesse's visits. She came to me at least once a day with meal scraps. I truly appreciated her efforts to feed me, though I found an odd truce with the edible plants. I could not grow a proper garden while in hiding, but I encouraged each plant to grow and replenish anything I took.

One evening, after dinner, the plants warned me of footsteps approaching. I pulled back my vine door to greet Jesse with a smile. Except she was not alone.

Jesse walked with a vine tied around her wrists and tears in her eyes. Gother held her bonds. Behind him, Charlotte the ogress snarled.

"Run, Emer!" Jesse cried.

Three steps. I managed three whole steps before Charlotte caught my arm. She yanked me back and roared at my face. Black eyes of hate glared at me. The harder I wriggled in her grasp, the tighter she held.

Charlotte the ogress growled at me. "You're mine now."

Chapter 25

Charlotte locked Jesse, Thachuma, and me in separate cells within the castle's underground storage room. It was, unfortunately, more secure than my bedchamber. No windows or firelight brightened our hopes. Charlotte's angry voice and heavy footsteps passed by us every couple of hours. Gother's voice responded, confirming his constant vigilance as our guard.

I lost track of time in the unchanging darkness. Was it days later, or mere hours, when Gother opened my cell? He pulled me by a new vine tied around my wrists to the front courtyard. The sun had barely crested the eastern mountains, announcing the beginning of a new day, giving light to my death scene.

Shinópu stood near the edge of the thorn thickets, having chopped a pathway almost to the end. In the middle of the courtyard, the large kitchen cauldron sat over a massive coal pit. An odd hissing came from the cold cauldron.

Jesse and Thachuma were brought by two other servants to stand beside me. I turned to whisper to Jesse, but Gother yanked me to the other side.

Charlotte grinned at each of us. "Which of the traitors should we eat first?" she asked.

I swallowed hard. What would hurt more: dying or watching my friends die?

Thachuma and Jesse shared a longing look, speaking volumes of the love between them. Whatever pain waited for me, it hardly compared to the pain either of them would suffer to watch the other die.

"Save me for last," I said, hoping to play to Charlotte's expectations. "Jesse and Thachuma betrayed me—they deserve to die first!"

Charlotte frowned. "That was my plan, but you know I can't give you what you want. What's the saying? Ladies first? I suppose in this case, it's princesses first."

She grabbed my arm and pulled me towards the cauldron. Jesse and Thachuma cried out for me. My insides clenched with every step closer to the massive pot. I took a small comfort that the cauldron was still cold. Would it slowly heat with a growing fire? Would it be like taking a bath and slowly falling to sleep?

Reaching the edge of the coals, I saw into the cauldron and the cause for the strange hissing noise.

Snakes.

Dozens of snakes writhed in the cauldron. No bath. Even if they slowly warmed the pot, I would be bitten all over and poisoned—again—before she cooked me.

"There," Charlotte said. "See what horrible death awaits you? I've been waiting a long time to remove you. Prince Seaver's obsession with you was unhealthy. I knew the only way I'd be happy with him as my slave was if you were dead. I didn't oppose his desires to find you. I wanted him to find you. Only then could I kill you. You've been a worthless thorn in my side ever since I first heard about you. Now, you're nothing more than a little weed between my toes."

Worthless. A thorn in her side. Little weed. Had Charlotte called me that before? How had I replied? Confident…bold…daring.

If this was my death, I refused to go out like a wilted and trampled flower. I wanted to be a rooted and blooming tree.

Summoning my past confidence, I dared to meet Charlotte's black eyes. "A weed is no more than a plant where it is unwanted." Then I reached within myself and called to the plants around me. "Help!"

I poured emotion into that single word. As I hoped, a thick root ripped from the ground. It grew a branch—no, a thorn—that raised a full fifteen centimeters in front of Charlotte. The needle-like branch froze my blood and movement, catching the ogress's attention.

She stopped and blinked at it.

"Hah. Hah!" She pointed at the root. "Is that the best you can do? Such a skill is wasted on one as weak as you!" Her laughter roared across the courtyard. My spirits shrank. I had used my last resource, my magic …and it was worthless.

If my spirit had begun as a sprout with birth, I was a tree in full bloom before my poisoning. Ever since waking, my tree had lost all its leaves and weakened, with decay building in my core. This moment splintered my center. My last hopes turned to ash, drifting away, impossible to catch.

Charlotte pulled me forward by my arm, but as her laughter softened, another sound grew. Horse hooves. I turned towards the noise.

Three horses charged between the trees, coming our way.

"Princess!" Caden's voice cried across the forest.

My heart's tree perked. Caden! He had come back for me! Just as he had in England! Except he was too late. I was too close to the hissing cauldron, and he was too far away to stop Charlotte.

He drew his sword and roared as his horse leapt over the thinnest part of the thicket, chopped down by Shinópu. "Charlotte!"

She paused and turned back, her face paling.

I spared no second thought. I might have lost my courage if I had. With Charlotte distracted, turned in Caden's direction, I broke the thorn from the root at

Charlotte's feet. I was unsure what to do with it until Charlotte picked me up with both her hands to throw me into the cauldron. I shoved the thorn into the ogress's chest with all my might. Sick regret sprang through me the moment blood grew from the wound. She dropped me and stumbled back. I knew what would happen. I knew what I had done, and a part of me felt sorry for doing it, even to an ogress who planned to eat me.

Charlotte's foot caught on the root, off balance from my shove. Her arms flailed, but caught only air. She fell into the cauldron. Hissing snakes swallowed her. I raised my shoulder and tied wrists to my ears, failing to block her wretched screams as the snakes ate her alive.

Woozy, I stumbled away from the cauldron. Bile rose in my throat, and I gagged. My ears were too clogged with the sound of Charlotte's screams to hear Caden's horse skid to a stop. My eyes were too blocked with the image of Charlotte's blood blooming from her stab wound—which I had created—to see Caden dismount his horse and kneel beside me.

But I felt him. His arms wrapped around mine, his hands held mine, his mouth spoke near mine.

I swallowed back a bitter taste to ask, "Pardon?"

"Are you alright? Are you hurt? Let's cut those bands." He continued to ramble as he slipped out a hunting knife and cut my bindings. "I came as soon as I heard. Thachuma sent me a bird and—"

He cut off as I threw my arms around his shoulders. He felt like home: warm, welcoming, and… somewhere I was valued.

My floodgates opened, and tears drowned any words.

Somewhere in the mess of Caden's arrival, Mica freed Jesse and Thachuma while Leo went after Charlotte's fleeing servants. Shinópu walked back to us and simply watched.

"Come on," Caden said, helping me to my feet. "Let's get you inside."

He walked me up the stairs and inside. He began to remove his arm from around my shoulders, but I grabbed his hand to keep him. Even if he was different from the Caden from England, I needed his comfort, his warmth, his stability.

The next thing I remembered was much later in the day as Thachuma handed me a fresh bowl of chicken broth. The warmth slowly brought me back to awareness.

"Princess?" Caden asked, still beside me.

He still valued me like a princess, but princesses were valued and treated differently than what I felt. My experiences said that I was unique from other "princesses." I had my own worth.

"Please, call me Emer," I told him.

Caden's blue eyes remained worried, though a relieved smile edged up his lips. "Of course, Emer. I'm so glad you're safe. Charlotte's gone. She can't hurt you anymore."

"I know," I said. "She fell into the cauldron."

"That's right," Caden said, holding me closer. "That must have been awful to watch."

After dinner, Shinópu brought out a small table harp and plucked out a slow tune. I watched the quiet former prince, former slave, now-freed man, wondering how he coped with it all. After a couple measures, he began to sing the lullaby lyrics of light breaking through darkness, seas rolling, wind calming, flowers blooming, animals cuddling, and lovers meeting before the land went to sleep.

Caden and Thachuma added harmonies, urging Mica to join them. He managed a full measure of off-pitched song before breaking into embarrassed laughter.

My own smile cracked like a sprout poking through cobblestone.

Caden requested the next song, "Say 'Tis Not Too Late." I blinked in surprise at his mention of the Somnus song. Did he know I had danced and sung that song to Caden in England?

My curiosity grew as Prince Caden offered his hand to me, to dance while Shinópu played. Something in his eyes said he understood how special the song was to me.

After our dance, Caden kept my hand in his to lead me out to the gardens. We left the firelight, but the stars shone brightly above us.

"My parents," he said, "gave me their blessing to search for your sisters. Of course, they hope that doing so will establish an alliance with your valley to help overthrow the ogres. We'll wake the other princesses, Emer. We'll save them all and restore both of our kingdoms."

"Thank you," I said, still a little dazed from the day.

"For what?" he asked.

"For coming back. For helping me to find my sisters. For the dance and the song. Why did you request that song?"

"Er." He paused to shuffle, unsure of his next words. "Dreams are…strange things."

Curious, I waited for him to explain.

"When you dreamed of me in the land called England, was Charlotte human?"

"Yes," I said.

"With bright blonde hair, an angled face, and she thought your favorite flower was a weed?"

"Yes," I confirmed. "Did you have more dreams of England?"

He nodded. "Ever since I kissed you, my sleep has been filled with the memories of another life. I merely spectate the events from the eyes of a lord's son, who acts rather foolishly at times. As frustrating as it is to

322

dream without control, I enjoy the moments spent with you, learning about you in ways no history accounts can describe."

He paused to slide his hands around mine. "I have a new appreciation for a cloudless sky of stars. I've gained a new thrill to this life of adventures and magic. I—er, you're worth the world to me, Emer. More than a research subject, more than someone I admire, more than an impulsive kiss because you're as beautiful as a poem. I'd follow you to the edge of the world, then cross worlds for you, because it hurts to be away from you. This is all happening so fast, and I understand if you don't feel the same way, but I need to say it because it kills me to think of situations where I never get the chance. So, what I'm trying to say is, I'm falling in love with you, Emer."

My heart skipped a beat, then skipped for joy. Yes, he was a different version of Caden, but similar in so many ways. There was enough of him in there to encourage my words. "I may be falling in love with you too, Caden."

He breathed and grinned with relief. Quoting his dream self, he said, "Emer, as a writer they say to show, not tell, right?"

"Please do."

Caden took me in his arms and kissed me with a tender passion. I knew that sleeping would be a struggle after we parted. Love made reality better than dreams.

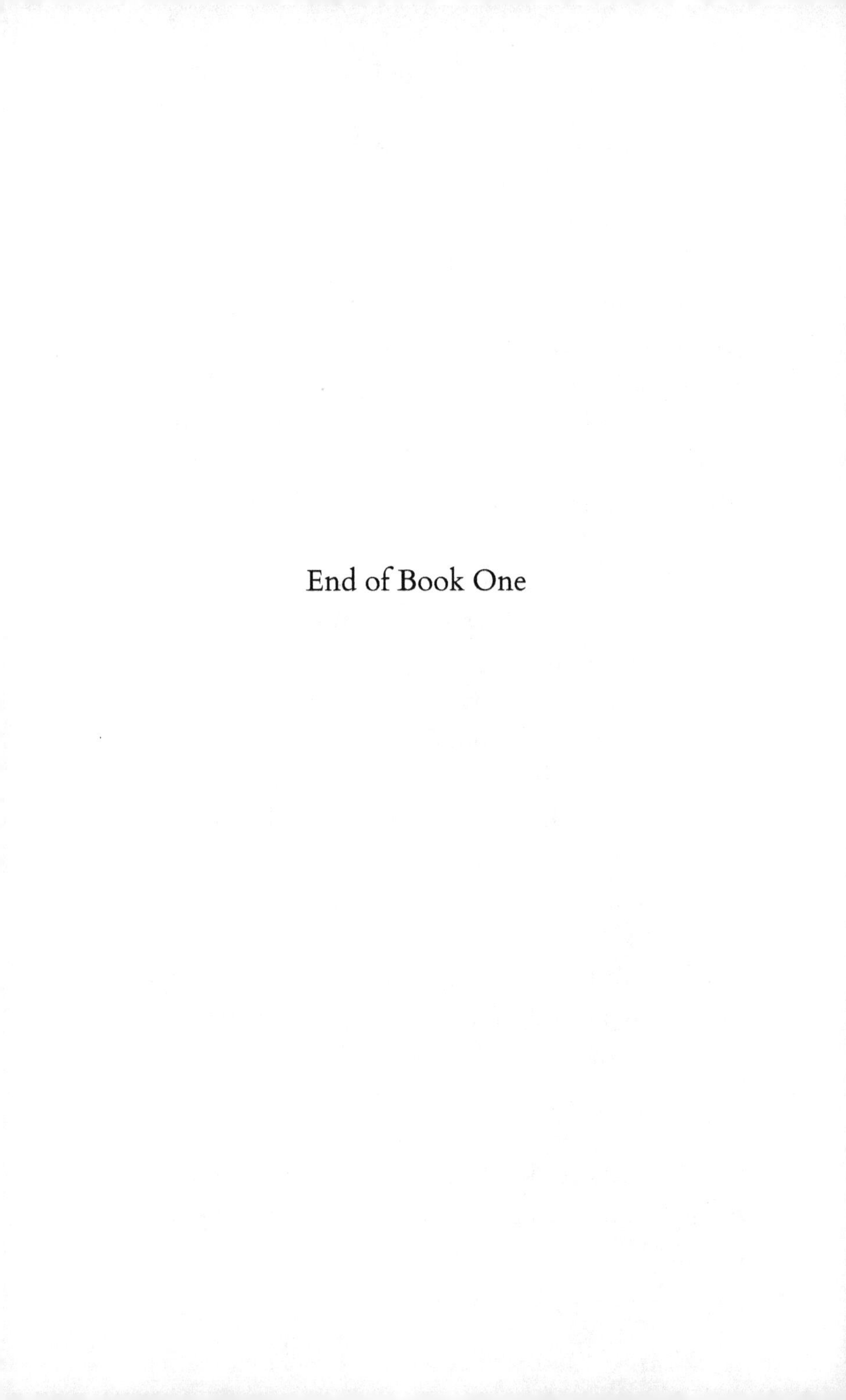

End of Book One

Acknowledgements

I'd like to start by thanking Charles Perrault for recording my favorite version of "Sleeping Beauty" (except this one, of course). As much as I love Disney (I even went to Disney World during the editing process of this book), "Sleeping Beauty" is the one story that I consider shortchanged by Disney's re-telling. Waking up was only the end of Part 1. So, I took on the duty to retell the full story from Perrault. I still thank and defend Disney for popularizing the tale of "Sleeping Beauty." After writing a twenty-five-page essay, no one can convince me that he wasn't the Perrault and Shakespeare of his time.

Speaking of twenty-five-page essays, I'd like to thank Professor Rudy from BYU's ENGL495 capstone class for starting my deep dive into English, French, and German fairy tales. Thanks for pointing me toward proper translations and research sources, such as the Norton Critical Edition of "The Classic Fairy Tales" (edited by Maria Tatar, 1998) and "The Classic Fairy Tales," by Iona and Peter Opie (1974). These university "textbooks" were actually fun to read and weren't outdated ten years later (unlike my husband's chemistry textbooks).

I'd also like to thank those who helped me during my revision process of "Don't Marry the Cursed" (book two of my Haunted Romance trilogy). Basing Theo's homeland on Grimm's fairy tales inspired me to research even deeper into the fairy tales and to experiment with retellings. This series wouldn't have been inspired without it.

As for my editors, all thanks go to Karie from CookieLynn Publishing.

If you love my cover, thank Arcane Covers. Also thank Shaela Kay for her advice and referral.

Special thanks go to Robyn Cheatham for Alpha reading (before *and* after the extended ending) and Jim Doran for his extensive suggestions. Other awesome Beta readers include Abby Smith, Lisa Gartner, Lexi Cooper, and E.W. Barnes.

As always, my biggest "Thanks" goes to Michael. He didn't read this one until it reached the Beta stage (which is much later than his usual), but he knew about every single adjustment in the writing and editing process. His listening ear and helpful suggestions were irreplaceable.

Lastly, I thank God, my Heavenly Father. I don't love writing about a polytheistic world, but I researched the biblical story of the Earth's creation a *lot* when creating the Rezhina Valley and the powers of the twelve princesses. Guess you'll need to read book two to find out how it connects.

About the Author

C Rae D'Arc has been involved in every stage of a book's life. As a writer, editor, retailer, reader, and reviewer, she has worked four part-time jobs at once. Thankfully, one of them actually paid her. She received her Bachelors in English from Brigham Young University, where she studied British and American literature, folklore, Shakespeare, and West European fairy tales. She now lives in the Tri-Cities of Washington with her husband and Aussie dog.

PS. To save you from hiccups, D'Arc only has one syllable.

www.craedarc.com
www.facebook.com/c.rae.darc
www.instagram.com/craedarc

9 781961 733039